P9-CKT-185

RUINED

A NOVEL

A NOVEL

PAULA MORRIS

Point

FOR REBECCA HILL

Library of Congress Cataloging-in-Publication Data available

ISBN 978-0-545-04214-7

12 11 10 9 8 7 6 5 4 3 11 12 13 14 15/0

Printed in the U.S.A. 40
First Scholastic paperback printing, August 2010
Book design by Becky Terhune

PROLOGUE

New Orleans, the summer of 1853. Yellow fever ravages the busy port city. Bells toll for the souls of the dead. Boats on the Mississippi River are placed in quarantine, their cargoes left to spoil, their crews felled by disease. Before the summer is over, eight thousand people will die.

In the city, yellow fever is known as the Stranger's Disease. Immigrants — Italian, Greek, German, Polish, new arrivals from the great cities of New York and Boston — have no resistance to the fever. The Irish, who'd traveled to New Orleans to escape their terrible famine, soon fall victim, dying within a week of the first sinister chill.

During the day, the streets are empty. At night, mass burials take place all over town. Graveyards fill; corpses lie rotting in piles, swelling in the sun. Gravediggers are bribed with alcohol to ignore the putrid smell and dig shallow trenches for the bodies of the poor. New Orleans's black population — slaves and the free people of color — have seemed largely immune, but in August of 1853, even they start to succumb. Native-born wealthy families — Creole and American — suffer as badly as poor immigrants.

The ornate tombs in the walled cemeteries, New Orleans's famous Cities of the Dead, fill with mothers and fathers, daughters and sons. At Lafayette Cemetery, on the new,

American side of the city, bodies are left at the gates every night. There is no room to bury these unknown dead, and many of the corpses are burned.

In the last week of August, in the dead of night, a group of men unlock the Sixth Street gates to Lafayette Cemetery and make their way by torchlight to an imposing family tomb. Two coffins of yellow fever victims, both from the same family, had been placed in the vault earlier that afternoon, one on each of its long, narrow shelves. According to local custom, once in place, the coffins should have been sealed behind a brick wall for a year and a day.

But the coffins are still unsealed. The men remove the marble plate, covering their mouths, choking at the smell of the bodies decomposing in the heat. Onto the top coffin, they slide a shrouded corpse, then quickly replace the plate.

The next day, the tomb is sealed. A year later, the men return to break through the bricks. The two disintegrating coffins are thrown away, and the bones of the dead covered with soil in the *caveau*, a pit at the bottom of the vault.

The names of the first two corpses interred in the vault that terrible August are carved onto the tomb's roll call of the dead. The name of the third corpse is not.

Only the men who placed the body inside the tomb know of its existence.

CHAPTER ONE

TORRENTIAL RAIN WAS POURING THE AFTERnoon Rebecca Brown arrived in New Orleans. When the plane descended through gray clouds, she could only glimpse the dense swamps to the west of the city. Stubby cypress trees poked out of watery groves, half submerged by the rain-whipped waters, flecked with snowy herons. The city was surrounded by water on all sides — by swamps and bayous; by the brackish Lake Pontchartrain, where pelicans swooped and a narrow causeway, the longest bridge in the world, connected the city with its distant North Shore; and, of course, by the curving Mississippi River, held back by grass-covered levees.

Like many New Yorkers, Rebecca knew very little about New Orleans. She'd barely even heard of the place until Hurricane Katrina hit, when it was on the news every night — and it wasn't the kind of news that made anyone want to move there. The city had been decimated by floodwaters, filling up like a bowl after the canal levees broke. Three years later, New Orleans still seemed like a city in ruins.

Thousands of its citizens were still living in other parts of the country. Many of its houses were still waiting to be gutted and rebuilt; many had been demolished. Some of them were still clogged with sodden furniture and collapsed roofs, too dangerous to enter, waiting for owners or tenants who never came back.

Some people said the city — one of the oldest in America — would never recover from this hurricane and the surging water that followed. It should be abandoned and left to return to swampland, another floodplain for the mighty Mississippi.

"I've never heard anything so ridiculous in my life," said Rebecca's father, who got agitated, almost angry, whenever an opinion of this kind was expressed on a TV news channel. "It's one of the great American cities. Nobody ever talks about abandoning Florida, and they get hurricanes there all the time."

"*This* is the only great city in America," Rebecca told him. Her father might roll his eyes, but he wouldn't argue with her: There was nothing to argue about. New York was pretty much the center of the universe, as far as she was concerned.

But now here she was — flying into New Orleans one month before Thanksgiving. A place she'd never been before, though her father had an old friend here — some lady called Claudia Vernier who had a daughter, Aurelia. Rebecca had met them exactly once in her life, in their room at a Midtown hotel. And now she'd been taken out of school five weeks before the end of the semester and sent hundreds of miles from home.

Not for some random, impromptu vacation: Rebecca was expected to *live* here. For six whole months.

The plane bumped down through the sparse clouds, Rebecca scowling at her own vague reflection in the window. Her olive-toned skin looked winter-pale in this strange light, her mess of dark hair framing a narrow face and what her father referred to as a "determined" chin. In New York the fall had been amazing: From her bedroom window, Central Park looked on fire, almost, ablaze with the vivid colors of the dying leaves. Here, everything on the ground looked dank, dull, and green.

Rebecca wasn't trying to be difficult. She understood that someone needed to look after her: Her father — who was a high-powered tech consultant — had to spend months in China on business, and she was fifteen, too young to be left alone in the apartment on Central Park West. Usually when he was traveling for work, Mrs. Horowitz came to stay. She was a nice elderly lady who liked watching the Channel 11 news on TV with the volume turned up too loud, and who got irrationally worried about Rebecca eating fruit at night and taking showers instead of baths.

But no. It was too long for Mrs. Horowitz to stay, her father said. He was sending her to New Orleans, somewhere that still looked like a war zone. On TV three years ago they'd seen the National Guard driving around in armored vehicles. Some neighborhoods had been completely washed away.

"The storm was a long time ago — and anyway, you're going to be living in the Garden District," he had told her. They were sitting in her bedroom, and he was picking at the frayed edges of her cream-colored quilt, not meeting Rebecca's eye. "Everything's OK there — it didn't flood. It's still a beautiful old neighborhood."

"But I don't even know Aunt Claudia!" Rebecca protested. "She's not even my real aunt!"

"She's a very good friend of ours," her father said, his voice strained and tense. "I know you haven't seen her for a long time, but you'll get on just fine with her and Aurelia."

All Rebecca could remember of Aunt Claudia were the jangly bracelets she had worn and her intense green eyes. She'd been friendly enough, but Rebecca had been shooed away after a couple of minutes so the adults could talk. She and Aurelia, who was just a little girl then, seven years old and very cute, spent the rest of the visit playing with Aurelia's dolls in the hotel bedroom.

And these were the people — these *strangers* — Rebecca was expected to live with for six months?

"Claudia is the closest thing I have to family — you know that. Everything's arranged. End of discussion."

"There hasn't been any *beginning* of discussion," Rebecca complained. Because her mother had died when Rebecca was small, and because she had no grandparents or any real family, she and her dad had always been a tight team — Brown, Party of Two, as they often joked. Now, all of a sudden, why was he acting in such a high-handed manner? "You never even asked me what I think. You're just shipping me off somewhere . . . somewhere dangerous. Haven't you heard about the crime in New Orleans? And there were, like, two other hurricanes this year!"

"Oh, Rebecca," her father said, his eyes murky with tears.

His whole body slumped, as though she'd taken a swing at him. He put his arm around her and pulled her close. His voice was soft. "Hurricane season is over, honey. I promise you, I won't let anything bad happen to you. Not now, not ever."

"Oh, Dad," Rebecca said, the words muffled by his shoulder. She couldn't remember him ever acting quite this way before. There were times when her father went quiet and broody, just sitting around the apartment gazing at photographs of her mother and looking morose, but she couldn't remember him crying. "I'm not really worried about bad things. It's just . . . I don't want to leave this apartment and my friends and school and everything, just to go somewhere messed-up and weird. It might be really boring."

"I hope we both have a very boring six months," he said. He drew back from her, and gave her a tired half smile. "Believe me, boring would be good."

Boring was exactly Rebecca's first impression of the near-empty Louis Armstrong airport. She'd wondered if she'd be able to see Aunt Claudia and Aurelia in the crowd, but trudging from the gate, listening to the piped-in jazz playing throughout the terminal, Rebecca spotted them at once. It would have been impossible to miss them, she thought, her heart sinking. Claudia was dressed in some sort of gypsy costume, including a bright headscarf and giant silver hoop earrings. She was darker skinned than Rebecca remembered, and her eyes were a strange sea green, her gaze darting around like a bird's.

Aurelia had grown — she was twelve now — into a round-faced cherub, her messy dark curls tied up in a ponytail. She was dressed far more formally than her mother: a black plaid skirt, a black woolen blazer emblazoned with a gold crest, white knee socks, and lace-up shoes. This had to be the school uniform for Temple Mead Academy, the school Rebecca would be attending as well. The uniform was even worse than she'd imagined. Her friends at Stuyvesant High School would die laughing if they saw that prim outfit, not to mention Aunt Claudia's Halloween-style gypsy getup. If this was what people here wore every day, Rebecca wondered, what did they look like at Mardi Gras?

She walked as slowly as possible through the security exit and fluttered the tiniest of waves in Aunt Claudia's direction. Her aunt's face brightened.

"Here she is!" she said, reaching out for an effusive, jewelry-rattling embrace as Rebecca approached. She smelled of lavender and something smoky and Eastern, like incense, or maybe charred satay sticks. "Baby, look at you! You've grown so tall!"

"Yes," said Rebecca, suddenly shy. Homesickness churned in her stomach: She would be living in a strange house for months on end, with this odd woman she barely knew. Nobody called her "baby" in New York.

"We have a car," said Aurelia, not bothering to wait for introductions or greetings. She was wriggling with excitement.

"That's nice." Rebecca wasn't sure if that was the right thing to say, but Aurelia beamed at her.

"We've never had a car before, *ever*," she explained. Aunt Claudia caught Rebecca's hand and drew her toward the escalator, Aurelia scampering down ahead of them.

"FEMA money," Aunt Claudia stage-whispered. Rebecca tried to remember what FEMA was exactly — something to do with the government, maybe. "I decided I needed it for work, before the streetcar started running again on St. Charles."

"You work in the French Quarter, right?" asked Rebecca. Her father had given her a few pieces of information, in his usual scattered way. He'd been completely distracted for the past two weeks, ever since he announced that he was pulling her out of school and sending her to the Deep, Deep South for months on end.

"In Jackson Square." Aunt Claudia nodded, breathless with the exertion of walking to the one baggage carousel surrounded by waiting passengers. "I read tarot cards. It was a quiet summer, but things are starting to pick up again. Tourists and conventions and all that."

"Oh," said Rebecca. Suddenly her aunt's outfit was making sense: It was her office wear, in a way. Though why her decidedly nonsuperstitious dad thought Aunt Claudia would be an ideal guardian was even more of a mystery.

"Your father called me from Atlanta," Aunt Claudia was saying while Rebecca hauled her heavy black duffel from the carousel, blinking hard so she didn't embarrass herself by crying. It was too soon to be missing home and missing her father, but she couldn't help it. They'd flown to Atlanta together, because he had to check in with his head office there before he traveled to China. They'd said a miserable goodbye, her father flagrantly sobbing like an overgrown baby.

Rebecca had to stop herself from thinking about how much she'd miss him and how useless he'd be without her.

Why he'd agreed to this stupid posting, she didn't know. Usually, he never went away for more than a week. The year she spent two weeks at summer camp in Maine, he looked like a crazy person, deranged with worry, by the time she got home.

"He goes to China on Tuesday," she managed to say. Traffic was hissing past the glass doors, rain thundering onto the road between the taxi stand and the parking garage. Aurelia helped lift the second of Rebecca's bags onto the cart, and they walked outside. Despite the rain, it wasn't cold at all, Rebecca realized, peeling off her NYU hoodie — her dad had promised her she could go to NYU for college — and looking around.

So this was New Orleans — small, wet, hot. The waiting cabs were black-and-white, really beaten up. Rebecca's father told her once that all airports looked the same, but she could tell she wasn't in New York anymore.

"Mama, should we wait for you here?" asked Aurelia, as springy as a raindrop herself. Aunt Claudia looked puzzled for a moment and then horrified.

"No, no! I don't want to leave you here alone! We'll all run across the road to the lot together. It's only a little . . . wet."

A grumble of thunder announced an even more intense burst of rain. Rebecca could barely see the grim concrete walls of the parking garage across the street. Her aunt was bedraggled as a patchwork rag doll by the time they found cover in the garage.

"Best to stay together," her aunt said in a quiet voice, almost to herself. She flashed Rebecca a bright smile. "Best to keep close. Only a little rain. Now, Aurelia, what does our car look like? Is it blue or black?"

During the drive in from the airport, the city didn't look promising. An empty, sand-colored canal ran alongside the highway for a stretch, and there were billboards — one for Louisiana seafood, one for a strip club in the French Quarter — that were obviously local, if kind of tacky. But much of everything else looked like most other American cities: signs along the highway for fast-food restaurants, tangles of on- and off-ramps, a clump of tall glass buildings downtown. In the distance, the white-lidded Superdome looked like a bright bulb on this rainy night. Strange to think of it as a place where thousands of people had been stuck, with very little food or water or hope, for a whole week after the hurricane.

But once they were off the highway and the crowded main roads, Rebecca could see something of the place her father had told her about. The Garden District looked as beautiful as he'd promised, its narrow side streets shadowed by giant oak trees, its houses pristine and picturesque. Many had tall white pillars, painted shutters, and black iron gates and railings. Some had long porches — galleries, Aunt Claudia called them — on their lower and upper stories, extending down one whole side of the house.

"And this street we're driving along is Prytania," Aunt Claudia explained.

"Britannia?"

"With a *P* — from the old *rue du Prytanée*. Based on the ancient Greek Prytaneum, the place they honored Hestia, goddess of the hearth. The sacred fires were kept burning at the Prytaneum. It was the center of village life."

"Here it's just the way we walk to school," Aurelia added. She tapped Rebecca on the shoulder, pointing to a magnificent coffee-colored mansion, set back from the street behind tall, wrought-iron gates. "That's it there."

Temple Mead Academy was grand all right, Rebecca thought, straining to get a good look at the sprawling pillared mansion. Although the building was only three stories, it seemed to peer down at its neighbors, calm and imposing, and a little snooty. It might be beautiful and old and all, but Rebecca wasn't especially looking forward to her first day there.

Now they were passing a small old cemetery, the domed roofs of its tombs visible above the cemetery's crumbling, mossy white walls. In New Orleans the dead were entombed in aboveground vaults like these, Rebecca's father had told her, because it was the French and Spanish custom, and people in New Orleans liked anything that involved showing off their money. He also said the city had a high water table: Bodies buried in the ground might bubble to the surface after a heavy rain. Rebecca shuddered, thinking of corpses peeping out of the wet soil like inquisitive worms.

The car jerked to an abrupt stop on Sixth Street, outside a house much smaller and shabbier than either of its neighbors.

"Home sweet home," announced Aunt Claudia, fiddling with the controls on her door: She couldn't seem to work out how to open it. "At least it's stopped raining."

Rebecca climbed out of the car and stood for a moment

on the damp sidewalk. The Verniers' wooden house was not only tiny — it leaned to one side in a perilous and possibly illegal way, almost touching the house next door. The ramshackle cottage was painted a faded yellow, and the shutters and front door were blue. A colorful hand-painted sign that read VERNIER in pink letters dangled above the door. The tiny front yard was a dense mass of greenery speckled with a few white flowers; and a banana tree, fat rain drops balanced on its glossy leaves, drooped onto the small front porch.

"Our cottage garden." Aunt Claudia gestured at the yard, her bangles rattling. Rebecca climbed the rickety steps to the porch and walked over to the rocking chair chained to the wooden railings. She didn't know about "cottage garden": It looked like weeds. The view from the porch was of the cemetery across the street — or rather its high, dirt-streaked walls. Just down the street was an entrance with tall gates. Aunt Claudia, fumbling inside her giant crocheted bag for the keys she'd had in her hand just a minute ago, followed Rebecca's gaze.

"Lafayette Cemetery's not a safe place," her aunt told her. "Unfortunately. You should keep away."

"Why?" Rebecca had a sudden vision of dead bodies reaching up to grab her, their stiff fingers dark with soil.

"Criminals and derelicts," said Aunt Claudia, pushing open the door. "They wait for tourists to wander in so they can mug them. Some poor soul was shot there just before the storm. Unless you're on one of the big guided tours, it's not a safe place. That's why all the gates are locked every afternoon. Really, you must promise me you'll never go there."

Rebecca resisted the urge to roll her eyes. Aunt Claudia was just as overprotective as her father. Didn't she know that Rebecca was used to catching the New York City subway, walking through Central Park, hanging out with her friends downtown?

Her aunt stood on the threshold, door ajar, key still in the lock, as though she was waiting for Rebecca's solemn promise before they could move inside.

"Here's Marilyn!" cried Aurelia. A small, long-haired, black-and-white cat bounded through the doorway, past Aurelia's outstretched hands and down the pathway. As though she'd been listening to their conversation, the cat scampered down the street toward the cemetery gate. Without hesitation, she squeezed under the gate's lowest rung and disappeared into the darkness. Rebecca couldn't help laughing.

"That cat is setting a very bad example," sighed Aunt Claudia, shaking her head. She seemed to have forgotten about making Rebecca promise things, which was just as well: Rebecca was hoping to follow Marilyn's lead sometime soon. She was from New York, after all: A small cemetery in a tiny city like this didn't frighten her.

CHAPTER TWO

"THIS," AUNT CLAUDIA EXPLAINED, WITH A JINGLY shake of the wrist, "is a shotgun house."

They were all crammed in the narrow hallway, just inside the front door, a panting Aurelia leaning against Rebecca's damp luggage. Rain clattered onto the roof, sounding as though it was about to break through at any second.

"It's *African*," Aurelia added, and Rebecca was confused until Aunt Claudia started talking about shotgun-house design coming to New Orleans with the big influx of migrants from Haiti, two hundred years ago.

"Some people will tell you it's called a shotgun house because you can fire a gun from the front door to the back, and it would pass straight through the house," she said, flapping one hand at the long hallway that stretched the length of the house to the back door. "Actually, it's derived from a West African word for 'house.' A true shotgun house doesn't have a hallway, of course. Just one room stacked behind another, in the Afro-Caribbean style . . ."

All the rooms of the house were off this skinny hallway, and there seemed to be a surprising number of doorways: The house looked small from the outside, but it stretched back forever.

"It may not be big as some of the mansions around here, but it's older than most of the other houses in the neighborhood." Aunt Claudia gestured into the front room, which Aurelia called "the parlor." Rebecca peered in. Clearly, her aunt's taste in home furnishings was as eclectic as her fashion choices. The living room — sorry, parlor — was a chaotic, dusty jumble of Victorian sofas and Asian statues, and the ancient-looking TV was shrouded with an embroidered shawl.

"We only get basic cable," Aurelia whispered, her mouth drooping into a pout.

"It was built in the early nineteenth century," Aunt Claudia called, bustling down the hallway, which was lined with gilt-framed still-life paintings, bunches of wizened dried flowers, and gaudy, glossy prints of various Indian gods. "For one of the many free people of color who lived in New Orleans. There were more free people of color here then than anywhere else in the United States — even New York!"

Rebecca felt herself bristling: She wasn't up for months of jibes about her hometown.

"And slaves, right?" she asked.

"Oh, yes." Aunt Claudia paused outside one of the doors. "A huge population of slaves. They far outnumbered the white inhabitants. New Orleans was a place where people were bought and sold, I'm sorry to say — the largest center of the slave trade. This is the kitchen, where we seem to spend all our time."

Rebecca followed Aunt Claudia into yet another cluttered space, lined with cupboards that looked as though they were last updated in the 1950s. A table topped with peeling Formica sat in the middle of the room, a battered tarot deck wedged between a saltshaker and a bottle of Alligator Bite hot sauce. Rebecca recognized it at once: Her father always kept a bottle of Alligator Bite in the fridge at home. She'd never thought about it being a Louisiana thing.

"There are still more black people than white in New Orleans," Aunt Claudia told her, filling a battered kettle at the kitchen sink. "Or at least there were before the storm. Nobody knows how many people live here anymore. Everything is still in . . . er, disarray. You hungry, baby?"

Rebecca shook her head. She felt too churned up to even think about food.

"*I'm* hungry." Aurelia pulled a drooping, chocolate-smeared box from the fridge. "Mama, can we have some cake?"

While the others argued about whether Aurelia should wait until *after* dinner for some cake, Rebecca gazed around the room. It was dilapidated and messy, the exact opposite of the tidy, modern kitchen in the Browns' New York apartment. And instead of a neat calendar hanging above the phone, plastered across the peeling walls of the kitchen were ripped pages that looked as though they came from one of those page-a-day desk calendars.

One page was for that day, October twenty-fifth. But all the other dates seemed entirely random: one in March, one in December, two in February — the twentieth and twenty-first — another in October, and one in November. All of the pages were blank, stuck on the wall in a slapdash manner, as though Aunt Claudia was in a big hurry. Rebecca wondered if she was patching holes in the wall, or if the entire calendar had once been posted, page by page, on the wall and wilted off in the damp. Nothing would surprise her in this place.

"Rebecca hasn't even seen her room yet!" Aunt Claudia tugged the cake box out of Aurelia's hands. "Go and show it to her, and then we'll all have a piece of cake — just a small piece!"

Aurelia grabbed Rebecca's elbow and steered her down the hallway: Her new room lay behind the fourth door on the left, between the bathroom and Aurelia's bedroom. It was not, Rebecca noticed, exempt from weirdness. The room was small with shuttered windows, quite dark because of the proximity of the house next door: It looked close enough to touch. The walls were painted a moody purple-gray color, and the bedspread was made from a slippery-looking, pale blue satin. There were bookshelves but no closet: All Rebecca's clothes would have to be folded and put away in a large wooden dresser, painted in black-and-white harlequin diamonds. Aurelia swung the door shut, and pointed to a clutch of wooden hangers dangling from an antique hook on the back of the door. One bore her new school uniform — that ugly black blazer and too-long plaid skirt.

Everything was much more old-fashioned than her room in New York, but it could have been worse, Rebecca decided, trying not to feel too depressed. The bed was large and seemed comfy, and there was enough space under the expansive dresser to line up her shoes. The worst thing about the room was the strange wall decorations. There were sinister devil masks and some kind of doll; on the top shelf of the bookcase sat a tiny skull with cavernous eyeholes.

"It's a monkey skull," Aurelia told her matter-of-factly, flopping onto the bed. "We use it to prop up the books."

Rebecca made a face. Aurelia leaned back, pointing to each object in turn.

"That's a carnival mask from Haiti — made from papier-mâché." And that's a *djakout*, which is basically . . ."

"A sack?"

"Yes. It's hard to explain exactly. That's from Haiti as well. But the gris-gris bag," she said, wriggling her fingers at a little red pouch hanging from the hook on the back of the door, "that's from here. You should really carry it with you. There are herbs and things in it to protect you."

"Do you really believe that?" Rebecca didn't want to be rude, but this all sounded like so much hocus-pocus. Just because she liked ghost stories and vampire movies didn't mean she was about to carry some voodoo pouch with her everywhere.

"Maybe," Aurelia sighed. She scrunched up her pert nose and giggled. "Maybe not. I like the Buddhist stuff better. The statues are cooler. Sorry you got stuck with the voodoo room."

"That's OK," Rebecca told her, startled when Aurelia scrambled to her feet and darted out the door. But within moments she was back: Her arms were full of Marilyn the cat, back safely from her cemetery adventure.

"Mama collects these to protect us from bad things," Aurelia explained, gesturing at the wall with an elbow. Rebecca squinted up at the demented rag doll on a stick, made from scraps of old fabric, and — worst of all — the rudimentary figure of an angel, hanging right above the headboard of the bed. "It's her big hobby."

"I think I need protection from *this* stuff," she told Aurelia. "Especially if that thing falls on me in the night. I thought hobbies were things like stamp-collecting or keeping guinea pigs or something."

Aurelia's eyes lit up.

"Did you have a guinea pig in New York?" she asked, stroking Marilyn's fluffy back. The cat's purr was as loud as an outboard motor.

"No, but I had a frog once," Rebecca told her. "And two goldfish, Leo and Orlando, but they didn't last long. My father's allergic to cats, and he says it's cruel to have a dog in an apartment as small as ours, especially with nobody at home all day."

"Your father is . . . Uncle Michael." Aurelia frowned. "And you lived on Central Park West."

"I *live* there — present tense. I'm just staying here while my dad's away."

"And your mother was Aunt Millie," said Aurelia, her face screwed up with concentration. "She was tall, like you. But she died when you were a tiny baby, and I never met her at all."

"You sound like you're about to take a test," Rebecca teased. She lay back on the bed, trying not to skid off the icy cover onto the floor. A water stain spread like a yellowing bruise across the ceiling. Nothing here looked or felt or smelled the way it did at home: She felt an intense pang of homesickness.

"Aunt Millie was my mama's cousin," Aurelia continued, squeezing Marilyn more tightly; the cat let out a plaintive little cry in protest.

"I don't think she was, actually . . ."

"Oh, I know." Marilyn kicked free from Aurelia's suffocating embrace and tore out of the room. Aurelia made a mock-sad face. "But we have to pretend. Otherwise the school won't let you in."

"Really?" Rebecca sat up. She knew the school was exclusive, but this seemed even more snobby than she'd feared. Aurelia nodded.

"Mama says so. Do you have any pictures of your parents?"

"Just one of the three of us together." Rebecca reached for her satchel and rummaged around for her wallet, flicking it open to show Aurelia the small photo tucked behind a plastic window. She took it with her everywhere. Everyone told her she looked like her mother — tall and dark, with the same uncertain smile.

"Dad says it was taken in Paris," she told Aurelia. "We lived there when I was small. . . . What?"

Her little cousin was looking puzzled, staring at the dangling wallet.

"There's nothing there," she said. "Has the picture dropped out?"

Rebecca turned her wallet around: Aurelia was right. The photograph was gone. She shook everything from her wallet onto the bed and flung the empty shell down in frustration. The picture was nowhere to be found in her satchel, either.

"But it couldn't just fall out," she said, more to herself than to Aurelia. "And it was definitely there when I showed my ID at LaGuardia. I remember looking at it before I put my wallet away."

"Maybe someone stole it?" Aurelia suggested. Rebecca shook her head, sorting through the contents of her wallet one more time, just in case.

"Who would steal a photograph and leave all the money?" She'd had her satchel with her the whole time since she left the apartment on Central Park West, aside from ten minutes in the Atlanta airport: Her father had offered to sit with her stuff while she browsed through some magazines. Surely he would have noticed someone rifling through her bag and removing a photo from her wallet? Unless . . .

Unless he'd taken it himself.

"It's too bad that you've lost it," Aurelia sympathized, and Rebecca nodded, unable to speak. Her father removing the picture from her wallet didn't make any sense; it was a copy of one he had sitting on the desk in his home office. He didn't need it. Why would he take away the only thing she had to remind her of home — and of her family?

CHAPTER THREE

THE WROUGHT-IRON RAILINGS SURROUNDING Temple Mead Academy were spiky — To keep the riff-raff out, Rebecca thought, walking toward it on her first day of school. Her stomach started twisting into tight knots as she and Aurelia climbed a flight of broad stone steps, especially when Aurelia stopped on the top step.

"I'm in the junior school," Aurelia told Rebecca, her usual cheerful grin fading. "That means we have all our classes next door."

She gestured at a modern building on the next lot, all sheer glass and hard edges, incongruous on this oak-lined street.

"But I'll see you at lunchtime, right?" Rebecca felt even more nervous. She didn't know Aurelia very well, but at least she *knew* her. And Aurelia was a friendly, bouncy little thing, clearly happy to have a visiting older cousin, of sorts, staying for a while.

"Different lunchtimes," said Aurelia, shaking her head. Chattering girls pushed past them, hurrying through the double doors. "But I'll meet you here on the steps, after school – OK?"

Rebecca nodded mutely, watching Aurelia scamper back down the stairs and across the stone-paved yard. Another wave of girls in plaid carried Rebecca through the doors and into a cool, dark foyer. A long staircase swept up to the next floor; paintings of pale young women wearing ethereal ball gowns lined the paneled walls. From the portraits to the chandelier hung high above Rebecca's head, it felt more like a palace than a high school.

The receptionist in the small side office told Rebecca to wait to see Principal Vale. Rebecca pressed herself against a wall to keep out of the way. Her new school uniform felt itchy and heavy. Normally in the fall she wore a uniform of a different kind to school – jeans, Converse sneakers, a sweater, and an amazing pale blue suede jacket she'd found in a vintage store downtown. All her books were loaded into the Chrome messenger bag her father had given her as a birthday present. But here everything was regulation, including the ugly shoes and bag. If her friends back home saw her, they'd think she was living in another era, not just another part of the country.

No matter how hot it was, the girls of Temple Mead Academy *had* to wear their blazers while walking to and from school. Aunt Claudia had impressed this on her last night. Today was mild and cloudy, and even the short walk from home had made Rebecca sticky with perspiration. She didn't know how the girls here put up with it in the spring and summer. But maybe they suffered in silence, like proper little ladies: Everything about the neighborhood seemed to belong in a different century.

Outside, rain had begun to fall again, and girls hurried in, shaking off wet umbrellas, pushing back hanks of damp hair. They all looked incredibly prissy, Rebecca thought. And there was another strange thing about the students at Temple Mead Academy: They were all white. Back in New York, the kids in Rebecca's class were black, white, Asian, Hispanic. Every ethnicity and religion and fashion fad in New York was represented. Here everyone looked the same.

The bell rang, and this made her smile, in spite of herself: Even the bell here was more genteel than the one at Stuyvesant — a ladylike ding rather than a crude electronic beeping. Suddenly the foyer was deserted, wet footprints the only sign of the throng of girls. Rebecca felt a surge of anxiety. Soon she'd have to walk into a classroom full of strangers and be introduced, have all these girls stare at her.

The front door pushed open again, and two people bustled in. One was a pale-skinned girl around Rebecca's age. She wore her dark hair in a loose ponytail tied with a black plaid ribbon. The Temple Mead blazer and skirt somehow looked more fashionable on her, as though it was a costume rather than an ugly uniform. Behind her stood an elderly black man, wearing a khaki raincoat, carefully lowering an umbrella.

"I'll be back for you after school, Miss Helena," he said, and the girl turned away without speaking. She looked at Rebecca and paused for a moment, a bemused and haughty look on her face. Rebecca didn't feel hot anymore: A chill rippled down her spine.

This Helena was very pretty, Rebecca thought, but there was something about her — something imperious or spoiled — that made her look unhappy. The girl said nothing; she walked up the sweeping staircase with slow, deliberate steps, clearly unconcerned about being late. The old man nodded over at Rebecca and then stepped outside again. She heard the umbrella click open and then footsteps slapping down the wet stairs. Surely he wasn't this girl's personal umbrella holder? Rebecca thought only narcissistic celebrities paid people to do things like that. It didn't seem possible that a girl her age would have someone to escort her to school in the rain. Why couldn't she carry her own umbrella?

Rebecca decided to ask Aurelia about her after school, although after she was ushered into the office of the principal — Miss Vale, a petite, elegant, middle-aged woman who seemed too busy to even *look* at Rebecca — and then led to her first class, she quickly forgot about Helena. There was so much to take in that first day. Her new teachers were OK — no one too mean, no one especially nice. The history teacher asked Rebecca where she came from and then wrinkled her nose at the words "New York." The math teacher grumbled for a while about Rebecca starting the semester so late, and the only male teacher she had all day, for French, looked distraught when he realized the class now had twenty-one students: He liked the girls to work on spoken exercises in pairs, he said, and then paused, as though he was waiting for Rebecca to offer to leave.

She felt the same way about the girls as she did the teachers — nobody was awful, but nobody was particularly friendly. Or maybe that was unfair: Maybe it was Rebecca who didn't feel very friendly. Back in New York, she was used to having a large group of friends, many of whom she'd known for years. The thought of starting all over again in a new place wasn't very appealing, especially as she'd only be here for a while.

Luckily, the principal had commissioned two other tenth-graders from her homeroom to eat lunch with her, so Rebecca didn't have to sit by herself. Temple Mead's lunchroom, with its corniced ceiling and shining floorboards, looked more like a ballroom than a cafeteria, though it had the same long skinny tables and beaten-up plastic chairs as Stuyvesant. Amy and Jessica, the girls looking after her, showed Rebecca where to pick up food, and then led her to a table near the window.

"Y'all have a lunchroom like this in New York?" Jessica asked her. She was a redhead with gold-rimmed glasses, and sometimes it was hard to tell if she was speaking or just giggling. Rebecca nodded, sipping from her bottle of iced tea.

"I'd love to go there," sighed Amy. She was Jessica's best friend, a skinny girl whose blazer looked two sizes too big. They'd been in the same class every year since they were six years old, they told Rebecca while they were standing in line. "Sometimes we drive to Houston to go shopping, but I wish we could go to New York."

Amy and Jessica had the same strange accent as everyone else Rebecca had met so far, and it wasn't at all drawly and Southern in the way she'd been expecting. It was true that they said "y'all," but she was surprised to hear that people in New Orleans sounded more like New Yorkers than hayseeds.

"We're going to Dallas at Thanksgiving, so my mother can get her dresses for the balls," Jessica giggled.

"The balls?"

"Yeah, you know."

Rebecca shrugged. None of the mothers she knew in New York went to balls — but then, none of them lived in white-columned mansions, either.

"During the season," Amy explained, putting down her grilled cheese sandwich. "Carnival. Mardi Gras."

"I thought that was all parades and stuff," said Rebecca, trying to think of the few things she knew about New Orleans.

Amy and Jessica exchanged bewildered glances.

"There are way more balls than parades," Jessica said. Her mouth twitched into a nervous smile. "And everyone here — all their fathers belong to a krewe."

"Like a rowing crew?"

"No!" they said in unison. Jessica slapped a hand over her mouth to stifle an eruption of giggles.

"Krewe with a *k*," Amy explained, enunciating carefully, as though Rebecca was slow in the head. "A krewe is like a club, a private club. Each krewe organizes its own parade during Carnival, and throws a huge ball afterward."

"The ball's the most important thing," Jessica agreed. "The old-line krewes — their balls are really exclusive. By invitation only. That's where the daughters and granddaughters of krewe members make their debuts. All the krewes wear costumes — and masks to disguise their identities. It's amazing."

Rebecca tried to look interested, but talk of masked old men and debutante balls made her feel even more out of place here. She didn't even know things like this still went on in America, and she couldn't really visualize them. All she could think of was Zorro and maybe the Ku Klux Klan dropping into a Jane Austen movie.

"The newer krewes *sell* tickets to their balls," Amy whispered, her eyes wide, as though she was communicating a shocking secret.

"We'll explain everything to you," tittered Jessica. She carefully licked the thin coat of ketchup off a french fry. "Don't worry."

"There's so much you need to know," Amy said, shaking her head. "About how things are done here, and what's important. School stuff as well."

"Like, we're not allowed on the back gallery during classes or in the side yard at any time unless we have gym. Or to sit on the front steps, ever," Jessica told her.

"Or to leave the school grounds during lunch unless we have written permission."

"And whatever you do, don't run along the street when you're wearing your school uniform. They hate that. We're supposed to comport ourselves as young ladies at all times."

"Young ladies," agreed Amy, her mouth full of sandwich, and both girls started giggling again. But Rebecca got the feeling they weren't laughing *at* the rules, exactly. They just laughed whenever they couldn't think of anything else to say.

Rebecca tried her best to smile back at them, but her heart was sinking. She didn't want to comport herself like a young lady or sit giggling with Jessica and Amy at lunchtime; Mardi Gras parades might be fun, but she didn't care one iota about the exclusive men's clubs that ran them. She missed her friends back home. And however much the Stuyvesant girls liked to complain about the boys at school — about how loud they were, and how they were only interested in boring things like baseball and Xbox — Rebecca kind of missed having those boys around.

"We have a formal dance every spring," Jessica was telling her, gesturing with another french fry. "You have to go with a boy from St. Simeon's . . ."

"You *have* to," agreed Amy. "Don't even think about going with a boy from another school. It's social death."

"What if you don't know any of the boys at St. Simeon's?" Rebecca couldn't help asking. Jessica and Amy stared at her.

"Well, usually your family knows his family," said Jessica, half swallowing her simpering laugh. "Or your brother or cousin or someone introduces you to a guy there. We could find someone for you, maybe. Someone who doesn't have a date already. Like Toby Sutton!"

Amy burst out laughing, and Jessica joined in; they were rocking back and forth, almost in tears. Rebecca didn't know what was so hilarious.

"Sorry," Amy managed to choke. She lowered her voice. "It's just . . . it's just that Toby Sutton is this really ugly, mean boy."

"Sssshhhh!" Jessica warned her.

"*You* brought him up!"

"He's Marianne Sutton's brother," Jessica whispered. "But he's not like her at all — she's real sweet. But he was almost expelled from St. Simeon's last year."

"Why?"

"They say he tried to set the school library on fire," hissed Amy.

"You don't know that for sure!" Jessica hissed back, nervously glancing around the room.

"And then the Suttons had to donate *half a million dollars* to the library restoration fund, so he could get let back into school."

"Really?"

"That's what I heard. Anyway, I'm sure we can find someone better to take you to the Spring Dance. Though it *is* the social event of the year. Apart from Helena Bowman's Christmas party, that is. Not that you'll get invited to that!"

They both started tittering again.

"I think I saw Helena Bowman this morning," Rebecca told them, trying not to be annoyed by their private jokes. "Is she tall, with dark hair?"

Jessica gave a long, solemn nod.

"She's dark and Marianne is blonde. They're both juniors. And best friends."

"Helena's more beautiful," said Amy.

"Marianne's nicer," muttered Jessica, but Amy ignored her.

"Helena lives in the best house. It's one of the biggest and oldest in the Garden District. All the tour buses stop there. Her ancestors were, like, one of the first families to live here. And her father is in Septimus."

Rebecca must have looked as puzzled as she felt, because both girls started talking at once, explaining that Septimus was one of the old-line carnival krewes and that their parade was one of the most spectacular every year. It even had a unique route, looping back along the river and curling up toward the Garden District, rather than ending downtown. The year after the storm they didn't hold a parade, but since then Septimus parades had been bigger and more spectacular than ever. They were planning a huge one this winter, the Friday before Mardi Gras.

"Helena's ancestors founded the krewe right after the Civil War," Jessica whispered, as though she was passing on classified information. "Only the oldest and richest families in this area are members."

That counted out Aunt Claudia, Rebecca thought. She wasn't rich, Aurelia's father was some Cuban who'd disappeared before he ever saw his daughter — or got around to marrying Aunt Claudia — and the little house on Sixth Street had only been in her family since the 1940s, when the Garden District was pretty run-down and the smaller houses, at any rate, were going cheap.

"So *you've* been to Helena's party?" she asked. Amy looked crestfallen, and Jessica gave a nervous giggle that turned into a hiccup.

"We're not in with — you know, Them," she explained.

"That's what everyone calls Helena and her friends," whispered Amy. "Them."

"Why?" asked Rebecca, pushing her plate away.

"They don't have the same rules as the rest of us," said Jessica. "They kind of get special treatment — better than the seniors, even."

"Like being allowed to arrive late?" Rebecca thought of Helena, strolling in this morning after the bell had rung.

"Yeah." Jessica nodded. "And after the storm, when the whole school evacuated to Houston for a semester, and we all had to go to classes there, Helena didn't have to show up. Someone said her family went to their place in Aspen instead."

"Make sure you don't annoy Helena," said Amy, raising her eyebrows. "Or Marianne."

"How could I annoy them?" Rebecca asked. This was a strange warning — Helena and Marianne were a year older, so that meant they wouldn't be in any of her classes. And somehow she doubted that Aunt Claudia moved in the same lofty social circles as "Them." In fact, she doubted that Aunt Claudia moved in any sort of social circle at all, apart from the circle of people who sat in deck chairs around Jackson Square, telling fortunes or selling souvenir watercolors.

"You're sort of, you know, an outsider," said Jessica, with a sympathetic shrug of her shoulders. "You might not know the right thing to do or say when you're around them."

"The *right* thing?"

"Just — if they talk to you, be real polite," advised Amy, leaning over her tray as though she didn't want anyone else to hear: Rebecca had to snatch at her arm to stop Amy from dipping one sleeve into some ketchup. "They could make a lot of trouble for you if they don't like you."

Rebecca said nothing, but she thought this was kind of ridiculous. She wasn't going to be intimidated by two snooty juniors. And what trouble could they make for her? Not invite her to their boring Christmas party? Keep her away from the lame-sounding boys of St. Simeon's?

"You don't have to worry about me," she told Amy and

Jessica, and gave them a false cheerful grin. They both looked relieved – probably for their own sakes, she decided later. If Rebecca was going to be some kind of social pariah, they didn't want to be dragged down with her. And even though this was just her first day, Rebecca had a niggling feeling that she wasn't going to fit in very easily here at Temple Mead and that Jessica and Amy would start avoiding her the second they realized this as well.

CHAPTER FOUR

BY THE END OF THE DAY, REBECCA FELT WORN-out and dispirited. The layout of the school was confusing: It seemed to be a maze of locked doors, roped-off staircases, and dark hallways that led nowhere in particular. Aurelia had all her classes in the more modern building next door, so she wasn't around to help point Rebecca in the right direction.

The rain had dwindled to an intermittent drizzle. Rebecca waited for Aurelia on the steps outside, relieved when she saw her little "cousin" bouncing toward her, another girl — blonde and grinning — in tow. If only Aurelia were older: She and Rebecca could hang out at school. But there was quite a division between what was called the junior and the senior school at Temple Mead, and Rebecca was realizing that they were never going to see each other during the day.

"This is Claire," Aurelia announced breathlessly. "She lives on Third Street. Her house is, like, three times as big as ours."

"But everything in it is so boring," Claire complained as

they all wandered toward the main gate. "You have all that cool stuff, like the monkey skull and the dried bat."

"I haven't seen the dried bat yet," Rebecca told her, thinking how disgusting that sounded.

"Marilyn ate it," said Aurelia breezily.

"My mother says Relia's mother is descended from a voodoo queen," Claire confided. "Which is why she looks all crazy. And why she 'Sees Things.'"

"Sees what kind of things?" Rebecca was curious. They passed the long line of luxury cars idling outside the school gates and strolled along Prytania.

"Oh, you know," said Aurelia, taking long steps to avoid cracks on the sidewalk. "Like the future and the past. Though sometimes she's not sure what she's seeing."

"My sister says she just makes it all up to get money out of tourists." Claire lowered her voice. "But my sister doesn't know anything. She's just a Pleb."

"A what?"

"A Pleb. Short for PLEB-ee-an. We learned about them in Latin."

"I think you pronounce it plib-EE-un."

"Whatever!" Aurelia was almost doing the splits, which was probably against school rules, Rebecca thought. "We say Pleb because it rhymes with Deb, and everyone is pretty much either a Pleb or a Deb."

"What are you talking about?" Rebecca was confused.

"Well," said Claire, dumping her schoolbag on the ground. "In Roman society, there were various classes, right? At the top were the patricians, who ran everything and got to be emperor. At Temple Mead, that's Them."

"Oh." Rebecca nodded. "I heard about 'Them' today. Helena Bowman, right? And Marianne . . . is it Sutton? Those are the names I remember."

"Not bad," Aurelia said approvingly. "Who told you about Them?"

"I had lunch with two girls from my homeroom. Amy and Jessica."

"Jessica Frobisher? She's my cousin!" Claire rolled her eyes. "She's a Pleb."

"Totally," agreed Aurelia.

"OK, so it's the Patricians and then the Plebs . . ."

"No. Between them there are two other classes. First, the senatorial class, who were all really ambitious and got to wear special togas."

"With purple stripes," added Aurelia, and Claire nodded. They were so in earnest that Rebecca couldn't help laughing.

"They're the Debs, see? They want to be Patricians, but they can't make it in. So instead they laud it over everyone else. They're on all the committees and boring stuff like that. And they're all obsessed with balls and parties. The thing they want most is to be queen of a carnival krewe the year they're debutantes."

"So that's why they're Debs and not . . . Sens?" Rebecca ventured.

"Exactly." Aurelia nodded. "And then there's the equestrian class. They're the girls who represent the school in sports."

"Tennis, volleyball, soccer," said Claire, sniffing. "Though they're not very good at any of them. We always get our butts kicked by Country Day and St. Louisa's."

"But the school loves them and gives them prizes and things all the time."

"And they wear those ugly bandages on their knees and elbows."

"So you call them . . . ?" The complexities of all this were overwhelming.

"The Cavalry," Aurelia and Claire said together.

"And then there are the Plebs, right?" Rebecca was starting to make some sense of their "class" system.

"They were the workers of Rome," Claire explained, scratching her messy blonde hair ferociously until a stray bobby pin tumbled onto the ground.

"The mob," sang Aurelia.

"The emperor made sure they stayed happy by arranging chariot races and gladiator fights. In return, the Plebs did their work and stayed in the background and didn't rebel or anything."

"And that's what Amy and Jessica are — Plebs?" Rebecca tried to suppress her smile.

"Practically everyone is," sighed Claire. "Except us, of course."

"What are you two?"

"Goddesses!" grinned Aurelia.

"Can I be a goddess as well?" Rebecca asked. She'd played some basketball at school, but doubted that she could make it into the Cavalry: She wasn't sure that Temple Mead even had a basketball team. The Debs wouldn't have her, and being a Pleb didn't sound very appealing.

"Hmmm." Claire screwed up her face. "You're from

somewhere else, so maybe you could be a goddess in another religion. Or — I know! You could be Cleopatra."

"I don't know about that," Rebecca laughed. "She ended up dying tragically, remember?"

"But she was glamorous and fascinating," said Claire, picking up her bag. "And Marc Antony gave up *everything* to be with her."

"Didn't do him much good," Rebecca said wryly, and both Claire and Aurelia looked sad, as though Marc Antony was a personal friend of theirs. "Humiliated in battle and then forced to kill himself."

"So romantic, right? Oh, no — I'm going to be late for ballet!" Claire sped away down Third Street, and with that Rebecca's Latin lesson came to an end.

But during lunchtimes the rest of that first week, when Rebecca either sat alone or managed to find a seat with Jessica and Amy — who made little effort to include her in any conversations — she realized that Claire and Aurelia might be onto something. A few members of the Cavalry stomped around the lunchroom, wearing their elastic bandages; a tableful of Debs conducted an overloud conversation on Who Was Wearing What to the first debutante ball of the season. The vast majority seemed to be Plebs — girls like Jessica and Amy who weren't going to win too many academic prizes, sporting accolades, or popularity contests, but were happy to cheer everyone else on. These were the girls who filled the ranks of what was known as the school's dance troupe, though

Rebecca quickly learned that "dancer" here meant a majorette without a baton who marched in a dozen parades during carnival season, accompanied — of course — by the St. Simeon's school band. And instead of gladiator fights and chariot races, the Plebs looked forward to the Spring Dance.

That Friday, Rebecca left the lunchroom early: She wanted to find the library and maybe take out a book or two on the Roman Empire. She thought she knew the way but, after several wrong turns, she was completely disoriented. Maybe her good sense of direction only applied in the streets of New York, where everything was on a grid: The long, dark hallways of Temple Mead made no sense to her. And then the bell was ringing, and the corridors and stairs filled with girls hurrying to class. The library trip had to be abandoned.

Climbing the stairs to the third floor, Rebecca heard someone calling her name. She turned her head to look, but couldn't see anyone in the sea of plaid uniforms that she recognized. Then she felt a hand on her elbow, drawing her away to the side. The girl pulling Rebecca over was a willowy blonde with wide, penetrating blue eyes: Marianne Sutton. And behind her, leaning against the banister and looking bored, as though she were waiting for a bus, was Helena Bowman.

"It *is* Rebecca, isn't it?" Marianne asked her in an imperious tone, and Rebecca nodded. "You're new here, aren't you?"

Rebecca nodded again. She couldn't quite bring herself to speak — not because she was intimidated by Marianne and Helena, but because she didn't want to act like she was yet another of their humble servants.

"And your last name is Brown?" Marianne asked, frowning.

"Yes." Rebecca figured she should speak rather than keep nodding, though she couldn't believe the rudeness of this girl. Marianne hadn't bothered to introduce herself — she'd just assumed that Rebecca would know who she was. She probably thought Rebecca would be honored by the attention.

"Do you have a middle name?" This wasn't the first time Rebecca had been asked this question. Some of her classmates had very strange first and middle names: There was a girl in biology whose first name was Buchanan, and Amy's middle name was Claiborne. Both Buchanan and Claiborne were family names — a mother or grandmother's maiden name. Amy explained that it let everyone else know where you came from, who your "people" were. It seemed really important to these girls that they were part of the history of the city and that everybody knew it.

"So?" Marianne sounded impatient. "What is it?"

Rebecca was tempted to say "Cleopatra," but she knew they'd never believe her. Helena, who had been staring off into the distance up until now, turned her cool gaze onto Rebecca. This look, combined with the tone of Marianne's voice, made Rebecca's blood boil. They weren't even pretending to be friendly: They were just being blatantly rude and nosy. Whoever Rebecca's "people" were, she knew they wouldn't be good enough for these girls.

"Actually, I have two," she said, trying to sound as frosty as Marianne. This was a lie: Rebecca didn't have a middle name at all. "Maria Annunciata."

"You're kidding." Marianne looked confused. Helena's pretty face hardened into a sneer.

"I'm named after my grandmother. My mother's from El Salvador," Rebecca continued, deciding to make her lie even more brazen. "She used to be a maid. That's how she met my father — he was a doorman at the same hotel."

Marianne said nothing, but dropped the hand on Rebecca's elbow. Rebecca knew this would happen: Both Marianne and Helena were huge snobs, just as she suspected. How dare they look down at her!

Rebecca hurried up the stairs away from them, her face hot with anger. But she couldn't help laughing when she thought about Marianne's amazed expression. At least, she thought, neither of them would ever bother her again. And she wouldn't have to worry about the pyromaniac Toby Sutton asking her to the Spring Dance, either.

The sooner the word got out at Temple Mead about her humble — if invented — Hispanic origins, the better. Rebecca didn't care what any of them thought of her. And she planned to spend as little time as possible thinking about *Them*.

CHAPTER FIVE

WHEN REBECCA AND AURELIA ARRIVED HOME from school that day, Aunt Claudia was still out, reading tarot cards down in the French Quarter. Rebecca was glad: She wasn't in the mood to answer any "how was your first week at school?" questions. Amy and Jessica sat with her at lunchtime because they'd been told to, but they were never going to be real friends. Nobody else talked to her much. And in all her classes, Rebecca felt out of step: The curriculum in Louisiana was completely different from the one she'd been following in New York. In every subject she was either way ahead and bored — or way behind and confused.

It wasn't hot — more like a mild day in spring rather than a late fall afternoon, something else to confuse and frustrate her — but Rebecca's school uniform felt as though it was stifling and scratching her half to death. Hanging up her blazer, she accidentally jostled one of the voodoo decorations on her bedroom wall, almost knocking the stick doll to the floor. These stupid things were just one more irritation.

"Right," she said aloud. "That's it."

Aurelia's curly head poked around the bedroom door. "Were you talking to me?" she asked, wide-eyed.

"I want to clear these things out of here," Rebecca told her, pointing at the gaping mask and a rough-edged hanging box added by Aunt Claudia just this week. "I'm sick of bumping into them, and they creep me out, anyway."

"We could put them up in the attic," suggested Aurelia. At least *she* was always friendly. "If you can help me get the ladder out."

Rebecca was surprised to hear a house this small had an attic, but once they'd climbed the stepladder, moved aside a panel in the hallway ceiling, and hauled themselves up into the triangle below the roof, she realized that "attic" was a slight exaggeration. This was an unfinished crawl space: Aurelia was small enough to walk around hunch-shouldered, teetering on the narrow beams, but Rebecca had to stay on her hands and knees, careful to stick to the grid of rafters so she didn't plummet through the insulation tiles into the room below.

The small space was already crowded with boxes and suitcases and a dusty trunk. With some difficulty, Aurelia held up an axe with a wooden handle to show Rebecca: This, she said, was there in case the Mississippi ever burst its banks and they had to escape into the attic and hack their way onto the roof to be rescued. As far as Rebecca knew, this was their one concession to a "hurricane preparedness" kit.

Rebecca pushed the cardboard box packed with the relics into one corner, getting more grumpy by the second. It was so stuffy up here, and her knees ached, crawling over the wooden rafters. Her fingertips brushed the spiky legs of a dead cockroach: It was all she could do not to cry out.

When the box was stashed in the corner, next to a dusty plaid suitcase that looked as though it had been there since 1962, Rebecca lay on her back for a moment, worn out. Aurelia sat down, too, picking at the fluff of an insulation pad.

"Guess what?" She looked at Rebecca and then glanced away again. "I know where Helena and her friends are going tonight."

Rebecca closed her eyes.

"I don't care about them, Relia. They're just mean snobs who need to get out of this town and get a clue." What was the point in knowing where Helena conducted her social life? It would just be another place for Rebecca to get snubbed or looked down on. She'd had enough of "Them" at school today.

"Not just Helena — boys as well. The ones from St. Simeon's." Aurelia lowered her voice and leaned toward Rebecca. "They go to the cemetery."

"Really?" This wasn't what Rebecca was expecting to hear.

"Last Friday, I woke up in the middle of the night because I could hear people laughing outside. And then I thought I heard Marilyn cry, the way she does when she's caught something she wants to show me. Sometimes it's a bird, sometimes a rat. So I got up to look for her and . . . and . . ."

Rebecca opened her eyes and gazed up at Aurelia: Her cousin was almost too excited to speak.

"And what happened?"

"I went to the front parlor and looked out the window. They were at the cemetery gates — Helena and some other girls and all these boys. They had a key for the gates. Helena was acting like a big phony, because she was pretending it was cold when it wasn't cold at all. She was shivering and jumping up and down until one of the boys put his school blazer around her shoulders. I don't know why she did that."

"She's a fake," said Rebecca, wondering how they got a key for the cemetery gate and what they got up to inside — drinking, probably.

"I think it was Anton Grey," Aurelia continued. "Everyone loves him the best. Claire wants to marry him, and I bet Helena does, too."

"Come on," said Rebecca, smiling at her. Presumably this Anton Grey was Claire's local Marc Antony substitute. "Let's go back downstairs before your mother gets home."

"Maybe they'll be back tonight," Aurelia whispered. "You can see for yourself, if you don't mind staying up really late and sneaking around the house in the dark."

That night, after everyone was in bed, Rebecca lay wide awake. It should be cold this time of year, she thought, but instead the night was almost sultry, too warm for sleeping. Her mind was whirring: She'd told Aurelia she wasn't interested in what Helena and her gang got up to in the cemetery, but Rebecca couldn't help wondering why the group chose there, of all places, to hang out. Her aunt had told her that the cemetery was dangerous and that it was locked every night, but rules didn't seem to apply to Helena, Marianne, and the other Patricians.

Rebecca tried closing her eyes and willing herself to go to sleep, and then she heard something outside the house — a surge of voices, the sound of not-too-distant laughter. She pushed off her bedclothes and glanced at her bedside clock: It was nearly midnight. Maybe the noise was just some neighbors coming home from a party, but there was no harm in checking. She opened her door carefully, so it didn't squeak, and tiptoed down the hallway to the room they called the parlor.

Aunt Claudia had been in bed for over an hour — Rebecca had heard her shuffle around as usual and the click of her door closing. Rebecca didn't want to wake up her aunt and have to answer questions about what she was up to. Not that her aunt was mean in any way: She'd been nothing but warm and kind all week, and Rebecca was already feeling guilty about removing the voodoo ornaments from her walls. Aunt Claudia seemed to be a good-hearted person, despite her many eccentricities, her odd choice in home furnishings, and her paranoia about unseen dangers.

In the parlor, transformed by the darkness into an obstacle course of sharp-edged furniture and dangerously teetering knickknacks, Rebecca pulled one curtain back far enough to peep out. She caught her breath: Just as Aurelia had said, a group of teenagers was gathered by the Sixth Street cemetery gate. Although none of them was wearing the school uniform, she recognized the four girls in the group from school — Helena, Marianne, and two other junior girls who were part of Helena's "Them" coterie.

Three boys were there, too, one of whom was already at the gate, rattling its bars and making the others laugh;

another balanced a carton of beer on his head. The third boy, the tallest of them all, seemed to be the one with the key. He waited until the others moved out of the way, then he clicked open the padlock and dragged out the chain holding the gates together. The group disappeared into the walled confines of the cemetery.

They'd left the gate ajar, Rebecca noticed, and in an instant made up her mind: She was going to sneak in and spy on them. Why not? She'd never been someone who scared easily, and anyway, if the cemetery was full of real dangers or horrific sights, snooty girls like Helena and Marianne would keep a mile away from it. Back in her bedroom, Rebecca pulled on sweatpants and her hoodie, quietly digging out her running shoes and slipping her house key into her pocket. It would be better if she had a flashlight, but her eyes would adjust to the gloom, she decided.

As Rebecca drew open the front door, Marilyn whooshed past her, streaking down the porch steps and out the front gate. The night was cloudy: It was hard to make out the moon and the stars, and Rebecca had to squint to see where Marilyn was headed. No surprise — the cat was darting through the open gates of the cemetery. All Rebecca had to do was follow her lead.

CHAPTER SIX

AS SHE STEPPED THROUGH THE UNLOCKED CEMetery gates, Rebecca swallowed hard. She'd come this far — she *had* to go on. The cemetery was pitch-black and eerie. The huge tombs with their towering urns and crosses — visible from the Verniers' house in daylight, just indistinct menacing shapes in the darkness — loomed over her. The place seemed like a scaled-down city in a blackout, with too many confusing alleys. Its pathways were dark tunnels, leading in every direction. She couldn't see or hear the group she'd followed: They'd left the central path and disappeared down one of the alleys. It was almost as though the cemetery had swallowed them up.

A sudden movement near her feet startled her, and it was all Rebecca could do not to shriek. Marilyn brushed against Rebecca's leg, giving her usual plaintive meow. When the cat trotted away down one of the overgrown pathways, Rebecca decided to keep following her. Marilyn was one of the cemetery's daily denizens: Maybe she knew where Helena and Co.

were hiding out. Anything was better than just standing at the entrance, not knowing what to do next.

Marilyn didn't stick to the path, so neither did Rebecca, tripping over stairs, raised edges, and cracked paving stones, doing her best not to fall down or cry out. Before long her eyes started focusing a little, so she stopped banging into things so much, and soon she could hear something more than the whispering breeze — the affected, tinkly laugh of one of the girls. Rebecca slowed her pace, gingerly making her way closer to the source of the sound. As she got closer, she heard the clink of bottles and one of the boys talking in a loud voice. When Rebecca was close enough to glimpse the top of someone's head, she ducked behind a giant boxlike grave. They mustn't see her: *That* would be the worst possible thing.

Rebecca crawled around in the shadows until she found a vantage point, squeezed between two tombs, that seemed relatively safe. The group was sprawled around the steps of a particularly imposing vault, one with intricate decorations — carved wreaths of ivy, as far as Rebecca could make out — and the name GREY etched into its central arch. Flickering candles stuck in empty wine bottles, rivulets of wax running down the glass, gave the scene a ghostly glow.

Three of the girls sat encircling the shortest of the boys; his face was animated, and he was speaking very quickly, despite the girls' constant interruptions and questions, about plans for something . . . maybe the next Septimus parade. Rebecca could only catch snatches of the conversation, talk of new "throws" and costumes. Carnival was three months away, she thought: Didn't these kids have anything else to think about? A second boy, beefy and redheaded, was trying to juggle two empty beer bottles. Helena sat a short distance from the rest, a flirtatious smirk on her face, fingering a silver cigarette lighter that the tall, dark-haired boy had handed to her.

Rebecca couldn't help staring at the dark-haired boy. His face was angular, and though he was tall, he didn't seem gawky or clumsy. Even in the semidarkness, she could tell he was better looking than the other two boys, and there wasn't any arrogance in his expression. In fact, he seemed quite preoccupied, leaning back against the neighboring tomb, staring off into space. Every few minutes he took a swig from a bottle of beer. She wondered if this was the famous Anton Grey, the one Claire was in love with: This had to be his family's tomb. It was a weird place to hang out, Rebecca thought, but then, these were weird kids.

"Yo, check this out!" The beefy kid threw the two empty beer bottles high into the air and managed to catch just one; the other smashed into pieces on the concrete ground.

"God, Toby!" hissed Marianne. "You're so immature."

Rebecca grinned. The wannabe juggler was Toby, Marianne's brother. Amy and Jessica were right: He *was* ugly and mean.

"Let me try with this," he said, grabbing at the silver cigarette lighter in Helena's hand. Rebecca, crouching low in her hiding place, couldn't see what happened next, but she could tell that Toby and Anton were having some kind of scuffle. No wonder, she thought: If Toby was ready to burn down the school library, he wouldn't think twice about setting fire to the bushes in a cemetery.

"Don't touch it again," Anton snapped.

"I know, I know," said Toby, his voice mocking. "It's a *family heirloom*. Chill out!"

"Hey, look!" said one of the girls — her name was Julie Casworth Young, Rebecca remembered. Amy had said that all the younger girls at school who idolized her, copying her hairstyle and buying the same bag, always referred to her as J.C. "It's that cute kitty again."

Marilyn had materialized out of the darkness, brushing against Anton's legs. Rebecca held her breath, hoping that Marilyn didn't bound over and reveal her hiding place. But before Marilyn could wander off again, Toby reached down and grabbed the cat. He raised her aloft, laughing maniacally, and then dangled her over one of the lit candles. Marilyn wriggled and meowed, her eyes glinting in the dark. Julie and Marianne were protesting, telling Toby to leave the cat alone, but Toby kept swinging Marilyn's writhing little body over the naked flame. Rebecca was so enraged she wanted to jump to her feet and smack Toby in the mouth. She didn't want these idiots to know she was spying on them, but Marilyn's snowy paws were dipping closer and closer to the flame: What was Rebecca going to do? Just watch?

"Cut it out," said Anton, and he shoved Toby so hard the redheaded boy staggered backward, dropping Marilyn. The scared cat shot away, speeding straight toward Rebecca's hiding place and managing, somehow, despite the tight space, to zoom past. Rebecca lost her balance, falling from her wobbly crouch onto the soft ground. Inadvertently, she gasped and then held her breath again, worried that she'd be found out.

"What was that?" This was Helena's voice, edgy and high-pitched. "Did anyone else hear that?"

"Did you lock the gate behind us?" Marianne asked.

"I thought so, but maybe not," Anton replied. "I'll go check."

He sloped away along the cracked concrete path. A wave of red-hot panic swept through Rebecca: She had to get back to the gate before Anton, otherwise she'd be locked in. The walls were too high to climb and — unlike Marilyn — she wasn't tiny enough to squeeze through the bars of the gate. But how would she find her way back through this maze of tombs?

She scrambled away as quietly as she could and as quickly as she dared, trying to remember the circuitous route she'd taken on the way in. Nothing seemed familiar in this confusing forest of stone; every one of these grand tombs looked and felt the same. Rebecca kept running, stumbling over broken slates, stubbing her toes on tree roots, but somehow managing to keep her balance. Yet there was no escaping the fact that she was lost. She had no idea if she was running in the right direction.

The cemetery's main path was shaped like a cross, each branch leading to a gate: What if she got completely disoriented and ended up at the wrong one? Anton was following the path, and he'd been here before. He was sure to reach the right gate before her. Rebecca would have to spend a miserable night alone in the cemetery and wait for the caretaker to unlock it in the morning. By then her aunt would have discovered she was missing, called the police, called her father . . . she would be in *so* much trouble.

Rounding a corner, Rebecca tripped on the protruding

edge of a paving stone and fell to the ground with a thump. She had fallen onto a path, she realized: Her hands stung where the concrete had scraped them, and she could hear the soft sound of approaching footsteps. Then the footsteps stopped. It had to be Anton, looking at her sprawled on the ground, and for a moment Rebecca was too scared, too annoyed with herself, to look up. The person standing right by her said nothing, and she felt even more nervous. What if this wasn't Anton at all, but one of the dangerous men her aunt said loitered in the cemetery?

Rebecca slowly raised her head. The clouds obscuring the moon moved, and a strange silvery light brought the tombs around her into focus.

The person standing over her wasn't Anton or any other guy. It was a black girl, about her age, looking down at Rebecca with curious interest. Her hair was long, hanging to one side in a loose braid. Her white blouse was ripped at one shoulder, and she was fingering her dark skirt, twitching it back and forth as though she was shooing flies.

The girl and Rebecca stared at each other without speaking; she looked about as startled as Rebecca felt.

"Do you . . . do you know the way out of here?" Rebecca asked, pulling herself to her feet and dusting herself off. Her voice was breathy: She was almost hyperventilating with anxiety. "The Sixth Street gate?"

The girl said nothing for a moment, gazing at Rebecca. She had a sweet, pretty face, her skin a flawless bronze; her dark eyes looked uncertain, as though she was a little afraid. She wasn't wearing shoes, Rebecca noticed, and her shabby blouse was thin: She had to be cold on a breezy November night like this.

"That way," she said at last, pointing. She gave Rebecca a slow, hesitant smile.

"Thanks," said Rebecca, backing away. It seemed rude to run off, but she had to get out of here before Anton locked her in or saw her making her escape. The girl was standing still, just gazing at her. Rebecca gave her a grateful wave and started running.

When she skidded through the gate and bolted down the sidewalk toward home, Rebecca wasn't sure what was pounding the loudest — her feet or her heart. Back on the front porch, she fumbled for the key and slipped inside without daring to look back. She closed the door, wincing when it clicked, and then tiptoed into the front parlor, to peek through the gap in the curtains.

The mysterious girl was nowhere to be seen. But there, standing at the cemetery gates, was Anton, tossing the key from one hand to the other. It was too dark to make out the expression on his face, but of one thing Rebecca was quite certain: He was staring straight at Aunt Claudia's house.

CHAPTER SEVEN

On Saturday morning, Rebecca couldn't stop thinking about the girl in the cemetery. What was she doing there so late at night? Maybe, like Rebecca, she'd wandered in through the open gate. Maybe the storm had made her homeless, and she had nowhere else to go. But three years was a long time to sleep in a cemetery, and the gates were locked every night, Aunt Claudia had explained, to keep the homeless out. The girl was lucky, Rebecca thought, remembering the bundled-up men who slept in doorways near her apartment back home, that it hardly ever snowed in New Orleans.

As soon as Aunt Claudia drove off to the French Quarter with her folding card table and striped deck chair, and Aurelia skipped over to a friend's house for a playdate, Rebecca decided to visit the cemetery again. The girl in the torn white blouse had done her a favor, helping her escape last night; maybe Rebecca could do something in return. The girl might be hungry or want something clean to wear.

For a minute, Rebecca wondered if the girl might be crazy or dangerous in some way, but this didn't seem likely. She had looked as frightened and surprised as Rebecca. Perhaps she was hiding from something — or someone — possibly the person who'd ripped her shirt. Whoever this girl was, Rebecca decided that she'd rather talk to her than to any of the snobby, self-involved girls at Temple Mead.

Rebecca walked to the open gates of the cemetery, and tried to retrace her footsteps from the night before. During the day, the cemetery felt like an entirely different place. It was an unseasonably warm day, the humidity almost thick enough to taste. Enclosed within its pale walls, the cemetery was a sun trap, its white tombs bright in the glare. It didn't feel like a looming forest of stone anymore, partly because of the little things Rebecca hadn't been able to see in the dark, like bunches of plastic flowers left in jars or pretty fleur-de-lis points on fences. A tour group meandered along the central pathway that linked the Sixth Street gate with its counterpart on Washington Avenue, everyone fluttering "Save Our Cemeteries" fans to try to keep cool.

The pathways she'd scrambled along last night — concrete giving way to grass, grass worn away to dirt in the cemetery's shadiest corners — were dusty and benign, though there were still too many of them, and some of the less-traveled routes were clumped with weeds and woven with knobbed tree roots. Rebecca couldn't even find her way back to the Grey family tomb, let alone remember her late-night path out.

Another tour group, all middle-aged people in ugly shorts and tragic sun visors, were stumping around after a woman in a yellow sundress; she was holding an umbrella aloft. Rebecca did her best to keep away from them. She couldn't see the girl in the torn blouse anywhere. In fact, the only other person she stumbled across was a drunken man asleep on one of the graves, one of his shoes — a bright green croc — lying nearby and an empty bottle encased in a paper bag drooping from his right hand. This freaked Rebecca out so much she sprinted away in the direction of the dreaded tour group again. They might dress like morons — a number of them were wearing purple, green, and gold plastic beads, she noticed, as though today was Mardi Gras — but at least they weren't scary.

Rebecca was lingering near the group, trying to catch her breath and deciding where to wander next, when she realized that the guide was talking about the Bowman tomb.

"That's the mansion, over there," the guide was saying, pointing to the gables of a tall charcoal gray house on Prytania Street, its upper floor visible through the trees. "Hard to believe there's a curse on it, right?"

People in the group were chuckling and shaking their heads.

"Looks like it survived the curse of Katrina!" one man shouted, and the tour guide gave a pained smile.

"It took a lot of storm damage," she said. "And work seems to be going on there all the time. But no, it wasn't destroyed. There wasn't any water in this neighborhood. And, according to the legend, it'll be fire, not wind, that brings the house down."

Rebecca stood on her tiptoes, straining to hear whatever else the guide had to say about this curse, but it was too late.

The group was moving on, ambling slowly in the searing afternoon heat toward the shade of a line of magnolia trees. Rebecca waited until they were out of the way before she walked up to the Bowman tomb.

It was fancy, just as she'd expected — big, like the Grey family's stone vault and topped with an ostentatious stone angel. The side of the tomb was etched with names dating back to 1850. Helena's name would be etched here one day, she mused, thinking how strange an idea that was. And then she corrected herself: Helena would get married one day and probably change her name. She'd marry someone like Anton Grey and end up etched on his family's tomb instead. Wasn't that the way things worked around here — all these rich families sticking together?

After another thirty minutes of walking around, Rebecca gave up. If the girl slept in the cemetery, she was nowhere to be found here during the day — or maybe she was just really good at hiding.

At school the next week, Rebecca decided to corner Amy and Jessica and see what information she could get out of them. At lunchtime, she slid her tray onto their table, noticing the way the girls exchanged unhappy glances when she sat down. Ever since she'd had that conversation on the stairs with Helena and Marianne, a lot of the Plebs had been kind of aloof to Rebecca. Helena and her friends must have spread the word that Rebecca was a lowborn outsider with a bad attitude, and nobody would dare contradict "Them," she suspected. Amy and Jessica were still friendly to her, more or less, but they weren't exactly inviting her to sit with them or inviting her to hang out after school.

"I wondered," Rebecca began, pausing to suck from her juice carton. "Have you guys ever heard anything about a curse on the Bowman mansion?"

Jessica nodded eagerly and then checked herself; Amy was giving her a disapproving stare.

"Well, sort of," she faltered, giving her usual nervous giggle. "I mean, you know. There's some old story."

"What kind of story?"

"An old voodoo curse," said Jessica. "Some old woman, like, a hundred years ago — she put a curse . . ."

"*Supposedly* put a curse," interjected Amy.

"Why?" Rebecca asked. She picked at her sandwich, trying not to look *too* interested.

"Someone was murdered there." Jessica lowered her voice. "And this old lady put a terrible curse on the family."

"The house," whispered Amy, jiggling in her seat. She seemed impatient with Jessica's version of the story. "It's the house that has a curse."

Jessica looked puzzled.

"But I thought there was something about . . ." She stopped talking abruptly, and bit into her sandwich, as though she couldn't trust herself to say another word.

"It's just some dumb old story," Amy told Rebecca. "Everyone makes up things like that about New Orleans and about the Garden District, especially. My father says they do it so there's a reason for tourists to come here. You shouldn't believe all the stories you hear."

Rebecca decided to try a different approach.

"Do people sleep in the cemetery?" she asked.

Jessica, her mouth full of sandwich, wrinkled her nose.

"Alive people, you mean?" she asked, and Amy pursed her lips.

"It's only open in the mornings," Amy replied. "And off-duty police patrol it. You could get locked in there, I guess. Nobody goes in that cemetery much but tourists and criminals, anyway."

The look she gave Rebecca suggested that one, or possibly both, of these labels applied to Rebecca herself.

But Rebecca didn't really need any help from the Plebs after all. That afternoon, walking home with Aurelia, she found her little cousin had plenty to say about the Bowman curse.

"They did some really bad things a long time ago," said Aurelia, dangling her almost-empty bag from one hand and jumping along the sidewalk to avoid the cracks. They were passing the long line of SUVs — Mercedes, Lexus, Porsche — that were parked outside the school every day, driven by the glossy blonde mothers of Temple Mead girls who lived farther uptown. "And they were cursed in perp . . . in perp . . ."

"In perpetuity?"

"Does that mean forever? Then, yes. And their house will burn down, and they'll all die, all seven of them."

"There are seven of them? But I thought Helena just had an older brother?"

Aurelia looked confused.

"I'm not sure about that part," she confessed.

"Will your mother know?" Rebecca asked, and Aurelia looked horrified.

"Don't ask Mama about this," she said, clutching Rebecca's sleeve. "We're not allowed to talk about the Bowmans, ever."

"Why not?"

"We have to . . . to keep away from them." Aurelia sounded less than certain. "Because they're not our kind of people."

"Well, I believe that," Rebecca said, "if you mean they're rich and snobby and —"

She stopped midsentence and came to a dead stop: There across the street, standing by the Prytania gate of the cemetery, was the girl she'd been looking for. In the daylight, her clothes looked even shabbier. She was dressed in the same waitresslike gear of white shirt and black skirt, and her feet were still bare.

"What is it?" asked Aurelia, who was still walking, but Rebecca didn't reply.

"Hey!" she called, waving frantically. The girl across the street glanced toward Rebecca, looking just as startled as she had on Friday night. Rebecca began crossing the street, walking toward her, but she had to wait for a moving truck to lumber by. By the time the truck had passed, and Rebecca could scamper to safety, the girl had disappeared.

For an instant, Rebecca thought she'd gone into the cemetery, but then she remembered that the gates were locked by this time every day. Could the girl have climbed over, somehow? She was nowhere to be seen along Prytania. Strange. Rebecca stood at the cemetery gate, peering through the bars, but the mystery girl was nowhere in sight.

"What are you doing?" Aurelia had followed her across the street. She gazed up at Rebecca, wide-eyed.

"I wanted to say hi to that girl," Rebecca explained. Aurelia looked puzzled.

"What girl?"

"The black girl standing right here. Didn't you see her?"

Aurelia shrugged.

"There's nobody around," she pointed out.

"Not now — she ran off. She's somewhere in the cemetery, I guess. Didn't you see her?"

"I didn't see anyone," said Aurelia, slowly shaking her mop of curls. "And the gate's locked."

"But you must have seen her!" Rebecca insisted. "She was standing there at the gate! I waved to her, and then she disappeared. She had long hair, and she was wearing . . . you *must* have noticed her!"

Aurelia shook her head again.

"Is this a game?" she asked Rebecca. "Are you trying to trick me?"

"Maybe you're going blind," said Rebecca, rolling her eyes.

"Or maybe you're seeing things," retorted Aurelia.

Maybe the girl had taken off so quickly that Aurelia didn't have time to notice her. Or maybe, Rebecca thought, her little cousin was right. Perhaps all those voodoo charms had worked their magic on her already, and she was going as crazy as Aunt Claudia, seeing things that weren't really there.

CHAPTER EIGHT

THAT FRIDAY NIGHT, REBECCA WAITED UNTIL HER aunt was asleep and then crept into the front parlor. As soon as Helena and her friends unlocked the cemetery, Rebecca was going to sneak back in.

All week, Rebecca had been planning this. If the strange girl was sleeping in the cemetery, she wouldn't want to be found out. That's probably why she ran away when Rebecca saw her during the day: Maybe the girl thought Rebecca was trying to get her into trouble or report her or something. But if they met again at night, when the cemetery was locked up and nobody else — no adults, at least — were around, she'd know that Rebecca was acting in good faith. Both would be somewhere they weren't supposed to be.

Sure enough, not long after midnight, the little band appeared again, headed for the Sixth Street gate. There were more kids than last week — eight, Rebecca counted — but no Helena. This wasn't really surprising: Helena had been out of school all week with the flu.

Once again, Anton let them all in with his key. Rebecca watched, holding her breath, to see if he would lock it this time. But after everyone stepped through the gate, Anton closed it and then, after a moment's hesitation, opened it again, leaving the gate slightly ajar. At first, Rebecca was relieved, but then she wondered if this was a trap. Maybe Anton was luring last week's intruder in, lying in wait to surprise her. She decided to hang around for a while, checking the time on her phone every few minutes until the longest quarter hour of her life had passed. Then she left the house, closing the door behind her quietly, and creeping down the street to the open gate.

This time Rebecca came prepared for her cemetery adventure. At the hardware store down on Magazine Street she'd bought a small flashlight. She paused at the entrance to the cemetery, shining her light in to see if anyone was around, and breathing a deep sigh when it revealed nothing but magnolia trees and tombs. Trying to make as little noise as possible, Rebecca made her way to the Grey family vault.

As she approached the tomb, Rebecca could hear the girls and boys talking and laughing as usual. Toby Sutton's obnoxious barking laugh boomed out, and she was well acquainted with Julie Casworth Young's annoying giggle by now — she sounded like a hyperventilating mouse. Rebecca clicked off her little flashlight, and ducked into the narrow, dank space between two tombs to make sure nobody could see her. All she wanted to do was make sure they were all there, all eight of them: Rebecca didn't want to bump into one of them when she began her exploring. And yes, the eight people she'd seen slipping into the cemetery all seemed to be there — nobody was waiting by the open gate to catch her, after all. Anton sat on the steps, his long legs stretched out, wincing at something Marianne was saying.

"I don't see what the big deal is," he said. "We spend all our time obsessing over these stupid things, when they're exactly the same every year."

"Excuse me if I don't see my best friend's party as *stupid*." Marianne sounded offended.

"What I mean is, all we talk about is Helena's party and the Septimus parade and the Spring Dance as though they're earth-shattering events, when the same people go to them every year and the same things happen every year. And there are so many other things we could be thinking about, you know?"

"Like what? Something manly like college football, I suppose?" Marianne was only pretending to be annoyed, Rebecca realized; really, she was trying to flirt with Anton. So much for Helena being her best friend.

"Look around you," Anton said, his voice serious. "This city is a mess. Three years after the storm and everything's still in chaos. Businesses are shut, houses are empty. Stoplights don't work. There are potholes as big as ponds in every street. The population's half what it used to be."

"Good riddance," sneered Toby. "We don't want poor people or criminals coming back to the city, anyway."

"You mean *black* people," said another guy, snickering. Rebecca tensed: These people disgusted her. How could Anton hang out with them? He seemed so much smarter.

"Oh my god," said Julie. From her hiding place, Rebecca

could only see Julie's feet; she was still wearing her school shoes, with their usual — decidedly nonregulation — purple laces. "You know, our gardener is living in Atlanta now, and the new guy my mother hired is from Mexico."

"Honduras," said someone else. "He's the same guy *my* mother hired."

"Whatever! He doesn't speak a word of English. I'm totally sure he's an illegal."

"Who cares? Someone has to cut the hedges!" said Toby, and Anton rolled his eyes, stirring as though he was about to get up. Marianne settled one long, pale hand on his leg.

"You can't drive yourself crazy about all this," she said in her silkiest voice. A slight breeze lifted wisps of blonde hair away from her face. "Remember what Helena says. We can't fix all the problems of New Orleans. They were there long before the storm, and long before we were born. But we *can* make New Orleans prettier and more fun."

"More fun for us, anyway," muttered Anton. He stood up, dusting down his jeans. "And that's all that matters, right?"

"I know you think parties and parades are silly. . . ."

"Yeah, but he still goes to them, don't you, buddy?" said Toby. He cracked open a bottle of beer and handed it to Anton. "He just likes to look down at everyone else."

"Shut up, Toby," said Marianne. Clearly, there wasn't much love lost between the Sutton siblings, Rebecca thought — or maybe Marianne really did have designs on Anton, and needed to take advantage of Helena's absence to make her big move.

"He's right," said Anton. He looked pensive, almost depressed.

"Don't say that!" cried Marianne, tapping him playfully, but Anton seemed morose now, swigging from his bottle and not saying anything else. This was Rebecca's cue to leave: She wasn't here to ogle Anton, however good-looking he was, and she certainly hadn't come here tonight just to eavesdrop on this horrible conversation. She was here to retrace her steps from last week, to try to find her mystery friend. Stiff from crouching behind the grave, she crept away.

It was hard to find the route she'd taken a week ago. Suddenly, Rebecca was in a blind panic, running and twisting and turning around, desperate to find the gate. Now she had more time, but even with the help of her miniflashlight, the cemetery in darkness seemed to have grown into something vast and mazelike. It took her a long time to come upon a stretch of concrete, and she wasn't sure at all if this was the spot where she'd fallen the week before.

Rebecca shone her pinpoint-sized light around, hoping to see something familiar. The light picked out some words etched into white stone — aha! She was standing at the foot of the Bowman family tomb.

With the moonlight obscured by a nearby oak tree, the Bowman vault seemed to tower even more than the Grey's. Its high walls were a sheer cliff face of white plaster. Rebecca lingered on its broad steps, shining a light up at the carved angel balanced on the vaulted roof. The angel had a pouty face, kind of like Helena, and she seemed a little cowed by her carved wings, as though they were too heavy for her slender frame. From this vantage point, the angel looked almost as big as Helena — and, Rebecca thought, just as stuck-up. She couldn't help laughing aloud at the thought of

Helena standing on the roof of the tomb, pinned down by giant, heavy wings. Helena was too lazy and spoiled to even carry her own umbrella to school.

"You don't think she's pretty?" said a voice from deep within the darkness, and Rebecca jumped, so startled that she almost dropped her flashlight.

CHAPTER NINE

PEEPING AT HER FROM AROUND THE SIDE OF THE tomb was the black girl, her eyes wide, her long dark braid velvety as the night sky.

"Who . . . who are you?" Rebecca stuttered.

The girl sidled a little closer, still touching the side of the tomb. She gazed at Rebecca, apparently more curious than scared.

"My name is Lisette." She sounded kind of foreign, Rebecca thought, but not in the same way as the French teacher at school. "Don't you remember me?"

"Yes! I tried to say hello to you the other day, when you were at the gates of the cemetery. I thought you saw me, but you disappeared."

"Oh." Lisette stopped moving. Rebecca waited for her to explain, but Lisette just stood, gazing at Rebecca's face with frank interest.

"I just wanted to thank you," said Rebecca. "For telling me how to get out of here last Friday night. That's why I came back tonight, to look for you."

"Aren't you with the others?" Lisette gestured with her head in the general direction, Rebecca assumed, of the Grey tomb.

"Them? God, no. I don't want them to know I'm here. That's why I was trying to get out, last week. I didn't want them to see me."

Lisette looked puzzled.

"You didn't come with them last week?" she asked. Her accent was hard to pin down. It was different from others Rebecca had heard so far in New Orleans — softer, in a way, and drawlier. Some of the Cavalry at Temple Mead sounded like they could work in the Brooklyn dockyards, but Lisette had a much more musical accent.

"No — I followed . . . Well, it's a kind of long and stupid story. I'm Rebecca, by the way." Rebecca stuck out her hand, but Lisette made no attempt to take it. She gave a shy smile, though, and at least this time, Rebecca thought, she wasn't running away. "Do you live here — in the cemetery, I mean?"

"Yes." Lisette nodded.

"Was your house destroyed in the storm?"

"Yes — well, it was damaged." Lisette seemed uncertain. "Part of the roof is gone. And there was some water."

"How awful!" It was bad enough being away from home for six months, Rebecca thought. But how could Lisette have slept in the cemetery for so long without anyone finding out or coming to look for her? "What about your family?"

Lisette shook her head. "I don't have any family. There was just me and my mother, and she's been dead a long time."

"I'm an only child, too," Rebecca told her. "It's just me and my father. We live in New York — well, we do usually. He had to go to China and I had to come here. That's another long and stupid story. Is your house — I mean, was it close by? I thought this area didn't flood."

"It didn't," said Lisette. "My house is a long way away, on the Creole side of town. It might be all right now. I don't really know."

This confused Rebecca. She didn't know New Orleans well enough to know where, exactly, the Creole part of town was. Maybe Lisette had to walk all this way just to reach dry land, though that seemed unlikely. And why take sanctuary in a cemetery, of all places? Why not go back to see if your house had been fixed? Maybe Lisette was hiding from someone. Maybe she was too scared to go home.

But before Rebecca could ask any more questions, Lisette's sweet smile disappeared and she held a finger to her lips. Above the steady singing of insects, there were other sounds — the crunch of leaves and twigs underfoot, the hum of talk and laughter, the clinking of bottles. Rebecca flicked off her flashlight.

"They come by this tomb sometimes," Lisette whispered. "Helena Bowman and the others."

"Do they talk to you?"

Lisette shook her head. "They've never seen me."

Rebecca's mind started racing: Like Lisette, she'd rather make herself scarce than face Marianne and her smug band of friends. Sure, over here she couldn't be accused of eavesdropping, but Rebecca didn't want to have to answer any rude questions. They might say she'd followed them in; Anton might have seen her running down the street last week. Maybe he'd recognize her and denounce her in front of his awful friends.

"Helena's not here tonight," Rebecca whispered back to Lisette, and then she wondered: Why did a girl from a far-off neighborhood — who spent all her time, apparently, hiding out in the cemetery — know Helena, of all people, by name?

"Good," said Lisette, half to herself.

"But we have to get out of here before the rest of them see us," said Rebecca, forgetting to lower her voice. The voices were getting closer, and Rebecca felt sick with anxiety, looking around for the best escape route. Strangely enough, Lisette didn't seem spooked at all. Didn't she always try to avoid them? "Quick — they're coming!"

Lisette gave an enigmatic smile, her teeth white as the moonlight. She reached out one hand to Rebecca.

"Keep still and say nothing," she said in a low voice, taking Rebecca's hand. Her grasp was surprisingly cool for such a warm and sticky night. "Believe me. They won't see you if you're with me."

Rebecca opened her mouth to protest, but it was too late. Anton and the others were approaching, swarming up the steps and around the tomb like invading cockroaches. Toby was ineptly juggling two empty beer bottles, and Julie was laughing at his near misses. Anton was deep in conversation with another boy, stopping just a few feet from where Lisette and Rebecca stood. Nobody said a word to them.

Rebecca's heart was hammering, and she realized she was gripping Lisette's hand very hard. She swung around to look at her new friend, and Lisette smiled, shaking her head, as if to remind Rebecca to keep quiet. But this was ridiculous: It couldn't be long before someone noticed them lurking in the shadows. However still Rebecca tried to stand, her legs were trembling like trees in a rainstorm. These kids might be self-absorbed — and some of them might even be drunk — but they weren't *that* dense. Sooner or later, they'd be spotted; maybe Marianne would scream, or Toby would grab them.

Part of Rebecca just wanted to make a run for it, to sprint away into the darkness and hide herself in the thicket of tombs. But something about Lisette's calm insistence that they wouldn't be seen made her stay put. And they were in this together, after all. Both were outsiders, sure to be derided by this group: Lisette because she was black and poor, and Rebecca because she would never belong to their social set — or to this city.

One of the boys staggered up to throw away his cigarette butt, leaning one hand against the tomb — just inches from her flinching face — and it was only then that Rebecca realized why Lisette was so certain they were safe, why nobody was going to find them. All of a sudden, it was obvious.

Nobody could see her, and nobody could see Lisette. They were invisible — as invisible as ghosts.

CHAPTER TEN

ANOTHER TEN MINUTES PASSED BEFORE Marianne, Julie, and the St. Simeon boys meandered off into the night. When the voices had receded, Lisette let go of her hand, and Rebecca slumped on the steps of the tomb, wondering if this whole adventure was just some strange nightmare. She was shaking so hard, she could barely speak.

"Why couldn't they see us?" she managed to croak, at last.

"We were invisible to them," Lisette said, sitting down next to Rebecca on the steps, stroking her dusty skirt as though it were a mermaid's tail.

"But *how*?" Rebecca asked. "I mean, I've never been invisible before."

"You should hold my hand more often." There was just enough moonlight for Rebecca to see the small smile creeping onto Lisette's face. "I'm invisible all the time. It's not so bad."

So that was why Aurelia couldn't see Lisette the other day: *Nobody* could see Lisette! But wait: Rebecca could see her perfectly well. This was just too weird.

"What do you mean you're invisible?" Rebecca asked. It wasn't that cold, but her teeth were chattering so much she could barely form a coherent sentence. "I can see you. And people aren't just *invisible*. It's not possible."

Lisette gave a soft sigh.

"People aren't invisible," she said, picking at a congealed spot on her skirt. "Living people, that is. Ghosts are invisible."

Rebecca shook her head hard, as though she was trying to clear water out of her ears: Something was clogging her brain, because she couldn't follow what Lisette was saying.

"So you're trying to tell me that *you're* a ghost and that's why you're invisible."

Lisette nodded. Rebecca slapped a hand against the stone step.

"But I don't believe in ghosts!" she protested. "At least — I've never really thought about it before. Ghosts are just something from . . . I don't know, horror stories. Creepy films. Ghosts are something you dress up as at Halloween. And you're not invisible — *I can see you*!"

"Other ghosts can see us."

Rebecca couldn't believe her ears.

"Oh my god," she said slowly, her heart thumping. "Can . . . can I be a ghost without knowing it? Have I died without realizing it? Is New Orleans hell or something?"

Lisette laughed.

"It's not heaven, that's for sure," she said. "But don't worry.

Sometimes other people can see us as well. You're not a ghost. By now I can tell the difference."

"Really?"

"It took a while, but I learned. Ghosts can be seen by other ghosts, but we can make our presence known to the living as well. There has to be a reason. Say, when some long-dead queen appears in a castle tower and someone sees her, it means she's trying to send him a message."

"What kind of a message?" Rebecca asked, hugging her knees, willing herself to calm down. Ghosts didn't exist in her world: They were just made-up things, like gremlins and elves and unicorns. Lisette might be a crazy person, telling her this ridiculous story. But then, those kids tonight in the cemetery were right there, just feet away, and they'd looked right through Rebecca and Lisette. What was going on?

"It could be a warning or a way of asking for help. And, you know, ghosts can only haunt particular places associated with their lives. With their deaths, especially. Otherwise, all the ghosts would head down to Grand Isle to sit by the sea."

"Or to Paris to sit in a café, I guess," said Rebecca. She'd never really thought about ghosts before or about ghosts being stuck somewhere they didn't want to be. This was all too much to take in.

"If we could go wherever we wanted, the entire netherworld would be crowded together in a couple of places," Lisette said drily. "And believe me — you don't want to see that! There are too many ghosts in New Orleans as it is. You should see them all in the Quarter, arguing over their territory. Sometimes it's comical. Sometimes it's scary."

"So, are you sending me a warning?" Rebecca asked, a little wary now. She wasn't sure how she felt about being singled out by a so-called ghost. In fact, she didn't know what was worse: being singled out by a ghost, or by a crazy person who *thought* she was a ghost. "Or do . . . do you need my help?"

"I don't know," said Lisette. She wriggled her toes — her bare feet were surprisingly clean. "People have seen me before, and I've always understood why. But I don't know about you. That's the reason I was so surprised last week, when you fell over on the pathway. I said something to you, but I talk to people all the time — they never hear me. But *you* could hear me, and then I realized you could see me as well."

"I can see a ghost," Rebecca muttered. "Really — you're a ghost?"

"Since August 1853."

"Are you serious? That's, like, a hundred and fifty years ago!"

"One hundred fifty-five and three months. It was during the great yellow fever epidemic. They couldn't bury us fast enough in this cemetery."

"You've been in this cemetery for a *hundred and fifty-five years*?" Rebecca whispered.

"Well, once a year, I walk to my house in Tremé. At the end of November, the anniversary of my mother's death. Walk there, then walk back."

"Why?"

"I don't know." Lisette shrugged, flashing her pretty smile. "Something in me makes me do it — I don't really understand why. I haven't been there since last November.

The house was still a mess. It's been that way ever since the big storm, the one they call Katrina. Since then, nobody lives there. Half the roof is gone. My mother would be sad to see it."

"Your mother's not a ghost as well?"

Lisette shook her head.

"The only way I'll see her again is, you know, in heaven. When I don't have to go a-haunting anymore."

"That's when I'll see my mother, too," Rebecca said, feeling an unbearable wave of sadness, though she wasn't sure if it was for herself or for Lisette. If Lisette was telling the truth . . . were there really all these unseen ghosts wandering the world? How many were there, Rebecca wondered — all those ghosts she couldn't see? Maybe her own mother was one of them.

"In the meantime," said Lisette, and her voice sagged with sadness, "the only other places I can go are this cemetery and the Bowman mansion."

Rebecca was about to ask why the Bowman mansion, of all places, when the silence of the night was broken by a distant — but distinct — cry.

"Rebecca! Rebecca!"

It was her aunt's voice, plaintive and breaking, calling for her from beyond the cemetery walls.

"Oh, no!" Rebecca leaped to her feet. "That's my aunt, looking for me. Oh god! She must have checked my room!"

"It's this way to the gate," said Lisette, getting up and walking down the steps. "Follow me."

Rebecca gathered up her flashlight, so flustered she dropped it again immediately.

"She'll call the police if she can't find me," she told Lisette. "And she'll go completely crazy if she finds out I've been in here."

"I could walk out with you, holding your hand. You'll be invisible, remember? She'll never know you were in here. I can't walk down Sixth Street with you, though."

"Why not?"

"I can only haunt certain places, remember? I don't know why — that's just the way it is."

Rebecca stumbled after Lisette's darting form, her mind reeling. Ghosts. Invisibility. Yellow fever. Hurricane Katrina. One hundred fifty-five years . . .

But when they arrived at the gate, and Lisette reached for Rebecca's hand, Rebecca came to her senses. She'd forgotten one important thing. Holding on to Lisette might make her temporarily invisible, but — unlike Lisette — she was a real-life, flesh-and-blood person, not a ghost. She couldn't walk through walls or doors or locked gates. With all the excitement and strangeness of the evening, Rebecca hadn't stopped to think that this week was no different from last. When the gang of "Them" left the cemetery, Anton had secured the gate behind them. Rebecca was locked in the cemetery.

CHAPTER ELEVEN

AUNT CLAUDIA WAS NOT AMUSED. SHE GLOWERED at Rebecca through the grille of the gate, her mouth set in a severe line.

"What are you doing in there?" she demanded, pulling one of her many voluminous patterned kimonos close around her. Her cat eyes looked worried rather than angry, but this only made Rebecca feel worse. "It's the *middle of the night*!"

"I'm so sorry," Rebecca said, and she really was sorry — sorry for getting stuck in the cemetery, sorry to drag Aunt Claudia out here onto the street *in the middle of the night*, and sorry to be caught. As soon as Rebecca dropped Lisette's hand, the ghost — if that's what she really was — had drifted away. "I was . . . I was looking for the cat, and the gate was open, and . . . I guess I got locked in."

"The cat!" Aunt Claudia raised one of her skimpy gray eyebrows. "The cat can look after itself. You, on the other hand . . ."

She rattled the tall gate ineffectually, frowning at its rust-dabbed lock.

"I'm sorry," Rebecca said again.

"How on earth am I going to get you out of there?"

"Maybe I could climb over the railings here," Rebecca suggested. She clicked on her flashlight. "Or maybe one of the other gates is open."

"Stay right where you are! This is a very dangerous place," her aunt scolded. "I'll have to call the police or the fire department. They won't be happy at all about this."

Rebecca wasn't too thrilled by that idea, either: The railings looked too spiky to scale, but she was sure there had to be some other way out, some tomb she could climb to get onto a lower section of wall. She'd rather Aunt Claudia invoke a voodoo charm than call the police, but now — her aunt ranting on about gates that should be locked and places girls should never go — didn't seem to be the time.

A gaslight flickered in the gated, cobbled parking area in front of the house near the corner. Only the gray slate roof of the house itself was visible from the street, the rest of its two stories protected from view by this front court — home to an Audi and a BMW — and, just beyond it, a high hedge. The gate squeaked open and someone stepped through, headed in their direction.

"The neighbors," Rebecca sighed under her breath. This was just what she needed: some outraged stuffed shirt come to add his or her voice to the chorus of disapproval. But as the figure got closer, she realized it wasn't some captain of industry, annoyed about being woken up so late at night. It was Anton Grey, loping toward them with his hands in his pockets.

"I'm real sorry, Miss Claudia," he said, not looking at Rebecca. He pulled out the key. "This is all my fault."

"Well, I'm sure it isn't, Anton." Aunt Claudia seemed flustered. Rebecca hadn't realized they knew each other: It made sense, she supposed, given the proximity of their houses. "And I'm sorry we've woken you up."

"No, no — I just got back. I was walking a friend home, and I heard . . . well, anyway. I can unlock the gate."

Anton's tone of voice was polite and apologetic, not cocky, but this didn't make the situation any easier. Rebecca felt intensely embarrassed. After spying on him earlier tonight, it felt strange to be this close to him, her eyes fixed on his long fingers sliding the key into place.

"We hang out here sometimes — a whole group of us," he was saying, still talking to Aunt Claudia. "I didn't know . . ."

"My niece." Aunt Claudia shot Rebecca a hard look, and Rebecca felt her cheeks burning. Anton's hair curled a little; she could see that now they were standing so close, separated only by the solid black bars of the gate.

"Your niece, right. Sorry, ma'am. If I'd known she was in the cemetery, I wouldn't have locked up." Anton caught Rebecca's gaze. He raised an eyebrow, the slightest glimmer of a smile in his dark eyes, and Rebecca glanced away, waiting for the gate to click open. This was totally mortifying: He must think she was spying on him and his friends! Why else would Rebecca be wandering around the cemetery so late?

"I didn't know she was in the cemetery, either," Aunt Claudia said. Anton jiggled the lock, and pushed; finally the gate creaked toward Rebecca. She wriggled through the slight gap, brushing against Anton on her way out.

"Thanks," she murmured, staring somewhere in the region of his collarbone while he relocked the gate. In New York, Rebecca hardly ever got nervous around boys: They were just there, in all her classes, being all smelly and sweaty and ridiculous. Occasionally, one was better-looking than the rest, but the only guys she'd ever had an actual crush on were movie stars. So why did the sight of Anton up close make her feel so tongue-tied and embarrassed?

It was this stupid situation, she told herself. He must be thinking she was a sneak and an idiot — stuck in the cemetery, getting berated by her aunt.

"I'm Anton, by the way," he said, pocketing the key. He stuck out a hand.

"Rebecca," she replied, but before she could shake his hand, Aunt Claudia had grabbed her by the arm and was hustling her away.

"Thank you," her aunt called over her shoulder to Anton. Rebecca was too ashamed to look back, to see if he was still standing at the gate or was wandering back along the street to his own house.

Aunt Claudia did not remove her vicelike grip on Rebecca's arm until they were both in the kitchen, the door closed so Aurelia wouldn't be disturbed. Rebecca sat in silence while her aunt boiled water for tea, setting two mismatched mugs on the table and, as usual, concocting her own strange blend from loose leaves stashed in a cluster of Oriental-looking tins in the cupboard that never closed properly.

Her aunt seemed preoccupied, as though she was thinking very carefully about what to say, and there was nothing Rebecca could do but wait for the inevitable lecture. It was sure to involve murderers, rapists, muggers, and the cemetery after dark, sprinkled with statements like "I'm so disappointed in you" and "Your father has entrusted you to my care." It was a speech, Rebecca decided, she could probably write herself.

The battered tin kettle on the stove began to sing, and Aunt Claudia snatched it off the heat at once, glugging boiling water into a teapot. She had quite a collection of teapots, but most seemed to be damaged in some way: This one was brown china, with a chipped spout. Rebecca had already decided to get her aunt a new, flawless teapot for Christmas, but maybe she should buy it sooner, as an offering of peace.

Her aunt set the teapot on the table, and rummaged in the dish rack for the plastic-rimmed sieve — used mainly to wash rice, which they ate with practically every meal, but summoned into double duty whenever they couldn't find the tea strainer.

"Now," she said, robe wafting as she settled into her chair like some aging butterfly, "I'm going to say something, and it's very important that you listen."

Rebecca nodded, trying to stifle a yawn: She wondered how late it was now and how long the lecture would be. She already had way too much information to try to process.

"You can't," Aunt Claudia began, one thin, blue-veined hand resting on the teapot lid, and then she stopped. "What I mean to say is . . ."

"Don't go to the cemetery, ever." Rebecca finished the sentence for her, awkwardly shifting in her seat.

"Obviously." Her aunt nodded, pouring tea into the cups — it was chamomile, maybe, with something lemony, and the hot liquid was the color of grass. "But more than that, Rebecca. You must stay away from the Bowmans. The Bowmans, the Suttons, the Greys."

"What?" That wasn't quite what Rebecca was expecting. "I'm not friends with any of them. I'm not part of that group that goes to the cemetery, if that's what you're worried about."

"I'm glad to hear it." Aunt Claudia took a tentative sip of the steaming tea. "But you see the girls at school, I presume, and now you've met Anton Grey. I know you're new here, and don't have many friends yet, but it would be a mistake to become one of their — what do you call it — group?"

"Why?" Rebecca knew why *she* didn't like Helena and Marianne, but she was curious to hear why her aunt objected to them. And to Anton, who tonight — all in all — was pretty polite and helpful. He didn't have to come out and open the gate. If it weren't for him, Rebecca would still be a prisoner now, waiting for the police to come and break the lock.

"They're part of a different world," Aunt Claudia told her. Without her usual dramatic makeup, she looked tired, careworn. "It's hard to explain to someone not from here, but these are families who've been here a long, long time, since this neighborhood was founded. Before it was even part of New Orleans."

"I know all that," Rebecca argued. Something about what her aunt was saying stuck in her craw, like an irritating throat tickle. Was Aunt Claudia trying to say these people were somehow *better* than Rebecca? Better than Aunt Claudia and Aurelia?

"But," Aunt Claudia said, laying one hand over Rebecca's, "you don't really understand, do you?"

Rebecca resisted the temptation to make a snide comment about her aunt's psychic powers.

"Their houses aren't any older than *your* house," Rebecca argued. "Just because their families have owned them for longer . . ."

"This isn't just about houses," interrupted Aunt Claudia. "It's about loyalties and allegiances. Who you're related to, and where your history lies."

Rebecca pushed away her tea.

"You know I don't care about any of that," she said. "All that debutante, high-society stuff. I just don't buy that they're of some higher social station, and that they're too good for us."

"I'm not saying that." Aunt Claudia sighed, and gestured at Rebecca to drink her tea. "I'm just trying to tell you that their world is a separate place, and if it seems as though they're welcoming you in, they're not. Don't trust them. Don't even speak to them, if you can avoid it."

Rebecca sighed with frustration. She didn't particularly want to have anything to do with Helena and her set — but that didn't mean she didn't mind being told she shouldn't, or couldn't. The social intricacies of this neighborhood made her sick. So the Bowmans and Suttons and Greys were rich; so they had big, old houses, and the slaves they used to own had been replaced with "staff." Their world wasn't that different from that of any number of wealthy people in New

York. They weren't special in some hereditary way: They could just afford to buy more things.

"I just don't see what the big deal is," she said. Aunt Claudia looked exhausted, pensively twisting her cup around and around on the scratched tabletop.

"I wish your father had told you more," she said at last: She sounded despairing, Rebecca thought, in an extremely over-dramatic way. "About the way things have to be, until . . ."

"Until what?"

"It's getting late." Aunt Claudia stood up, clattering her cup into the sink. "You can take your tea with you to your room, if you like. Really, Rebecca — try to get some sleep."

But it was hard to get to sleep that night. That evening two strangers had come to her rescue — one a black ghost who she shouldn't be able to see, the other a Patrician white New Orleanian she'd been told to avoid. Perhaps she'd never see either of them again. And if she did, Rebecca knew one thing for certain: Aunt Claudia would not approve.

CHAPTER TWELVE

REBECCA SLID INTO A CHAIR AT THE CAFÉ Lafayette, dropped her bag on the floor, and pulled a postcard out of her blazer pocket. It was from her father, delivered to the house on Sixth Street the day before. She'd read it more than a dozen times already, though it didn't say much: He was working hard; November in central China was really cold; he missed her.

She missed *him*. Just seeing his familiar spidery writing made her feel depressed and homesick. This would be the first time in her life they wouldn't be together for Thanksgiving. At least she had plenty of homework to keep her busy: The Temple Mead teachers were piling on extra work, talking about the time they'd all lose during Mardi Gras, when school was closed for a week.

This week she'd started doing her homework in the café on Prytania. Aurelia was busy with piano and singing lessons, getting ready for her holiday recital, and being home alone in the little yellow house made Rebecca feel even more depressed: The strange decorations loomed over her like dusty, arcane exhibits in a museum, and there was nowhere to study apart from the kitchen table. The house was too gloomy, in a permanent shadow cast by the cemetery walls, the oak trees, and the tightly packed row of houses. All she ended up doing was thinking about Lisette.

By contrast, the Café Lafayette was bright and noisy, housed in a small mall-like building that was also home to a cluttered bookstore, an expensive hair salon, and a place rich people could take their dogs for grooming. The café looked kind of like an elegant bar, its walls painted blue-gray, with big windows on two sides and black-and-white artsy photographs of Lafayette Cemetery hanging on the back wall.

That afternoon every table was taken by the Plebs and Debs of Temple Mead, all drinking over-sweet tumblers of bubble tea and vying for spots in the window, so they could squawk and gush whenever boys from St. Simeon's walked by.

Rebecca and the rest of the serious homework crew were stationed along the back wall, laptops plugged into electrical outlets or books spread across the table. She tried to block out the café chatter, though she couldn't help laughing when someone at Amy's table — not Jessica, who'd inherited Helena Bowman's flu — giggled so much she choked on a tapioca pearl. One or two St. Simeon boys wandered in, but they didn't stick around. To Rebecca's relief, none of "Them" dropped by. It was too Plebby a hangout, she decided, for someone like Helena Bowman.

From her seat in the café, she could keep an eye on at least one of the cemetery's entrances. Maybe, just maybe, she'd see Lisette again. Was she *really* a ghost? Did the dead really haunt their old familiar places? And did that mean Rebecca's own mother might be wandering somewhere, with nobody to talk to but other ghosts and random strangers?

Rebecca fingered the postcard, wishing it was the family photo that had mysteriously disappeared from her wallet. In an e-mail, she'd asked her father about it: He'd played dumb, saying that it must have fallen out somewhere. Maybe he was right. But without the picture, Rebecca felt as though her mother's face was fading somehow. She didn't remember her at all: Millie Brown had died when Rebecca was a toddler, knocked over by a speeding car while she crossed a Paris street, Rebecca in her arms. Her mother was killed instantly. Rebecca had somehow rolled to safety and had no memory of the accident at all.

And now no photograph of her mother and father.

She set the postcard on the table, next to her plastic bottle of water, and started rummaging in her bag for her history homework. Someone was dragging the spare chair away from her table — she could hear them! — without even having the courtesy to ask her if that was OK.

"Hey!" she said irritably, sitting up. These girls prided themselves on being Young Ladies, but this was kind of rude. . . .

Oh.

The person pulling the chair away wasn't a young lady. It was Anton Grey.

"Hey — Rebecca, isn't it?" He smiled at her and held out his hand. "Anton Grey. We didn't get to shake hands last time."

"No — I guess we didn't." Rebecca took his hand, feeling shy all of a sudden, aware that the eyes of all the Temple Mead girls in the place were boring into her right now. It felt extremely weird to be holding Anton Grey's hand across the table, and he must have felt the same way: He pulled his away sharply, and Rebecca felt her face flushing.

"Do you mind if I sit down?" he said. So he wasn't taking the chair away: He was pulling it back from the table so he could sit down. Rebecca swallowed hard.

"Go ahead," she said, trying to sound casual and wondering why it was such an effort.

"I hope I'm not interrupting your homework," he said, a smile flickering: There weren't any books on her table at all. Just the postcard, which Anton was eyeing with interest. Rebecca swiped it off the table and dropped it into her bag.

"It can wait." She shrugged, and then she didn't know what else to say. The café seemed very quiet all of a sudden. Rebecca wished she had some bubble tea, so she could suck on the straw instead of grasping for some sensible and interesting conversation. All she could do was stare at the bottled water sitting on the table — you had to buy *something* here to justify taking up a table for ninety minutes — and try not to fixate on the polished brass buttons on Anton's school blazer.

"Miss Claudia was pretty mad on Friday," Anton said, picking at one of the buttons: He must have noticed her staring. "I hope you didn't get in too much trouble."

"Oh, no," said Rebecca quickly. She glanced up at him. His cheeks were rosy; maybe it was just stuffy in here. His eyes were intensely dark, almost black, and his lashes, she thought, were as long as a girl's. But his face was too lean to be pretty, and across his chin, following the line of his jaw, were the faint white traces of a scar.

"I wouldn't have locked the gate if . . . you know." He smiled at her apologetically.

"It's OK," she told him, embarrassed to be talking about it still. What she didn't want was Anton asking her why she was in the cemetery that night. "My aunt worries about me because I'm new in town."

"From New York, yeah?" Anton's face brightened, and Rebecca was relieved to talk about something else for a while. He seemed very interested in hearing all about the city, a place he'd visited just once, when he was a child. He had lots of questions for her — about her school, and places she hung out, and where her apartment was.

"At this time of year, you can see one of the ice rinks in Central Park from our living room window," she told him. "I go there nearly every weekend. Or, at least, I went there. I guess I won't be doing much ice-skating this winter."

"That sucks," he said, and she told him about her father working in China for months and months. "That postcard you were looking at — that was China, right?"

She nodded.

"That's another place I'd really like to go. Too bad you couldn't go with your dad."

"I know," she said, glancing at the whispering Plebs with distaste: Amy's eyes looked ready to pop out of her head. Going to school in China would be beyond hard, but at least she'd be far, far away from the Roman class system.

"Well, there are some cool things that go on here over the winter. You know, once the parades start. Before that, there are lots of parties and dances and . . ."

His voice trailed off, and Rebecca felt uncomfortable

again. He was probably thinking how Rebecca wouldn't be invited to any of these parties. What was it Aunt Claudia had said? *They're part of a different world.*

"But it's not exactly New York, I guess." His grin was rueful. "Hey, do you want a coffee or something?"

"I don't really drink coffee," Rebecca told him. Personally, she thought spending the better part of five dollars on some frothy, sweetened coffee drink at Starbucks was a total waste of money, and she would always tease her self-proclaimed coffee-addict friends in New York for trying too hard to be adults.

"Neither do I," Anton admitted. "And that bubble tea stuff — I just don't get it."

"I get enough tea at home," said Rebecca. She glanced over to one of the window tables, where all the girls were sucking intently on straws, staring over at Rebecca and Anton as though they were exhibits at the zoo. She lowered her voice. "Aunt Claudia is nuts about anything herbal, and the more it looks like hedge clippings, the more she likes it."

"My mother's the same! She thinks it speeds up her metabolism or something."

They talked for a while longer, long enough for Rebecca to find out a few things about Anton: He was an only child; his father ran the family law firm downtown; before the storm, Anton had a small sailboat at the docks on Lake Pontchartrain, but it had been smashed to pieces and sunk by the wind and the waves.

"I haven't been out to the lake at all," Rebecca told him. "I haven't even been to Audubon Park yet."

She hadn't done much sightseeing of any kind, partly because Aunt Claudia was busier than ever on weekends now that convention season was in full swing, and partly because nobody at school ever invited her anywhere. She'd been down to the Quarter a few times with her aunt, wandering its pretty, narrow streets and browsing in the little stores, or exploring the museum and the cathedral, while her aunt told fortunes on Jackson Square. There was so much to see down there — balconies and courtyards, buskers and artists. She didn't need to hang out at dull parties with stupid girls.

"The streetcar's running along St. Charles again," Anton said, almost as though he was thinking aloud. "Maybe we could take a ride to the park sometime?"

"Sure," Rebecca said quickly. Aunt Claudia had told her to have nothing to do with Anton, but he seemed friendly and straight-up, not like Helena and Marianne. Apart from Lisette, he was the only person in New Orleans who'd seemed interested in talking with her. And he probably knew all sorts of things about the families who owned those grand mansions along St. Charles Avenue: It would be an insider's tour.

And, she had to admit, he was really cute.

"How about tomorrow, after school?" Anton suggested. "We could go now, but I've got this tutor who comes to the house. My parents are obsessed about me getting into Tulane."

He rolled his eyes.

"Sure — whenever," she said. Aunt Claudia didn't have to know about this. Nobody had to know, in fact.

"I'll meet you . . . on the corner of St. Charles and Sixth Street," he told Rebecca. So maybe he didn't want anyone to see them, either, she thought. "And we'll be back before . . ."

Before someone wondered where they were. Rebecca understood. Aunt Claudia didn't want her to spend time with Anton, and maybe Anton's family didn't want him hanging around with someone like Rebecca. They probably thought Aunt Claudia was some kind of gypsy or witch, her small tumbledown house lowering the tone of the neighborhood. Not every house in the Garden District was a mansion, but even the smaller houses were perfectly manicured — and none of them had a "cottage" garden.

"I'll see you then," she said, so he didn't have to finish the sentence.

After Anton left the café, Rebecca tried to get on with some homework, but her mind was bouncing around. A lot of the whispering and giggling going on at the window tables was directed her way, she knew. The weird girl from New York had been sitting with *the* Anton Grey; they'd been talking for half an hour! What was up with that? How could she possibly know him? Why had he come looking for her in the Café Lafayette? What made *her* so special?

Rebecca drained the last of her water and packed up her books, trying to suppress a smile. Let them all talk, she thought. She didn't even care if it got back to Helena and Marianne. It would give them another reason to dislike her, but that was OK. She didn't need them to like her. Soon it would be Christmas; before too long after that it would be Easter. The end of the school year would roll around, and she'd be out of New Orleans. They'd live and die here.

CHAPTER THIRTEEN

BY THE NEXT DAY, THE WEATHER HAD TURNED into something approaching a New York November, cool and gusty. Wind blew leaves and litter across the street, the giant oak trees rustling and whispering to each other. Rebecca rushed home from school, pulling her blazer tight around her, glad that Aurelia and Claire were staying late for choir practice so she wouldn't have to *explain* anything.

From the hook behind her bedroom door, Rebecca pulled out her pale blue suede jacket; she tugged on a pair of jeans and the gray cashmere sweater she bought at the last J.Crew sale. She stuffed her phone, keys, and a tight bundle of cash into her jacket pockets, just in case: There was no need for a bag. Maybe she could take some photos on her cell phone and send them to her father or to her friends; maybe she could even take a picture of Anton. She had to do *something* to keep in touch with her New York friends: After just a couple of weeks away, Rebecca was only getting occasional texts and e-mails. Everyone was busy with school, busy with their lives. She wasn't part of that world anymore.

The wind blew the front door shut when she stepped onto the porch: It was blowing up from the river, bringing with it that strange, dirty New Orleans smell — a little of garbage, a little of mold, a little of overripe fruit or a blossom rotting on the ground, overlaid with the tang of grease and sea. At this very moment, that wind was probably blowing Aunt Claudia's tarot cards all over Jackson Square.

Out of habit, on her way past the cemetery's open gates, Rebecca glanced in, just in case, hoping — as ever — to spot Lisette. It was usually closed on weekday afternoons, but today the gates were wide-open, a City Parks van parked on the central path.

And there *she* was, walking along the central pathway, her back to Rebecca.

"Lisette!" It was so long since Rebecca had seen her. Anton could wait: She *had* to talk to the ghost — if that's what Lisette really, truly was.

The torn tail of her skirt dragging along the ground, her long black braid bobbing, Lisette turned off the path and disappeared behind a row of towering white vaults. Maybe she was headed for the Bowman tomb, Rebecca thought, jogging after her along a cracked concrete path. A small tour group was wandering out through the Washington Avenue gate, pointing at the bold striped awning of Commander's Palace restaurant. There was nobody else around, apart from a groundsman wearing soundproof earmuffs and swinging a power trimmer, oblivious to Lisette's presence, nodding at Rebecca as she passed.

Approaching the Bowman tomb, Rebecca jumped over a wizened tree root; she skidded to a halt on the worn grassy path and stepped over the low rusted railings, looking for Lisette. Her friend was huddled at the back of the tomb, just the shards of her skirt visible from the pathway.

"I've been looking for you!" Rebecca exclaimed, clambering around the vault. Untouched by the weak, late-afternoon sun, its sheer sides were cold to the touch.

Lisette shrugged, and gazed down at her bare feet.

"I've been around," she said. She sounded listless, Rebecca thought. It had to be quite boring, being a ghost. There was nothing to do in the cemetery except maybe talk to other ghosts and hear the same tour guides tell the same stories, day after day.

"Do you get sick of it?" Rebecca leaned against the side of the tomb, arms folded, the wind licking her hair. "Sick of being a ghost, I mean."

"Most of the time, not much happens," Lisette admitted.

"Are there other ghosts for you to talk to?"

"In the cemetery? Not as many as you'd think. Along by the river — now *there's* a place to see ghosts. Mean ones, mainly. Mad and mean. A lot of them have been drunk for two hundred years. And the Quarter is full of ghosts as well. Right along Claiborne Avenue. In Faubourg Tremé, Faubourg Marigny — ghosts everywhere."

"I wish I could see them," Rebecca sighed. Lisette moved over, making room for her, and she sat down next to her on the stone steps.

"Just get someone to murder you and then cover up your death." Lisette gave an arch smile. "You'll see other ghosts all the time."

Rebecca smiled back, wanting to ask how Lisette died, but

the question seemed so rude. And what if Lisette didn't like talking about it? What if there was some kind of ghost etiquette Rebecca didn't understand?

"Anyway," Lisette said, shrugging. "You can see me. And when you hold my hand, like you did that night in here, you can see what I can see."

"Really?" Rebecca couldn't believe this. "So why didn't I see the other ghosts in the cemetery?"

Lisette held up one finger.

"Ghost. There's just one of them here, apart from me. He's a gravedigger — *was* a gravedigger. He's over there, by the firemen's tomb. We can go over and see him sometime, if you like. He never leaves that corner of the cemetery. If I get really lonely, I go and talk to him, but all he does is sing old songs and tell stories about the old days."

"When did he die?" This was a test: Rebecca wanted to see if Lisette stumbled over the answer at all.

"Nineteen-ten. He was moving a body into one of the vaults, and someone hit him on the back of the head with a shovel."

"A grave robber?"

"Maybe. Someone he owed money to, that's what *he* thinks. It wasn't his time to die, anyway. That's why he's still haunting the cemetery."

"Rather than some house, you mean?" Rebecca was trying to work out ghost-world rules.

"You don't choose where you haunt." Lisette gave a tired sigh, barely louder than a breath. "The place has to mean something. It has to relate to your life and your death. That's what I think, anyway, judging from the other ghosts I've met, and what I know of the places my feet lead me. The places I can't get away from."

"When you saw me that first night in the cemetery, how did you know *I* wasn't a ghost?"

Lisette laughed softly, shaking her head.

"Ghosts can't get lost," she said. "And they don't say 'ouch' when they fall over!"

Lisette bent down over her knees, smoothing her thin, almost threadbare skirt. One of her sleeves was ripped so badly it hung off her shoulder, and there was something that looked sticky and dirty at the back of her head, under her hair — a dark wound, perhaps, the hair over it matted and thick.

"Of course," Lisette continued, "I won't be a ghost forever."

She sat up and looked at Rebecca, her pretty face frowning.

"How does it end?"

"Once the curse is broken," Lisette told her. Her face relaxed, its worried creases disappearing. "Then I'll be able to rest in peace. You won't see me anymore."

"The curse?" Rebecca sat up straight. The stone was too cold for nonghosts to sit on, she decided, scrambling to her feet. "I heard about a curse on the Bowman family — or on their house or something. Is that what you're talking about?"

Lisette looked around, the way Amy and Jessica had glanced nervously around the lunchroom the day Rebecca asked them the same question.

"It's such a *long* story," Lisette said. She stared up and down the next line of tombs, starting the way Marilyn the cat did when she heard something in another room. "Someone's coming."

Rebecca listened: Lisette was right. She could hear footsteps, girls talking. She took a step down, hemmed close to the tomb by its miniature iron fence.

"Do you think . . ." Rebecca began, turning back to talk to Lisette: But the ghost girl was gone. Just like that, she'd disappeared off somewhere — why, Rebecca didn't know. If only she'd taken Rebecca's hand, they'd both be invisible right now. Instead, Lisette was nowhere to be found, and Rebecca . . . well, she was clearly, completely, totally visible.

And standing in the grassy alley, looking extremely startled, were Helena Bowman and Marianne Sutton. They were both still in their school uniforms, Helena clutching a perfect posy of waxy white flowers.

"What are *you* doing here?" Helena sounded outraged. "How dare you climb all over my family's vault?"

"I'm not . . . I'm just — sorry." Rebecca lumbered over the boundary fence, almost losing her balance and knocking her elbow against the neighboring tomb. She'd never thought that Helena or anyone else might visit this place during the day, but of course they did: Their family members were buried here. Helena must be bringing fresh flowers to leave at the gate of the tomb. "I was just looking around."

"Then take a tour." Marianne gripped Helena's arm as though her friend needed propping up. Helena *was* looking wan, and a little frail, with dark circles under her eyes. "This isn't a playground! People are *buried* here, you know."

Rebecca hated being caught like this: There was nothing she could say to explain why she was on the wrong side of the railing, and she'd already apologized. Something in the tone of their voices made her reluctant to apologize again.

"I have to go," she said, and clambered onto the pathway, weaving to avoid bumping into Helena. She walked away as quickly as she could without running, before either of them could say another word. Rebecca might be late to meet Anton, but she didn't want Marianne and Helena to see her running. She didn't want them to think they'd scared her away.

CHAPTER FOURTEEN

ANTON WAS WAITING FOR HER: HE SEEMED relieved rather than annoyed when Rebecca ran up, burbling her vague excuses. How could she tell him the truth — that she'd spotted a ghost in the cemetery and darted in for a quick chat, only to be turfed off the Bowman family grave by Anton's BFFs, Helena and Marianne? It was easier to say she'd had to stay late at school.

"The last two streetcars have been full. Some car-dealer convention," he told her. "Like they have anything to celebrate! Do you want to just walk?"

"Sure!"

"The only thing is, it's about three miles to the park, so I don't think we'll make it all the way. I can't stay out too . . ."

He didn't finish his sentence, and Rebecca didn't press him. They weren't supposed to be out together, end of story. Today they were both in disguise, in their civilian gear: Anton had traded his St. Simeon's blazer for a brown MAKE LEVEES, NOT WAR T-shirt and an American Eagle hoodie, so he almost looked like a normal teenage boy rather than some Patrician heir.

They strolled along the center of the broad avenue, walking down the disused streetcar tracks — a sandy lane rimmed with grass lush from all the rain. Joggers thudded past them, some of them running in chattering pairs, some pulling dogs on leashes. Anton pointed out the plastic beads dangling high in the oak trees, relics of this year's carnival parades.

"The parades run along — what is it, the south side of the street?" Rebecca asked him, trying to get her bearings.

"The river side," he corrected her. "And over there is the lake side, and what we're walking on right now is called the neutral ground. North and south don't mean much here. Most of the West Bank isn't really to the west of us at all, because of the way the river curves. And now, though we're really following the river, we're walking into Uptown — and it's called that because it's upriver of the Quarter."

"Confusing," she told him, and he shrugged: He was used to this, she guessed, having never lived anywhere else, but Rebecca had grown up in a city where streets were on a grid. "Are you a member of Septimus? Do you get to sit on a float?"

"*Ride*," he said, grinning at her. "I'm not a member, but my father and grandfather are, and I usually ride on one of the floats."

"Usually?"

"OK — always." He leaned toward her and lowered his voice. Rebecca's heart started thudding; she hoped Anton couldn't hear it. "Don't tell any of your cool New York friends, but for years I was one of the pages, riding with the king. I had to wear a blond wig and white satin pantaloons."

"Nice!"

Anton told her more about the Septimus parade, in between pointing out some of the more grandiose mansions lining St. Charles Avenue; a number of them were in the process of being decorated for Christmas. Outside one austere, sprawling stone place, men wrapped skeins of fairy lights around the wrought-iron fence, securing them in place with large red bows. Another house, he told her, was famous for filling its entire front lawn every December with hundreds of pots of white poinsettias.

Septimus, she discovered, was an all-male krewe, like the vast majority of old-line organizations. The only women in the parade were the queen — always young, always a debutante — and her maids, who wore elaborate beaded costumes so heavy and tall the girls had to be roped into position on the floats. Septimus differed here from some of the other krewes: The maids in Septimus were usually younger girls, not other debutantes. So both Marianne and Helena would be maids this year, riding on the same float. Rebecca made a mental note to skip the parade. She had enough of being looked down on by those two at school.

"And old-line means?" she asked.

"That it started just before or after the Civil War," he said, scuffing at the soft ground with one shoe. "In the nineteenth century, anyway. But when people talk about 'old-line' this and that, they usually mean the families. Everything here is about family."

"So I understand." Rebecca sighed.

"But it's all so . . . the thing is," he said, his expression earnest and intent, "it's kind of ridiculous. Everyone prides themselves on being one of the 'old-line' families. But none of us are really from here. When the Garden District was laid out, it attracted the newcomers to the city, the people who weren't part of old New Orleans — that is, the French-speaking, Creole-Catholic part. My great-great-great-whatever grandfather, the one who built the house we live in?"

"Yes?"

"He was a coffee trader who'd been living all over the Caribbean. But he was born in London and grew up in New York. And the Bowmans were originally the Baumanns from Boston — they were German. Protestants, like most of the people who moved into the neighborhood. The Suttons were Irish immigrants originally. Everyone rich and successful, of course — cotton brokers, or bankers, or big-time merchants. But they were outsiders once as well, and a lot of them were self-made millionaires. In other words, not exactly old money."

"You know a lot about the history of the place," Rebecca told him. The wind blew grit into her mouth, and strands of hair lashed her face; she wished she'd tied it back. But she didn't want the walk to end or for Anton to stop talking.

"It's who we are," he said, speaking so quietly she almost missed it. He looked at her, his dark eyes serious. "If it's so important to people, they should at least know the truth. Most of the black people in this city have got longer lineages than we have. They're the descendants of slaves."

"Or the free people of color," Rebecca reminded him, glad she knew something of the city's history.

"Absolutely." He smiled at her. "Or the people who moved here from Haiti or other places in the Caribbean. They were all here before us. If Katrina showed us anything, it was how easily what people have built here can just disappear."

Rebecca thought of Lisette's house on the other side of town, flooded and damaged by the wind.

"So what I'm saying is — I'm a New Yorker, too!" Anton nudged her with his elbow.

"An outsider," she said with mock solemnity. Maybe this was why he seemed to like her, she thought: He didn't *want* to be part of the in-crowd. He knew a lot about his family history, but something in the tone of his voice suggested it oppressed him. He didn't sound proud or arrogant at all.

"I don't belong here any more or less than you do," he agreed.

"But not really — right?" They stopped while a car cut across the tracks, making a turn onto the other side of St. Charles. "You guys have all known each other forever."

"Like you and *your* friends, probably."

"Except I met my friends at school. Their parents didn't know my parents. They didn't all go to the same colleges and work in the same businesses and marry each other."

"See this?" Anton pulled the silver cigarette lighter out of his pocket and handed it to her. Rebecca pretended to be surprised: She didn't want him to know she'd seen it before, when she was spying on him in Lafayette Cemetery. "It was a wedding gift from my great-aunt to Helena's great-grandfather. They got married in 1925."

"And you carry it around with you . . . because you're a smoker?" Rebecca made a face.

"Nope."

"Because you plan to give it to Helena on *your* wedding day?" she teased, feeling herself blush. Now it was Anton's turn to make a face: Helena might be part of his group, but obviously she wasn't the girl of his dreams. "If that's even legal," she added hastily.

"Anything's legal in Louisiana," he told her. "If you know the right people. Actually, I don't really know why I carry it around with me. I just do."

"It's a beautiful thing," Rebecca told him, stroking the lighter: It was warm to the touch, etched with a delicate fleur-de-lis pattern.

"But not something I'll ever need or ever use." Anton grabbed onto a ridged iron lamppost, spinning himself around it. "It's just a relic of another time."

Rebecca waited until he'd finished jumping around, smiling because the wind was blowing his curly hair into clownlike clumps. Then she handed the lighter back.

"I wish I had something of my family's to carry around," she said, thinking of the photo that had disappeared from her wallet. "We don't have any heirlooms." This was true, though she hadn't really thought much about it before. Maybe some things in the New York apartment had belonged to long-dead grandparents, or great-uncles and aunts, but her father had never pointed them out. "We don't have much family history. We don't have much family, actually. Not like you, anyway."

"Really?" He looked at her quizzically. "You're lucky."

They stood for a moment in the dirt of the neutral ground, looking at each other, Rebecca thought, as though they were aliens from different planets meeting for the first time. Anton was the one to break the silence, nervously clearing his throat.

"I wanted to ask you — would you mind going to this Christmas party with me? If you can't, it's OK . . . it's just . . ."

"A Christmas party?" Rebecca wondered if they had some sort of school dance at St. Simeon's, though surely Amy and Jessica would have alerted her to such a pivotal social event.

"The Bowmans have it every year. It's in December, but I wasn't sure if you were going to head back to New York as soon as school finishes, or . . . or . . ."

"No, I think I'll be here." Rebecca was hoping to go home for Christmas, but her father was being annoyingly vague about when and if he was returning from China. And was Anton actually inviting her to Helena's party? Did he have no clue about the contempt Helena felt — and made no effort to hide — for outsiders like Rebecca? Helena wouldn't dream of inviting Rebecca to her party. She'd rather her house was overrun by an angry mob of Plebs, Rebecca suspected, than admit an outcast from Planet Elsewhere.

"So you'll come?" Anton's face brightened. Rebecca hesitated, wondering if she really wanted to put herself through the ordeal. She'd like to get dressed up and go out somewhere with Anton, but the thought of Helena and Marianne's reaction when she walked through the Bowmans' front door made her instantly start dreading it.

On the other hand, it would serve both of them right. Their pretentious party wouldn't seem quite so exclusive if *she* managed to infiltrate it.

"Sure," she told Anton. She gazed over at a three-story house where a Hispanic man in paint-splattered overalls was attaching an elaborate Christmas wreath — gray eucalyptus leaves, bloodred berries, and twisted tails of ivy — to the blue front door, while other workers busied themselves removing carved pumpkins from the steps and the Halloween spider's web from the manicured hedge. Holiday decorations had to go up early here, Anton had explained, because the day after Christmas everybody couldn't wait to toss their trees onto the sidewalk and put up all their Mardi Grass banners and lights. And the holidays meant all the serious parties, the events that went on all winter and culminated in the great balls of Carnival, were beginning. The Bowmans' party was one of the first of the season. Wonder of wonders: Rebecca Brown would be there.

"Sure, I'll go," she said again, and he flashed her a broad smile, throwing his silver cigarette lighter high in the air and catching it with his left hand.

"I guess we should probably start walking back," he said, and Rebecca nodded her agreement. She didn't want to make Aunt Claudia suspicious by arriving late for dinner. Because telling Aunt Claudia about this walk with Anton — or about the invitation to the Bowmans' party — was out of the question. She would just get upset and might say that Rebecca couldn't go. It was better if Rebecca kept this particular secret to herself.

CHAPTER FIFTEEN

REBECCA SHOULD HAVE SAID SOMETHING TO Anton: She should have told him to keep his date for the Bowmans' Christmas party a secret. At lunch on Monday, Jessica — her nose still red from the flu — materialized by Rebecca's side in the food line.

"Feeling any better?" Rebecca asked. Jessica seemed marginally more friendly than Amy, though that wouldn't be hard: On Friday, approaching the lunch table with her tray, Rebecca had seen Amy making a *god-it's*-her-*again* face.

"Not really." Jessica sniffed, irritably fiddling with her glasses. "But I can't afford to miss any more school."

"I can fill you in about what you missed in history, if you like."

"Yeah, yeah." Jessica sniffed again. "And I heard . . . I mean, is it true that you're going to Helena Bowman's party?"

"Yes."

"With Anton Grey?"

"Yes."

"He asked you?"

"Yes."

"To the party?"

"Yes."

"To Helena Bowman's party?"

"Yes!"

"Why did he ask you?"

"I don't know," said Rebecca, feeling kind of sorry for the other girl. Jessica looked so forlorn, as though she'd missed out on winning the lottery or something. Maybe she'd been dreaming for years about going to the Bowmans' party on the arm of some dashing St. Simeon's boy, and now here was this outsider, not particularly pretty or popular, waltzing in and getting it all handed to her.

"How do you even *know* him?" Jessica absentmindedly loaded three packets of salad dressing onto her tray.

"I met him at the café." Rebecca wasn't about to confide in Jessica about her late-night cemetery lock-in, or her walk with Anton along St. Charles, or their excursion on Friday after school. He'd taken her to a cool, ramshackle place in the Irish Channel called Parasol's to eat roast beef po'boys, and there — sitting across from each other, grease dripping from their fingers, condensation on their water glasses dripping onto the vinyl cloth — they'd talked more about that night in the cemetery. Rebecca had asked Anton not to tell people about her getting shut in, and he'd agreed at once. He'd said nothing to anyone, he reassured her; his parents could be funny about who went into the cemetery after hours, and anyway, it was nobody's business but his and Rebecca's.

But clearly he'd told *someone* that he was taking her to the Bowmans' party.

"Amy said she saw you at the café together," sighed Jessica. She leaned close to Rebecca; her eyes were bloodshot and teary. "Some people are kind of annoyed about it, you know."

"Annoyed about what?" Rebecca didn't get it. "About us sitting together?"

"About you going to the party," Jessica whispered.

"Jessica!" Amy was standing up at a crowded table, waving frantically. "I've saved a seat for you!"

She glowered at Rebecca, as if to say, There's no seat saved for *you*.

"*I'm* not annoyed about it," Jessica said quickly. She shot Rebecca a rueful smile and giggled nervously. "I'm just kind of jealous, you know?"

"Is it that big a deal?" Rebecca picked up a container of yogurt and resisted the urge to smack it onto her tray.

"It's that big a deal," Jessica whispered. The smile faded from her face. "Watch your back, OK?"

Rebecca ate her lunch alone, at the end of a table packed with shrieking freshmen. She could barely taste her food. Her forehead was pounding, as though tom-toms were playing in her brain, echoing through her body. These girls were so petty: Just because she got a party invitation they wanted, she was getting warnings to watch her back? What she did in her own time was none of their business.

She didn't want to dawdle here a minute longer than necessary. There was still half an hour until her next class began: She'd spend the time in the library.

With its robin's-egg blue walls, tall shuttered windows, and long table of new MacBooks, the library was one of

Rebecca's favorite places in the school — now that she'd finally worked out how to get there.

She settled on the floor between the stacks and started flicking through books in the Louisiana history section. In an architectural book on the Garden District, she found pictures of Anton's house. And there was Helena's, and Marianne's: Just as Anton said, the houses had been owned by the same families since the 1850s. There was no mention of the curse anywhere, of course. Maybe Amy was right, and it was just a fake story made up to entertain tourists.

"Hard at work?" The thin form of Helena Bowman loomed over Rebecca. Helena crossed her arms over her chest, leaning against one of the stacks. Her face was pinched and mean, Rebecca decided — not pretty at all. Helena seemed to live in a constant state of petulance these days, as though she had nothing to be happy about. What was the point of being so rich and admired if it brought you no pleasure?

Rebecca said nothing, staring up at Helena and — of course, appearing behind her like a faithful shadow — Marianne. The way Helena looked at her was so insolent, so contemptuous. Perhaps it was because Rebecca was from somewhere else, and didn't care about their hierarchy and status. More likely, it was because Anton was paying her attention.

The librarian — in her usual tailored blue cardigan suit, a silver fleur-de-lis brooch primly pinned to her lapel — walked past the end of the row and paused, as though she was about to tell Helena off for talking. Then there was a glimmer of recognition, and she walked on without speaking.

Typical, Rebecca thought. One rule for most of the girls, and another for Them.

"People are saying you're coming to Helena's party," Marianne hissed, making an effort to lower her voice.

"It can't be true." Helena sniffed, as though something in the library smelled bad.

"Then I guess it isn't." Rebecca pretended to go back to reading her book, but the words were swimming. All she wanted was to be left alone.

"So you're *not* coming?" Marianne stage-whispered. She pushed a cloud of fair hair off her face, squinting at the dust motes dancing in a slim shaft of sunlight.

"Well, Helena just said it's impossible." Rebecca wasn't about to give them a straight answer. Helena sighed impatiently, shaking her head at Marianne.

"Anton says he's bringing you," Helena snapped. "So you can stop playing coy."

"I'm reading, not playing." Rebecca gestured with her book. "Would you mind?"

"Well, I guess I can't *stop* you from coming to my house," sighed Helena. She looked even more pained than usual. "If Anton insists on inviting you . . . well." She glanced at Marianne: It was a smug, spiteful smile.

"It's just, you might not enjoy yourself very much," Marianne told Rebecca earnestly. "You won't know anyone there."

"I'll know Anton," said Rebecca defiantly, gripping the closed book, wishing she could use it to smack their plaid-covered knees. She scrambled to her feet, aware that getting up in such a narrow space made her look about as elegant as a newly born calf. But at least standing up she'd be as tall as them, not gazing up like some groveling servant. Helena gave her a pitying look.

"Oh, you don't know Anton *at all*," she said, backing away, and she and Marianne rustled off, noses in the air. Rebecca didn't know what Helena was talking about: She didn't want to know. Was she implying that Rebecca was being duped somehow, that this was an elaborate trick Anton was playing to humiliate her?

Rebecca stood with her back to the shelf of books, doubt about Anton and his motives making her stomach churn. She usually had good instincts about people. Aunt Claudia, for example — she might be batty, but Rebecca had felt right away that she was a warm, good-hearted person. Amy wasn't malevolent: She was just a bottom-feeder in the shark tank that was Temple Mead Academy, and this had been perfectly obvious to Rebecca her first day of school. Jessica was nice enough, but immature and easily led — that had been clear as well.

But with Lisette and Anton, Rebecca wasn't so sure. Maybe they were both playing her. Maybe Lisette wasn't really a ghost; maybe Anton didn't really like her. They acted friendly enough, but it seemed as though the rules of normal life — *real* life — didn't apply to them.

Stop it.

She was going to drive herself crazy worrying about all this. If Rebecca wanted to find out exactly who (and what) Lisette was, they needed to spend more time together. And Helena was just trying to make mischief, she decided. In Helena's mind, Anton was theirs — hers and Marianne's, part of their exclusive group. They'd say anything to keep Rebecca out. All she had to do was dust off her skirt, slot her book back into place on the shelf, and get to her next class on time. At least they were a year ahead of her, and she didn't have to look at their snooty faces during classes every day. Nothing they said should matter — not to Rebecca, anyway.

Walking to the café after school, Rebecca followed the line of the cemetery wall, ducking around the corner to peer through the Washington Avenue gate. Lisette was nowhere to be seen. Rebecca leaned against the locked gate, dropping her bag onto the ground and pulling her phone out of her blazer pocket to check on messages. No calls, no texts. She hadn't seen or heard from Anton all weekend. That wasn't a big deal, she thought: Maybe he'd drop by the café today. If he wanted to see her, he knew where to find her. She dropped her phone back in her pocket and bent down to scoop up her bag.

A shoe smacked down on the bag handles, pinning them to the ground. A thick-soled, heavy black shoe, at the end of a black-panted leg. Why Anton was creeping up on her like this, and acting so aggressively, she didn't know.

Rebecca squinted up at the boy. It wasn't Anton.

"Waiting for someone?" Toby Sutton's bright orange hair looked like a brush fire in the late afternoon sun, the pale moon of his face pocked with acne marks. He scowled down at her, still not lifting his foot from the handles of her bag.

"Could you move?" Rebecca jiggled the trapped handles, fuming. They'd be muddy now; she wouldn't be able to carry the bag without getting her hands dirty. Toby was an oaf.

He didn't move. Rebecca heaved an exasperated sigh and stood up straight: She'd had enough today of cowering at the feet of Sutton family members.

"I said, *move*." Rebecca had never fought a boy before. She'd never fought anyone in her life. But if she had to shove Toby Sutton to get his stupid foot off her personal property, she would.

"We've all been talking about you at school," he said, ignoring her demand. He grinned, his eyes glimmering. "Everyone thinks it's pretty funny, the way you're chasing after Anton."

"I'm not chasing after anyone," Rebecca spat back. This was outrageous. Anton was the one who'd sought *her* out in the café; the walk along St. Charles and the visit to Parasol's were *his* idea.

"That's not what I hear." Toby was a lot more aggressive than Marianne, Rebecca thought: The blonde girl always seemed like a watered-down version of Helena, someone who might be almost OK if she wasn't in thrall to the Queen of Them. But Toby — he was just nasty. He folded his arms and sneered at her. "So maybe you should take my advice and stop embarrassing yourself."

"Take your advice? I don't even know who you are!" This wasn't true, exactly, but Toby didn't know that. He didn't know about Rebecca's nighttime visits to the cemetery, unless Anton had said something. And Rebecca couldn't believe Anton would have told the others about her getting locked in, not when he promised to keep it to himself.

"You know who I am all right," Toby sneered, and Rebecca's stomach shimmied with unease. Maybe she'd been wrong to trust Anton. "Don't play dumb. Just do yourself a favor and keep away from Anton. Keep away from all of our friends, OK?"

"I think that's for Anton to decide, not you." Rebecca tried to sound braver than she felt. There was something intimidating about Toby's broad, looming presence. She couldn't stand the fact that he was scaring her.

Toby shook his head, a cold smile stretching across his face.

"We move as a group," he said, his voice quiet. "That's the way it is. And we don't let in outsiders — especially nobodies like you."

"You're the nobody," she said with contempt. She slammed a foot onto the bag handles, right next to his, staking her claim. "Look at you — standing around here trying to bully a girl!"

Toby started to laugh. He staggered back a few steps, releasing Rebecca's bag, swinging his own bag high on his shoulder.

"If you think *this* is bullying," he called, still walking backward, "you really *don't* know what you're messing with. Think of this as friendly advice."

"Yeah, *real* friendly." Rebecca's face sizzled with rage. Tears prickled her eyes, though she was determined not to give him the satisfaction of seeing her cry. She grabbed her bag, trying to ignore the grit scouring the palm of her hand.

"You've been warned," he said, turning away. He stuck his hands in his pockets and walked down the street, gazing up at the striped awning of Commander's Palace and whistling. Rebecca felt an intense loathing — for him, his sister, and everyone they knew. Even Anton. How could he be friends with people like this? Why did he possibly want to "move as a group" with them?

She rubbed away hot tears with the back of her free hand, and stalked off in the opposite direction. She couldn't go to the café looking — or feeling — like this. There was nobody she wanted to see this afternoon, not even Lisette. And especially not Anton.

CHAPTER SIXTEEN

REBECCA! AURELIA! DINNER'S ALMOST READY!"

Rebecca emerged from her room reluctantly: She'd shut herself away in there ever since arriving home from school. The horrible incident with Toby Sutton had shaken her, and she'd tried to distract herself with texting her friends in New York. But everyone had been too busy to talk: Ling was taking the kids she babysat to the zoo in the park; Jenny was tutoring at the after-school homework center; Miranda was at a French lesson. And then, because of the one hour time difference, everyone was at dinner. Even the time zones were conspiring against her, Rebecca thought, trying not to feel sorry for herself — not least because if she was in New York right now, *she'd* be busy, too, not hiding out in some dark bedroom.

In the kitchen, its wood-framed windows misted up with steam, Aunt Claudia was wildly stirring something at the stove. She looked frazzled, as ever, by the demands of cooking.

"Table, please!" she said as Rebecca skulked in. Rebecca pulled a handful of cutlery from the drawer that always stuck and then went about her other tasks in silence: pouring water into mismatched tumblers and plopping down a cloth napkin at each place.

"Is everything all right?" her aunt asked, giving Rebecca an appraising look.

Rebecca shrugged. She knew it was rude, but she was tired of everything today.

"Aurelia!" Aunt Claudia called. "Where is that child?"

Aurelia wandered in clutching a squirming Marilyn, showering kisses over the cat's small, pointed face.

"Please put that animal down and wash your hands," Aunt Claudia scolded. She dolloped spoonfuls of white rice onto plates, apparently not noticing when sticky clumps dropped onto the table. The sight of more rice didn't fill Rebecca with much enthusiasm: She'd never eaten so much of it in her life. She might as well have gone with her father to China.

Monday nights they usually ate it with a thick, sloppy sauce — Aunt Claudia called all sauces "gravy" — of red beans, from which chunks of spicy sausage poked like slime-covered rocks in some sea on Mars. Other nights they ate it with shrimp, or with crawfish, or stuffed into charred green peppers or something similar called a *mirliton*. Sometimes her aunt served up spicy "dirty rice," flecked with scraps of meat, along with fish of some kind or a roast chicken from the grocery store. There was even rice in the gumbo — a dark, stewy kind of soup that in the Vernier household seemed to provide a watery grave for any number of unidentified leftovers. There'd probably be rice with their Thanksgiving dinner next Thursday.

Tonight Aunt Claudia had finished work in the Quarter early, so she'd had time to "make groceries," she told Rebecca, at the big supermarket down on Tchoupitoulas Street, by the river. From the number of pots on the stove, Rebecca had guessed her aunt was cooking Shrimp Étouffée, one of her more elaborate concoctions: This dish was actually one of Rebecca's favorites. It really reminded her of something her father made sometimes, though he called it Shrimp Surprise.

But dinner tonight turned out to be a mysterious medley of catfish, green peppers, green onions, and a couple of cans of tomatoes, simmered in a sauce so hot and gloopy that it stuck to the roof of Rebecca's mouth.

Aurelia seemed intent on shoveling in dripping forkfuls of dinner. Until she gave a start, as though she'd just woken up, or remembered something important.

"Becca, are you really going to Helena Bowman's Christmas party?" she asked, scooping up a puddle of pink sauce with a sawn-off chunk of French bread.

"What?" Aunt Claudia's fork clattered onto the table.

"Everyone's talking about it." Aurelia grinned at Rebecca. "Are you really going with Anton Grey?"

Rebecca shrugged, as though it was the last thing on her mind, although Toby's nasty words were still rattling around in her head. *Nobodies like you*. All she wanted to do was go back to New York, get away from these people and never see them again.

"Rebecca?" Her aunt wasn't about to let the matter drop — that was clear.

"He might have asked me if I wanted to go," she said,

aware she was using the "sulky" voice her father occasionally complained about.

"And you said no, I hope."

Rebecca stared down at her plate, stabbing with her fork at a bloated pink shrimp.

"Because," Aunt Claudia continued, "the less you have to do with those families, the better. As we've discussed. Aurelia, you have gravy all down your arm."

"I don't want to go, anyway." This wasn't really a lie. The thought of being snubbed at the party by the daughter of the house and her friends wasn't that appealing, and Toby had made all those threats, hinting that something awful would happen if Rebecca showed up. And as for Anton: Maybe his silence over the weekend meant something. Maybe he'd changed his mind and realized he should take someone more socially acceptable.

"And when is this party, exactly?" Aunt Claudia was speaking to Rebecca, but she was gazing into space or at some spot beyond Rebecca's shoulder.

"In a couple of weeks," she said, trying to sound casual.

"What day?" Rebecca realized what her aunt was doing — she was scanning the blank, random calendar days hanging by the door, the humidity half molting them off the wall.

"It's on December fifth, I think," Rebecca told her.

"That's all right then," Aunt Claudia mumbled, speaking to herself, then she cleared her throat and dabbed at her plate with a sliver of bread. "Anyway, good. I mean, you're not going. We're agreed."

"I'd go anywhere if Anton Grey asked me," sighed Aurelia, looking at Rebecca as though she was crazy.

"You would do no such thing." Aunt Claudia frowned. "Rebecca, I hope you've made it very clear to Anton that you have other plans that night."

"I thought you liked him," Rebecca couldn't help saying. "You know, when . . . when . . . I mean, he was quite helpful. And polite."

She didn't want to talk about the specifics of the cemetery lock-in with Aurelia there.

Her aunt glanced over at Aurelia, who was now preoccupied with dropping something from her plate onto the floor where Marilyn was lurking.

"Anton is . . . well, he's who he is," she said to Rebecca, and her voice sounded sad. For the first time, Rebecca wondered if Aunt Claudia had been pushed around by these families, the way Rebecca was now. She'd lived here all her life, after all. "He's as polite as he should be. But he's no more free than any of us."

"What do you mean, he isn't free?" This didn't make much sense. Anton was his own person, surely, just like Rebecca.

"Free to be someone he's not." Her aunt rubbed her hands together, grinding the silver rings that adorned almost every one of her long, thin fingers. "And now, Aurelia — please stop encouraging that cat and clear the table."

That night, Rebecca lay awake in her room, wondering why her aunt had started talking in riddles, and whether what she'd said was right. Nobody was free, according to Aunt Claudia — at least, not free to be someone else. But didn't people reinvent themselves all the time? Every infomercial

Rebecca had ever seen featured people who'd transformed themselves — their shape, their skin, their look, their marriage, their personal fortunes. If Anton wanted to break out of the Patrician set, he should be able to. This was America, after all. Or was New Orleans its own weird country — pagan and decadent and hierarchical, like the Roman Empire?

On Saturday morning, Aunt Claudia headed off to the Quarter as usual. Over breakfast, she told Rebecca that there were usually a lot of tourists in town the weekend before Thanksgiving, and she was hoping for a lot of business. That was another strange thing, Rebecca thought, sweeping the front porch clean of its accumulated leaves and dirt as her aunt jerked the car into the street: Aunt Claudia never offered to tell *her* fortune or read *her* tarot cards. Maybe she didn't like bringing her work home with her — except that deck of cards was always there on the kitchen table. Rebecca wondered, not for the first time, if Aunt Claudia was really the descendant of a voodoo queen, or if she was just a crackpot who made up all her "fortunes."

Farther up the street, at the cemetery gates, someone was waving. Rebecca blinked, and whoever it was disappeared. Then a familiar smiling face peeked around the gatepost, beckoning to Rebecca with an outstretched arm. Even at this distance, Rebecca knew it was Lisette. She leaned the broom against the porch rail and jogged down the street.

"I'm sorry I haven't been around," Rebecca told Lisette, glancing around to make sure nobody else was anywhere nearby and sidling around to the back of the nearest tomb. Enough people thought she was strange already: If Lisette really was a ghost, visible only to Rebecca, she didn't want to add "seen talking to herself in public" to her list of supposed crimes.

"I thought maybe you'd left," said Lisette, and Rebecca filled her in, quickly, on the way Toby Sutton had accosted her outside the cemetery after school.

"Ugh!" Lisette declared, perching on a protruding tree root. "*That* doesn't surprise me. The Sutton family have been horrible for more than a hundred and fifty years. And I should know!"

"Aren't you supposed to be making your big walk soon?" Rebecca asked her. Lisette nodded, picking absentmindedly at her ripped sleeve.

"Next Saturday. That's the anniversary of my mother's death. She died in 1853, so it's been one hundred and fifty-five years. How many years for you?"

"Thirteen," said Rebecca, with a rueful smile: It wasn't very long at all, compared with Lisette. But at least Lisette had known her mother. At least she could remember her. "How far is it?"

"About four miles each way." Lisette wriggled her bare toes. "It's not so bad. I get to see all the other ghosts along the way."

"Do you talk to them?"

"Of course." Lisette smiled up at her. "I hardly ever get a chance to talk to *anyone*. The night you and I met . . . well, before that I hadn't spoken in months to anyone but that crazy old gravedigger."

"There must be so many of them," Rebecca said, trying to imagine the streets of the city thronged with ghosts. It was impossible to visualize. The city of New Orleans was almost three hundred years old: If Lisette was to be believed, there had to be ghosts everywhere.

"More every year," Lisette told her, "though some disappear, of course."

"They disappear?"

"If they find peace. You know, if their death is avenged at last. It doesn't happen too often, though. A lot of those ghosts have been around much longer than I have."

"I wish I could see them!" Rebecca leaned her head back against the chilly tomb.

"You could," Lisette said casually, brushing at her legs, though why, Rebecca wasn't sure — no insects could land on her, surely, and dirt never seemed to stick. "If you came with me, that is."

"I could come with you?" Rebecca lifted her head.

"It takes a long time," Lisette warned her. "Four miles there, four miles back. And some of those ghosts — well, they like to talk. They don't have a thing in this world to say, but they surely like to talk."

"Really — I could come with you?" Rebecca's mind was zooming with the possibilities. "And I could . . . I could see the ghosts?"

Lisette nodded.

"Remember? When you hold my hand, nobody living can see you. And you can see all the ghosts."

Invisible to the real world. Able to see the spirit world. If this was true, Rebecca decided, those miles would be the greatest four miles — actually, eight miles — of her life.

"But maybe it's not a good idea," Lisette reasoned. "It might scare you. Some of them — well, they don't look so pretty. And sometimes they're not too happy, either. You understand."

"I guess," said Rebecca, wondering how upset *she* would be if she had to wander the streets forever, unable to rest in peace. "But I want to go, Lisette. I *really* want to go." New Orleans was still a mystery to Rebecca, a small place that got her all twisted around, a town of neighborhoods with long-forgotten names. But with Lisette, she'd get to see much, much more of it firsthand. And even better than that, she'd be able to glimpse its lost, secret world of ghosts.

"Next Saturday, then," Lisette said. "I'll wait for you by the Bowman tomb."

CHAPTER SEVENTEEN

FOUR MILES DIDN'T SOUND LIKE A LONG WAY. Rebecca had walked miles and miles in New York City on any given day — when she didn't want to wait for a crosstown bus, say, or when she and her friends decided to loop the park, or go for a major wander downtown, or see how many times they could walk back and forth across the Brooklyn Bridge.

But four miles in New Orleans was another matter entirely when you were dealing with the spirit world.

Lisette hadn't been lying: The city was thronged with ghosts. Three hundred years' worth of ghosts, all of them wearing the clothes they died in, many of them bearing — all too visibly in some cases — the injuries that killed them.

That next Saturday, with her hand firmly clasped in Lisette's, Rebecca could see them all. And this sight was so amazing, so overwhelming, it was all Rebecca could do to keep her mouth from hanging open in surprise.

Some of the ghosts were white; many more were black. Some spoke French or Spanish. A little girl in a ragged dress, skipping up and down the street, sang to herself in German. Rebecca heard some snatches of languages she thought she recognized, like Italian, and others she couldn't identify at all.

Most of the ghosts wandered around their little patches alone, but many hung out in strange mixed-century gaggles. Near the corner of Terpsichore Street in the Lower Garden District, a black man wearing nothing but a cutoff pair of torn trousers, raw marks from chains or handcuffs worn into his thin wrists, stood leaning against a lamppost. Deep in conversation with him were two white women, one in a flimsy 1920s-style evening dress with a blood-soaked back, the other a soccer mom in jeans and a mangled purple LSU sweatshirt. The man waved at Lisette as they walked by.

"He was a slave, flogged to death," she whispered to Rebecca. "He's been around almost as long as I have. Not sure about why he was killed — he doesn't like to talk about it. That woman in the pretty dress joined him in 1929, I think. Her boyfriend murdered her in that house up there."

Lisette pointed to a leaning house on the corner, its windows boarded up.

"And the other woman?"

"She's been there for the last four or five years. Head-on collision at the intersection with a drunk driver."

Walking along the highway underpass, Rebecca saw some very strange sights. The area used to be a neighborhood, Lisette explained, until thirty or forty years earlier. Now traffic thundered above them, and the vacant space below was used as a parking lot. But the neighborhood ghosts still had no choice but to hang around, even though their streets and houses were gone. A kid with an Afro and flared jeans lay back on the hood of a car, and when a curious Rebecca turned to look at him, she had to stop herself from crying out loud: His face was a red and black contorted mess. He'd been shot, Lisette told her.

Several black men dressed kind of like Native Americans prowled around the underpass; Rebecca heard snatches of chantlike songs, and one of them drummed from time to time on the trunk of a car.

"Mardi Gras Indians," Lisette said. "From one of the old Uptown gangs. One of them's been here a long, long time, and the other two joined him after one of those wars. Oh, which one was it? The second one, I think."

"The Second World War?"

Lisette looked uncertain.

"Is that what they call it? All of them were stabbed in different fights on Mardi Gras. I don't see too many of them, though, even up on Claiborne. Maybe they don't fight these days."

A fat black woman in a long, shapeless dress, her face badly bruised and nose broken, called out to them.

"Have you seen my baby? Have you seen my baby?"

Her voice was so plaintive, and her smashed-in face so grotesque, that a chill shuddered down Rebecca's spine; for a moment she was tempted to let go of Lisette's hand, just to make the awful faces of the ghosts disappear. She didn't know what she was expecting of the spirit world, or even if she'd truly believed she'd see *anything* out of the ordinary — but here, on the streets of New Orleans, there were too many sad and ugly sights. History was a mess, thought Rebecca.

"No, Miss Ella, I haven't seen your baby," Lisette called back, pulling Rebecca's arm to hurry her up and leaning close to whisper. "She's been asking me that for seventy years."

In the Warehouse District, Rebecca didn't know where to look: Nineteenth-century dockworkers with rope burns around their necks mingled with a businessman who'd been killed by gunmen robbing his office ten years ago, and a gaggle of brassy prostitutes — from a variety of different eras, judging by the various lengths of their skirts — who all waved and hooted at Lisette. A man dressed in the style of an eighteenth-century fop, complete with white-powdered wig and silk breeches, paced up and down the cobbles of Julia Street, gazing into the windows of art galleries.

"He was visiting from Havana, when this was all still someone's plantation," Lisette told her. "They said he caught yellow fever, but actually he was poisoned by his cousin, because they were fighting over some land. He told me the story when I was first a ghost — he'd already been here for a hundred years then. He's been much happier since all the art galleries moved in. Now he has something new to look at."

Crossing busy Canal Street was hard, because Rebecca couldn't tell who was a ghost and who wasn't. Nobody could see her, but she could see *everybody*. And, unlike Lisette, she had to dodge the real world: They couldn't just walk right through Rebecca any more than she could walk through walls — or locked cemetery gates.

She wildly ducked past anyone walking her way, sometimes noticing only at the last minute — to her horror — that the Asian guy in green hospital scrubs had a small wound in his chest — stabbed during a carjacking, Lisette told her — and that the nun pacing the neutral ground wasn't waiting for a bus or a streetcar: It was a man dressed as a nun, and he'd been strangled late at night one Halloween sometime in the 1980s.

In the Quarter, with its Saturday crowds, Rebecca couldn't help it: Her invisible self was bumping into startled people all over the place.

"That mimosa I had at breakfast must have been strong," she heard one very-much-alive woman tell her husband, after Rebecca careened into her. "I'm banging into things I don't even see. I think I must be drunk."

Lisette dragged Rebecca into the road, because cars were easier to avoid than people. Some ghosts were very easy to spot, like the woman with dark ringlets wearing a flowing blue ball gown, picking her way back and forth across Royal Street, gazing up at a flower-bedecked balcony. She didn't have any shoes on, Rebecca noticed, so she nudged Lisette.

"She died before the streets were paved," Lisette explained. "Before there were even *banquettes*."

"What?" Rebecca didn't know what bang-kets were.

"You call them sidewalks."

"So people walked around without shoes on?"

"Ladies did, when it had been raining and they were going to a dance." Lisette tugged Rebecca around a group of tourists ogling a silver-painted human statue. "They had their servants or slaves carry their shoes for them, because the roads were so muddy. See all the mud around the hem of her dress?"

Rebecca looked back, peering so hard at the dark tidal

line around the bottom of the beautiful gown that she walked straight into a bicycle chained to a lamppost.

"Ow!" she moaned, Lisette's hand almost slipping free from her grasp.

"Watch out," Lisette warned her. "We should turn here. If we keep walking this way, we'll run into all the Sicilian guys from the market, and they're still really angry. Down by the river it's bad, as well. Lots of people died in fights there. And there's a mean drug addict down on Ursulines — he's been there since the 1950s, and I try to keep out of his way. He says terrible things about black people."

"Ghosts can be racist?"

"Ghosts are the people they always were. Death doesn't change you. It just . . . well, it freezes you, I suppose, in a moment in time. People who were crazy or mean before are still crazy or mean after they're dead."

There weren't so many of the living up on Rampart Street, at the edge of the French Quarter, but there were plenty of ghosts — Spanish-speaking soldiers playing some sort of marbles game with brass buttons ripped from their coats; slaves of both genders and all ages; a sallow-faced man in a frock coat clutching a dueling pistol; and a sullen teenager sitting on the curb, a nasty, dark wound blooming across the side of his head like some exotic flower. He was wearing low-slung jeans and a baggy white T-shirt; his sneakers were Nikes.

"He wasn't here last year," Lisette whispered as they crossed the street. "He must be a recent arrival. It takes a while to get used to being a ghost. Sometimes people are unhappy about it for a long, long time. That's why everyone's leaving him alone, see?"

Rebecca had seen Armstrong Park before, because Aunt Claudia always parked near Rampart Street when she came down to the Quarter, and they drove past it on the way home. But Rebecca hadn't realized before today that this used to be a neighborhood as well — another black neighborhood, torn down years and years ago.

"That was Storyville," Lisette said, gesturing with her free hand. "You know, where all the bad places were. The clubs, they call them, where they play music. And the *brothels*."

"Where they played jazz, right?" Rebecca remembered hearing something about this, or maybe reading something in one of the local history books. "Didn't Louis Armstrong grow up around here? And Jelly Roll Morton?"

"Are they ghosts?"

"Well — not exactly. I mean, they're dead, but I don't think they died here. And I don't think either of them was murdered or anything."

"I recognize that first name — I think one of the ghosts up here used to say he'd played with him back in the day. He pronounced it 'Lewis,' in the Anglo way. I don't know where that ghost is now. Someone must have avenged his death. I haven't seen him for years and years."

That was another thing Rebecca hadn't realized until today: Lisette really only knew about history before her death. Unless some other ghost had explained something to her, the world after 1853 was a mysterious and complicated puzzle. She only knew little pieces of things. For example, she knew all about Storyville — which grew up after her death — because she'd spent years walking through it, and she knew about a historical figure like Abraham Lincoln because she'd heard a lot of ghosts talking about him during the Civil War. But when Rebecca asked her about other historical events — like, say, the sinking of the *Titanic*, or the atomic bomb dropped on Hiroshima — Lisette didn't have a clue. No other ghost had ever mentioned them.

"Mainly they like to talk about themselves," she explained.

Once they'd crossed Rampart and cut down a street alongside the park, Lisette started pausing more often to chat with a ghost or two, and though Rebecca said hello to them, nobody ever spoke to her.

"Who dat, baby?" one woman asked Lisette, nodding in Rebecca's direction. "She not one of us, now."

"It's a long story," Lisette told her.

"Save it for next year," said the woman, sashaying up the stairs of a small green house and disappearing — literally — by walking through the wall.

"They can see and hear you, but they can't speak to you," Lisette explained. "We can see the living, but we can only talk to other ghosts."

"And the people you haunt," Rebecca reminded her.

"The people we haunt." Lisette smiled. "Even if we don't know why."

"How far is it now to Tremé?" Rebecca asked. It felt as though they'd been walking for hours. She was exhausted, overwhelmed with everything — and everyone — she'd seen. The ghostly version of New Orleans was crowded with more strange costumes and ghoulish, bloody sights than Greenwich

Village during the Halloween Parade. One thing was sure: Rebecca would never doubt Lisette again. She was a ghost, all right.

"This is it!" Lisette squeezed her hand. "But we have to walk a ways further."

This part of Tremé looked just like the French Quarter, Rebecca thought, its streets jammed with small, shuttered houses — Creole cottages, she thought they were called — painted in pretty colors. As they walked farther, the style of houses didn't change all that much, but she started to see the difference between the wealthy Quarter and this neighborhood. Homes were a little shabbier, a little creakier, some leaning and peeling, some in a state of obvious disrepair. The "real" people — that is, nonghosts — of the neighborhood were out and about, some sitting on their stoops or riding bikes, others working on their houses. Everyone Rebecca saw was black.

"I read how this is the oldest African-American suburb in the country," she told Lisette, but her friend didn't reply. She seemed focused now, quickening her pace as they walked up St. Philip Street.

"They complaining about a foot of water!" one ghost in a bloodied sailor's uniform shouted to them. He gestured with his head at some people carrying a fat roll of moldy carpet down their front steps. Rebecca couldn't believe that they were just cleaning the house out now, three years after the storm. "I want to tell them, walk a ways up there, up toward Broad Street and see what the water did. They got nothing to be muttering about."

Rebecca smiled at him, but the sailor seemed to look right

through her. Lisette didn't say a word. In fact, she didn't speak at all until she came to an abrupt stop outside a house that looked as though it was about to fall down.

It was a small house that once, long ago, must have been a clean sky blue, but now its paint had rubbed away; it looked scoured by years of wind and rain. Weed-spouting cracks splintered its foundation. One shutter hung broken from its hinges; the others were missing. The roof had caved in, and the remnants of a ragged blue tarp were loosely fixed over its gaping hole.

"This is my house," Lisette whispered. They stood staring up at it.

"And this is what the storm did to it?" The house was a depressing sight. It looked as though it was about to collapse.

"Not just the storm. My mama, she took care of it. It was *her* house. But for years it's been getting this way. People buy it, but they don't live there — they rent it out and do nothing to keep it together. Every year it looks worse and worse. And since Katrina, nobody lives here at all. Nobody bothers to fix it. One of the ghosts down on St. Claude told me there was talk of pulling it down. 'Houses are coming down all over,' he said. 'Easier to wipe them away than put them right.'"

"That's terrible!" Rebecca thought how sad it had to be for Lisette, coming here year after year and seeing the home she grew up in and loved crumbling into a ruin. "But aren't historic homes protected here? This house must be nearly two hundred years old."

Lisette shrugged.

"All those houses in Storyville were old," she said. "And up there — see?"

She pointed up the street, and Rebecca looked. Ahead of them stretched another branch of the interstate, humming with unseen traffic, its overpass running above what Rebecca thought was Claiborne Avenue.

"That used to be a beautiful street," Lisette said. "Big oak trees, just like St. Charles Avenue. It was the heart of Tremé — the green heart, some people said. But they pulled down all the old houses and the old trees so that the big road up there could go in. Lots of ghosts there are real unhappy still. All they got to haunt is a pile of concrete."

"It's strange to think of how the past gets swept away," Rebecca mused. She wondered how long it would be before Lisette's house was demolished, cleared away with no trace, like all those houses and streets in old Storyville.

"The past doesn't go away." Lisette gazed up at her house. "You just can't see it anymore."

"I don't know about *your* past," Rebecca told her. "Not really."

Lisette glanced over: Her dark eyes were glittering, her cheeks flushed. Her skin was the color of burnished gold, Rebecca thought. Where her sleeve was ripped away from her shoulder, Rebecca could see a small, purplish hint of a bruise.

"Perhaps now's the time," Lisette said. "On our walk home. If you have the stomach for it."

CHAPTER EIGHTEEN

"I DIDN'T DIE FROM YELLOW FEVER," LISETTE TOLD Rebecca. "That was what they said to my mother, and to the notary, but it wasn't true."

Rebecca could barely breathe. At last, Lisette was going to tell the story of how she became a ghost.

That summer, Lisette explained, not long before her seventeenth birthday, another yellow fever epidemic descended on the steamy city, its first outbreaks recorded at the docks, and soon taking hold of the neighborhood people were starting to call the Irish Channel. Before long, people in the wealthier, leafier Garden District were falling sick as well.

Business wasn't good during the times of the fever and her school was closed, Lisette said, but she and her mother were getting by. One day, when they were both working in the small front parlor of their house, starting work on the trousseau of the daughter of a Creole family up on Esplanade Ridge, a note was delivered.

"I never read the note, but I could tell from my mother's face it was something bad," Lisette said. She paused so they could cross Rampart without Rebecca getting run over. "And that evening she asked me if I would consider going to nurse someone who was sick. Someone who'd been very good to our family, who'd just fallen ill."

"Why would she send you?" Rebecca was aghast. "Wasn't she worried about you catching yellow fever as well?"

"You don't catch it from other people," Lisette told her. "We knew that much, even then."

"Of course — duh." Rebecca was ashamed of the lapse in her scientific knowledge.

"And I'd already caught it — when I was five," Lisette told her. "It wasn't so bad — lots of children had the fever and lived to see the next week, especially children of color like me. Something in our genes, I think, from Africa. So after that I was immune."

Although she'd never worked as a maid or nurse of any kind before, Lisette agreed to go — even though the house she'd be staying in was a long way away, on the American side of the city.

"Everyone we knew spoke French, or something like it," she said. "A mixture of French and English, most times. Upriver was a different world to me, like a foreign country. That was my one and only time on the St. Charles Avenue streetcar, that day."

"There was a streetcar then? What — was it pulled by horses?"

"Not then. It was the New Orleans and Carrollton Railroad, pulled by a steam engine. It was loud and smelly, and it moved quite fast. There were too many people pressed together inside. I didn't like it at all. But my mother held on to me, and I knew nothing terrible would happen if she was there. I was right about that, I guess."

Lisette gave an enigmatic, sad little smile. "But my mother left me at the gate. She didn't come into the house."

"Why?" Rebecca asked, but Lisette just shook her head. She didn't say anything at all for a while, so Rebecca tried a different sort of question. "Who did you have to look after?"

"Two people. A wealthy man — he was a sugar factor. . . ."

"A what?"

"A go-between, maybe? Or you would say a broker? He bought sugarcane from the planters upriver and sold it on. And he arranged loans for them, investments. He was from New York, but he'd lived in Mississippi, coming back and forth to New Orleans for almost twenty years. He'd made a lot of money. Just that year, he'd built this big house in the Garden District for him and his wife, and his son and his daughter. It wasn't even really finished, but they were already living there. The son was away for the summer, and they told him to stay away. The man was sick, and so was his daughter. She was not much older than I was. That winter she was going to make her big social debut."

Lisette was used to much smaller houses and a very different kind of neighborhood. Everyone who worked in the house was a slave, and, unlike the black people she'd grown up around, none of them spoke French. They regarded her, she said, with some suspicion.

"My skin was light, and when I told them my grandparents had come from Haiti, and that my mother had her own little business, and that we lived in Faubourg Tremé — well, they acted as though they didn't know *what* I was doing there. And I didn't know myself, really. I knew a few Americans, but I'd never met this man in my life. But he knew me."

"Really?"

"He said my name when I was taken to his bedside. He tried to smile at me. But he was already very ill, shivering and soaked with sweat. His lips were cracked, like a dry riverbed." Lisette shuddered at the memory. "Already yellow with the jaundice, but his tongue was dark, almost purple, as though it was rotting away in his mouth. I could see he didn't have long."

"But how did he know you?" Rebecca wasn't worried about bumping into other people now: She was intent on Lisette's story.

"At first, I didn't understand. All I knew was that my mother had said *she* would go, but that was not possible. And this man, he'd asked for me. But to everyone else in the house I was a stranger. I had to sleep in the building out back, where the kitchen was, and it was so hot — so very, very hot. The cook did not like me. She said I had fancy ways. And the lady of the house, she didn't like me much, either. She never called me by my name. I was in the house less than a week, and on the last night she said I had to sleep on the floor by the daughter's bed. Things were very bad by then. The girl was vomiting up the black blood. I had to hold her down when she was sick, even when the blood sprayed into my face. The father, he was already dead."

"How horrible!" Rebecca had read a little about yellow fever: It sounded like a painful, ugly way to die.

"That day was so hot, so terrible — totally still." Lisette raised her face to the sky.

There was no warmth in the sun this afternoon, Rebecca thought. The sky was darkening to gray, as though rain was coming. She hoped they made it home before it started.

"And no breeze was almost a relief, in a way," Lisette went on, "because the wind brought the smell of the river. Everything on the ships and barges, they were going bad. The stink of death was everywhere. Each morning, outside the cemetery gates, there were bodies. Their faces all sunken, agonized. It was horrible. We kept the shutters closed so we did not have to see, but we could still smell them. This is a bad thing to admit, but all I wanted was for the girl to die so I could go home again."

"But she didn't die?"

"Oh, no, she died." Lisette sighed. "In the night, she died. The mother, she was mad with grief. Screaming, pulling and clawing on the drapes. The doctor and his son came, and the lawyer came — men in black, swarming through the house like flies. The bodies needed to be buried quickly in the family vault, they said, before they swelled up in the heat and burst open."

That's disgusting, Rebecca thought, waiting for Lisette to go on. But she was distracted, it seemed, by someone who *had* to be a ghost, sitting slumped on the front steps of a narrow house. He was wearing a tight-fitting black suit and a sharp trilby-style hat; his shoes were pointed. He was looking at Rebecca and Lisette with interest.

"Hi, Marco," Lisette said as they approached. Marco sat up a little, but his hangdog expression didn't change.

"I never took no money," he said. "I never took no money from nobody. But this is what they did to me!"

He opened his jacket to reveal a blackened gash down his shirtfront. Rebecca recoiled: She'd seen plenty of congealed blood today, but this seemed a particularly large and jagged wound. Marco seemed pleased with her reaction.

"Dat's right," he said. "I never did nothing, and this is what they did to me."

Lisette pulled Rebecca along the sidewalk, picking up her pace.

"Hurry," she whispered. "Otherwise he'll ask me to touch it."

"Yuck!" Rebecca said, though she couldn't resist glancing back. Marco had settled back against the steps and was rebuttoning his jacket. "At least he didn't die from yellow fever."

"The doctor kept saying you couldn't catch the fever from a dead body," Lisette continued, "but no one else in the house believed him. We didn't know then, exactly, what brought yellow fever to the city summer after summer."

"Mosquitoes carry it, right?" Rebecca was trying to make up for her earlier brain freeze. "Like malaria."

"That's what some ghost told me, years ago — Johnny, remember him?" Rebecca nodded, thinking of the guy in scrubs pacing back and forth along Canal Street. "But back then we thought it lived in the city, in the hot air, in the dirty streets. We thought it was the price we paid for living here."

Lisette fell silent, the only sound now the slap of Rebecca's feet along the sidewalk — Lisette, she noticed, walked without making noise of any kind — and the surge of passing cars. Lisette's grip on her hand grew tighter, as though she was steeling herself for the next part of the story. Rebecca didn't want to ask any questions or push her too hard. She knew that what was coming was the saddest part of all.

"I was stripping the sheets off the bed," she said softly. "Taking all the linens to be burned. The first coffin had already been carried over to the family vault, and some of the servants were on their way down the back stairs with the daughter's. I should have gone out through the back gallery, but I didn't want anything else to do with that body. And besides, I was curious. Downstairs there were raised voices, and I could hear the lady shouting something over and over. So I crept down the front staircase, and though the doors to the parlor were closed, I could still hear what they were saying."

"What was she shouting?" Rebecca was almost whispering now. It seemed incredible to her that while Lisette was telling her this story, they were still walking, still holding hands — incredible that around them the citizens of New Orleans were still going about their Saturday-afternoon business. Just across the road, someone was walking out of a chiropractor's office, rubbing at his neck; someone else was doing a terrible job of parallel parking his car. A woman was hanging red and green plastic beads from the railings of her porch, talking in a high-pitched baby voice to a little dog.

"She was shouting, 'Who is she? Who is she?' I could hear her screaming this. And then the lawyer's deep voice would go on for a while, and she would start screaming again. She didn't sound sad anymore. She just sounded angry."

"Were you frightened?" Rebecca asked her. It must have been so hard for Lisette — in this strange part of town and strange house, with dead bodies, and an enraged woman screaming.

"I wasn't scared — not then, anyway." Lisette had stood with her ear against the heavy door, trying to make sense of the lawyer's low drone. "I thought — *why doesn't this woman know who her own daughter is? Why is she asking this lawyer*? But then I realized she wasn't talking about her daughter. They were going over her husband's will, and that's why she was asking this question. I heard the lawyer say my name — Lisette Villieux. She was talking about me."

CHAPTER NINETEEN

REBECCA FELT FEVERISH WITH EXCITEMENT: SHE could barely take in what Lisette was telling her. She no longer cared about looking out for ghosts or asking about how they died: All she wanted to do was barrage Lisette with questions about her own life. How did the lawyer know her name? Why did the dying man send for her? Why was everyone arguing about her after the man was dead?

"In his will," Lisette said, her pace slowing again. "I was mentioned in his will. And my mother — I heard her name as well, Rose Villieux. That was why I couldn't move away from the door, you see? I had to stay and listen. I wanted to know what they were saying about us, and why."

"I understand," Rebecca told her. She would do exactly the same thing, she thought, even if her brain was telling her to run for her life out the front door.

"It took a while for me to make sense of what they were saying, but eventually it was clear. The dead man — he was my father. Our house in Tremé, he'd bought it for my mother and me. In his will, he gave it to her. That's what the lawyer was telling his wife — that was why they were speaking my mother's name. And there was some money for me, so I could keep going to school."

"You were his *daughter*?" Rebecca couldn't believe it.

"Natural daughter, as we used to say. It was the way things went back then. Lots of men in New Orleans had two families, one white and one black. Some of the girls I knew at school had rich Creole fathers who gave them gifts and saw to their education. Some of them had fathers who spent a lot of time with them and their mothers."

"But where did they all meet — these white men and black women? Were the women originally their servants? Their slaves?"

"Sometimes. Sometimes they met at one of the quadroon balls in the Quarter. If you were a young woman of color, you could meet some fine, rich young Creole at a ball and your mama, she would make a deal with him. To get you a house, and money for life."

"That sounds like prostitution, almost!" Rebecca said, instantly regretting it: She didn't want to insinuate anything about Lisette's mother. But although Lisette was shaking her head, she didn't look offended.

"It's no different from the way white girls met their husbands at balls and parties." She pulled on Rebecca's hand to draw her back onto the sidewalk; a pickup was careering around the corner in front of them. "And weren't *their* parents doing the same thing, making sure they had a nice house and things for the rest of their lives? It was just that black and white people couldn't get married, by law. So some gentlemen, they never married at all. They just spent their time with their colored wife and family."

"But your father . . ." Rebecca began, and then stopped. It was too awkward to say: *Your father had nothing to do with you.*

"He was an American, not a Creole," Lisette said quietly. "Maybe it was hard for him, having that double life. That day he sent the note to my mother, I think he knew he was dying. Maybe he wanted to see me one last time. Maybe he saw me many times when I was growing up, and I didn't realize. I mean, maybe he saw me in the street and knew me. I think about this a lot — how I didn't know him, but he knew me."

Rebecca imagined Lisette's father, watching her from afar — looking at her as she skipped to the market, swinging a basket; looking into her little classroom from the hallway, making sure she was hard at work.

"So did he meet your mother at one of those balls?" she asked. Lisette shrugged.

"I don't think so. My mother was too dark-skinned to go to them, and she told me she'd never allow me to attend one. Maybe she'd done some work for him, some tailoring — I don't know. I never had the chance to ask her. One moment, I was standing outside the parlor doors listening, thinking — here is this secret that my mother never, ever told me. Thinking that the man who just died was my father. And then the doors burst open, and suddenly the lady is there. And she's wild."

"Wild as in crazy?"

"Crazy, angry. Her eyes red and big." Lisette widened her

eyes. "Pulling at her hair. When the doors burst open, they almost knocked me over. And when she saw me, well . . ."

Rebecca waited. She wasn't sure if Lisette could go on. Her friend was looking away, trailing her free hand along the neat hedge outside one of the Prytania Street houses.

"She flew at me," Lisette said, her voice so soft Rebecca had to twist closer to hear clearly. She gave Lisette's hand a comforting squeeze. "Shrieking, arms flailing. She was beating me, ripping at my clothes. She ripped my sleeve off, almost."

That's why it was torn, thought Rebecca. The woman married to Lisette's father had practically clawed it off Lisette's body.

"Didn't anyone try to stop her?" Rebecca asked.

"The lawyer man tried," Lisette replied. "But she was like a woman possessed. In that moment, I think, she hated me. Maybe because her own daughter had just died, and I was still standing there, young and healthy. Or maybe it was because she'd just found out this terrible secret, that her husband had another woman — a black woman — and another child, and a house he'd bought for them on the other side of the city. Maybe she even knew my mother somehow, and that's why my mother said *she* couldn't go to nurse him when he was ill. I think about these things over and over. I wish I could ask my mother."

"So she attacked you, right there in front of the lawyer."

"And the doctor — he'd been out back checking on two of the manservants, because they'd just taken ill as well. He was running up the hall, I remember. She shook me and shook me, and I was backing away, trying to get free of her and her claws and her angry face."

"But you couldn't?" The houses they were passing were starting to look familiar, Rebecca realized. They must be back in the Garden District.

"There was nowhere to go. I tripped on the bottom step and fell, and she was still over me, shaking and shaking me. She slammed my head against the stairs. It must have hurt, though I don't remember the pain at all. It's a funny thing, the way we don't remember the pain. Just the sensation of hitting, and then a smoky kind of darkness. And then I was standing up, but at the same time I could see myself lying on the stairs. My body was still, and my eyes were open, but they were just staring at nothing. My head was leaning in a strange way, and a dark spot, like spilled ink, was growing on the stair carpet. That woman was still shaking me, trying to bash my head against the wood another time. And the men — one of them had his hands on her shoulders, pulling her way. The other was shouting something — 'For the love of God!' I remember that."

"And you could see all this?" Rebecca was imagining what it would be like to see your own lifeless, bleeding body.

"Oh, yes. I could see it. I could walk down the stairs. I could watch them all and hear them all. And that's how I knew."

Lisette looked at Rebecca, her eyes as dark as the inky blood she'd just described.

"Knew you were dead," whispered Rebecca.

"Knew I was a ghost." Lisette stopped short in front of a locked gate, gesturing with one shoulder to its broad front gallery, the old-fashioned gaslight by the door, its narrow white pillars. Lumber and scaffolding were piled all over the yard at the corner; it looked as though construction was underway on an addition of some sort. A solarium, thought Rebecca, and a swimming pool. She knew the details, because she'd heard all the talk about it at school.

It was the Bowman house.

Rebecca must have flinched, or tightened her grip on Lisette's hand, because Lisette hurried to reassure her.

"They're not here this weekend," Lisette told Rebecca. "They always go away for all of Thanksgiving — I don't know where. They wouldn't be able to see you, anyway."

"Of course," Rebecca said. Something about this house provoked such a strong, visceral reaction in her.

"The place you died," said Rebecca, gazing up the steps. "It's this house, isn't it?"

Lisette nodded.

"And the woman who killed you," Rebecca said slowly, "was Mrs. Bowman?"

Lisette nodded again. All the warmth had disappeared from the afternoon. A few drops of rain spattered the sidewalk. Rain had no effect on Lisette: It just hit the ground she walked on, as though she wasn't there — because, of course, she wasn't. But Rebecca shivered, anticipating the coming storm.

"My death had to be covered up, of course," Lisette said, stroking the iron railings. A breeze was picking up: Leaves danced down the sidewalk, and the big oak tree on the corner started rustling, as though it was warning the Bowmans of their presence. "They knew my mother would be around asking questions before too long. I wasn't one of their slaves. So the doctor said he would declare me another victim of yellow fever, and sign all the necessary papers. His name, you know, was Sutton."

"Really?" So Helena and Marianne's families *had* been friends a long, long time.

"And late that night, the lawyer and the doctor came back for me. My body was wrapped in a sheet. They carried me across the road to the cemetery — they had keys, of course, to the gate. I followed them over, to watch what they were doing. I was thrown into the family tomb, on top of my father's coffin, and my sister's."

"Didn't your mother demand to see your body? You know, when she found out?"

"They told her I'd been buried in a communal grave in the cemetery with other fever victims. Too many people were dying every day by then. When she went to the cemetery, the grave was filled in and the Bowman family vault — well, it was all sealed up."

"Of course," said Rebecca. They stood together, safely invisible, looking up at the Bowman house. It was hard to believe such a terrible thing could have happened in such a beautiful house. On a night like this, with clouds tumbling in the sky, and the low growl of thunder in the distance, the house looked calm and solid, a refuge rather than a place of danger. A place of secrets, sickness, murder. "It must be awful, having to look at this house every day."

"Sometimes, I even go inside," Lisette said.

"Really?" Rebecca didn't know that *she* would want to come here more than she absolutely had to.

"Not very often. But this year I'm coming to the party."

"You are?"

"Mmmm," murmured Lisette, staring up at the house. "It's time."

Rebecca didn't know what that meant. Lisette was pulling away from her now, dropping Rebecca's hand. She started walking off alone toward the cemetery: Rebecca was standing — suddenly visible again, she realized — outside the Bowmans' wrought-iron gates.

"I'm coming to the party, too!" Rebecca called after her, not caring that any neighbors looking out their windows at that moment would see her talking to no one in particular. Lisette glanced back at her, smiling.

"Look for me at ten o'clock," Lisette said. She looked exhausted, spent with the walk and with the story she'd told.

Rebecca nodded, watching Lisette amble away. Now she understood why Lisette haunted the Bowman house. She understood why for the past one hundred fifty years she'd drifted around in the long shadow of its quiet, oak-shaded galleries. It was the place she'd died, murdered at the age of sixteen — and it was her father's house. Villieux may have been her mother's last name, but Lisette was a Bowman.

CHAPTER TWENTY

IT TOOK SOME PLANNING, AND SOME LIES, AND the enthusiastic cooperation of Aurelia and her coconspirator, Claire, but Rebecca was going to the Bowmans' party whether Aunt Claudia — or anyone else — liked it or not.

A week had passed since the walk with Lisette, and all Rebecca had been able to think about was getting inside the Bowmans' house, and seeing the place where her friend had been murdered. She and Anton had communicated by text only: Rebecca didn't want anyone to see them together. She *had* to take this opportunity to at least see the staircase at the Bowmans'. Helena was hardly going to invite her around for dinner.

The afternoon of the party, her aunt arrived home from her day in the Quarter, complaining about patchy business and out-of-tune buskers. Rebecca made her some tea and mentioned, in an oh-so-casual way, that she was going to the movies that night with Aurelia and Claire.

"You know, that Reese Witherspoon thing," she said,

watching her aunt count out the day's meager takings onto the stained Formica table. "It's on at the Prytania."

"I thought Aurelia was just having a sleepover at Claire's," Aunt Claudia said, smoothing out crumpled notes and shuffling them as though they were a floppy deck of cards.

"Oh, she is! But first we'll go to the movies together . . . and I may go back with them for a while. To hang out."

This sounded so lame and implausible that Rebecca had to turn toward the window and pretend to be intent on rinsing old tea leaves out of the strainer. As far as her aunt was concerned, Rebecca spent all her spare time doing homework in a café or reading books in her room. The idea of her hanging around with that high-energy twelve-year-old twosome, Aurelia and Claire, both as fizzy as a whole bottle of Alka-Seltzer . . . well, it wasn't a very compelling lie. But Aunt Claudia seemed just distracted enough to buy it.

"Do you want me to drive you there, baby?" she asked.

"Yes, please," said Rebecca. This was all part of the plan, so her aunt wouldn't suspect anything. And anyway, as Rebecca had realized, her aunt thought the party had already taken place. Inadvertently, she'd given Aunt Claudia the wrong date — December fifth, which was the day before. "Claire's mother is going to pick us up afterward and take us to her house. I'll just walk home from there. I won't be home late — ten-thirty or so, I guess."

"I'd rather Claire's father walk you home," her aunt said. "Just to be safe."

"I'm sure he won't mind," Rebecca told her. Of course, Claire's parents knew nothing about her coming over to their house, because she wasn't *going* to their house. Claire and Aurelia had been sworn to secrecy on the lives of the entire cast of *Gossip Girl*.

That night, after Aunt Claudia let them out of the car outside the Prytania — an old redbrick movie theater that seemed completely out of place on its residential street — Rebecca shepherded her giggling charges up the stairs, bought tickets from the guy in a black SAVE NOLA T-shirt sitting behind the arched window, and waved good-bye to her aunt. Inside, she bought the girls tubs of popcorn and bottles of water — at the same inflated price they commanded in New York, she noticed — and left Aurelia and Claire to find seats in the cavernous, shabby old theater.

In a tiny stall in the women's bathroom, Rebecca opened her shoulder bag and removed its contents: her one decent dress, which was black, strapless, and carefully folded; a pair of strappy black sandals with kitten heels; some dangling silver earrings bought at one of the little boutiques in the Quarter; and a small makeup bag crammed with mascara, lip gloss, and eyeliner. She had fifteen minutes — fifteen minutes to tug off her jeans and American Eagle checked shirt (while trying not to crack her elbows on the walls of the toilet stall), to wriggle into her dress and make up her face, and to meet Anton in the street outside. And she made it, in perfect time.

"You look great," he said, holding open the passenger door of a silver Audi. Anton had turned seventeen a month ago, so he could drive without a licensed older driver in the car — not that his parents had ever been sticklers about that kind of thing, from what Rebecca could gather. They'd left him alone this weekend altogether, with only the housekeeper for company: His father was on a business trip in Chicago, and his mother had gone along to do some Christmas shopping.

"You don't look bad yourself." Rebecca slid onto the leather front seat, blushing because it sounded more flirtatious than she'd intended, and hoping it was too dark for Anton to notice her red cheeks. He *did* look good, very mature, in Ralph Lauren pants and a button-down shirt, his pale blue tie flecked with a tiny fleur-de-lis design; a navy blazer lay across the backseat. But he also looked as embarrassed and awkward as *she* felt.

"It seems like ages since we, you know . . . saw each other," he said, driving slowly along Prytania, back toward the Garden District. "I thought maybe you'd changed your mind about . . . you know . . . hmmm."

His voice trailed off into a choked sort of cough.

"Oh, no!" Rebecca said quickly. "I mean, I really want to go."

That sounded way too eager, she thought. She didn't want Anton to think she was some giggling Pleb, desperate for a St. Simeon's boyfriend.

"What I mean is, I really want to, you know, go to the party. To see the house and everything. I didn't mean — ah, anything else."

"Oh," he said, frowning a little and drumming his fingers on the steering wheel. "OK."

Now she was worried she'd offended him. It was so much easier to talk when they were walking down St. Charles, Rebecca thought. Sitting here together in this confined space was way too hard. It felt like . . . well, a real date.

People were going to see them in public together for the first time, if you didn't count that day at the café. A wave of anxiety washed over her.

"Well, this is it," Anton said at last, parking on a quiet block of Fourth Street, in a pool of yellow cast by the antique streetlight.

A lot of people were parking nearby, on that block and the next, hurrying toward the Bowmans' mansion on Prytania. Most of them were older, Rebecca noted as Anton locked her bulging shoulder bag in the Audi's trunk: The women wore long dresses and carried pashmina wraps; the men wore elegant jackets. She wished *she* had some kind of wrap or jacket — the night was clear and getting colder. Rebecca didn't recognize the younger people ahead of them on the sidewalk, but that might have been because she was used to seeing everyone in a school uniform.

Beyond its tall wrought-iron gate, the Bowman house quivered with light: Miniature storm lanterns, each sporting a tiny, flickering candle, lined the pathway and dangled the full length of the front porch. Very little progress seemed to have been made on the dug-up side yard, and lumber was still stacked at the foot of the broad side gallery, draped with a giant canvas. But the construction didn't detract from the imposing grandeur of the house, and once she was inside the double doors — opened by the dignified elderly black man Rebecca had seen on her first day of school — she soon forgot about the less-than-perfect garden. There was so much else to take in: the spacious central hallway with its black-and-white tiled floor; the towering Christmas tree, every decoration glinting silver or pristine white; and, sweeping up to the next floor, the long dark swirl of the staircase.

Rebecca stood at its foot, one hand caressing the ornate post, ignoring the rush of people around her. This was it: the spot where Lisette had been killed, her head smashed open on the blunt edge of one of these steps. Rebecca was transfixed. The house looked so elegant, as though nothing bad could ever happen there. How many of its guests knew about this terrible guilty secret?

Anton's hand was on her arm, drawing her toward the doors of the double parlor: Those were the doors where Lisette had hunched, listening! Rebecca reluctantly followed him into the long, high-ceilinged room — two rooms, really, the edges of their tall dividing pocket doors just visible. The sofas and some of the art on the walls were modern, but Rebecca doubted that much had changed in these rooms in the last century and a half. The looming windows with their open shutters, the ceiling rosettes from which sparkling chandeliers hung, the ornate carved fireplaces, the wide, creaky floorboards — they were all relics of the house Lisette must have known.

Rebecca had been to adult parties before in New York — her father insisted on dragging her to them, so she could learn, he said, how to be "civilized." But rooms were smaller in New York; everyone they knew lived in an apartment. In the Bowmans' house, everything was larger than life. Rebecca wondered how they even got a Christmas tree so large into their foyer.

A waiter approached, and Anton picked up two glasses of champagne. Rebecca took a sip of hers, wincing when the bubbles rushed up her nose, and followed him through the crowd and its miasma of perfume. He led her through the front rooms and through another set of double doors, into an even bigger, grander space. Silk curtains puddled on the floor at each window; the only furnishings were a few dark, red-cushioned chairs, and some indoor palms splayed against the windows.

A makeshift bar was set up in one bend of the curving room, waiters in white shirts and black pants pouring out glasses of champagne and juice. In another bend, a jazz trio — also dressed in black and white — played in front of the marble fireplace, though nobody seemed to be listening to them. Everyone was talking and laughing and shouting and drinking. The only black people at the party, as far as Rebecca could see, were the men serving drinks and the musicians. It was just like one of those quadroon balls, Rebecca thought: She'd been doing some more reading in the library at lunchtimes. The only black men allowed to attend those were the musicians. Most of the women at the balls looked white — they were quadroons, which meant a quarter black, or octoroons, which meant an eighth.

These fractions mattered back in those days, when mixed-race marriages were strictly forbidden. Perhaps here, tonight, there were women who wouldn't have been allowed to marry their husbands. Or perhaps that was why everyone was so obsessed with names, and bloodlines, and keeping marriages within a select group of families. They didn't want any skeletons in the closet — though at least, Rebecca thought, laughing midsip and accidentally inhaling a glug of champagne, all skeletons were white.

Anton led her around, whispering to her about various older guests who were friends of his parents, and in no hurry, apparently, to go off in search of his friends. She could see several girls she recognized from Temple Mead, all from the grade above hers. Julie Casworth Young was wearing a jade-green taffeta cocktail dress, her fair hair tightly wound in a chignon. When she spotted Rebecca, she looked bemused, then annoyed, darting off to whisper in Marianne Sutton's ear. Marianne frowned and looked a little confused for a moment. But soon, Rebecca noticed, Marianne had started acting up; she stood with a gaggle of her friends, shrieking with laughter, or was busy draping herself over a boy Anton identified as Paul Robichon. Paul had graduated from St. Simeon's that spring and had just arrived back from his freshman semester at Duke.

Maybe Marianne was trying to make Anton jealous, Rebecca thought, but it didn't seem to be working. He seemed more affected by the way Toby Sutton and the other guys from his year at school were keeping their distance. It was pretty clear they were avoiding him. In the dining room, where platters of crab cakes, deep-fried oysters, stuffed figs, garlic shrimp, and delicious cornbread muffins were crowded onto a dining table that seated twelve, Anton and Rebecca lingered for a while, standing by the windows to eat. But nobody came over to talk to them. They might have been as invisible as Lisette.

Helena flitted in and out of every room, wearing a floaty short dress of silver and white. She looked like one of the Christmas decorations, Rebecca thought, surreptitiously licking garlic butter off her fingers and picking her champagne flute off the windowsill. When Helena brushed past them without even a glance in Anton's direction, Rebecca realized the gang was all intent on snubbing him. This was her fault, she knew. By taking her as his date to the party, Anton was a social pariah.

Rebecca didn't care on her own account, but she felt awful for Anton. He was looking more and more preoccupied, more uncomfortable, as the evening went on. She squinted over at the clock on the mantel, trying to check the time, but the guests swarming the buffet table kept getting in the way.

"We can go any time you like," Anton told her; he must have seen her looking at the clock. "I know you have to get home and all."

He sounded depressed, and Rebecca couldn't blame him. She was here tonight to see the house, and to see Lisette, not to hang out with friends, but for Anton, this was one of the biggest events in his annual social calendar. He knew practically everyone here — in fact, most of their conversation tonight had involved her asking about people on some sofa or standing in a cluster and Anton telling her their life stories. Lots of the adults had come over to chat with him and to smile politely when he introduced her as "Rebecca Brown, who's visiting from New York." It sounded so glamorous and sophisticated, as though she'd just flown in for the party.

"Oh, really?" one lady with a plastic surgery–tight face asked her. "Aren't you just precious? Where are you staying while you're here?"

"With my aunt," Rebecca told her. "On Sixth Street. Her name is Claudia Vernier."

"Oh!" The lady's face would have registered surprise, Rebecca thought, if it were possible, but her face was too fixed in place for her expression to change. Instead, all she could do was sound icy and take a step back. "Well, well."

And that was the end of the conversation. Rebecca wasn't sure if the woman knew Aunt Claudia and thought she was a weirdo — very possible — or if she'd never heard of such a person and knew, instinctively, that this meant Aunt Claudia had to be a social untouchable. Also, all this talk of her aunt being descended from a voodoo queen had made Rebecca wonder: Most of those olden-days voodoo queens were black women, French speakers who fled the turmoil in Haiti during the revolution there. Maybe Aunt Claudia was an octoroon.

"We should stick around until ten or so," Rebecca told Anton. "I don't have to be home until ten-thirty."

"How about we go sit out on the porch?" Anton asked her, handing his empty plate to a waiter. "If you get cold, I can give you my jacket."

"Sure," Rebecca agreed. Poor Anton — all he wanted to do was get away. Out on the porch, she'd still be able to see Lisette dropping in. And before they left, she could squeeze in a "powder room" break or two — just to get another good look at that staircase. At some point in the future, Anton would make up with all his snobby friends, she was sure, but Rebecca had a feeling she would never cross the threshold of the Bowman house — by invitation or by choice — ever again.

CHAPTER TWENTY-ONE

OUTSIDE, ANTON AND REBECCA SAT CLOSE together on a wooden porch swing that faced the ballroom, its back to the broad side yard. They could still hear the band, which was playing some jaunty call-and-response number in French called "Eh, La-Bas," and hear the high-pitched talk and laughter from inside the house. Some guy in a pinstriped suit was dancing with Helena over by the closed French doors, spinning and dipping her out of time to the music. She was giggling theatrically and leaping about with more energy than anyone would expect from a girl who'd been too sick to come to school half the semester.

It was nicer outside, away from the clamor. Tea lights sparkled along the curving gallery railings, brighter than the muted moonlight. Anton pulled off his jacket and draped it around Rebecca's bare shoulders, and the slight rock of the porch swing tilted them together.

"You shouldn't have brought me," she said softly. The champagne had gone to her head: She felt kind of dizzy. "You're not having a good time."

"I'm having the best time," he said, turning his head toward her, and they both laughed.

"That's a *big* lie," Rebecca said.

"What I mean is, I'm having the best time right now. We should have come out here earlier."

"We should have just stayed out here the whole time, you mean?"

"That's exactly what I mean. We could have sent in for champagne, and told the band to play louder."

Their shoulders were brushing and, with every lilting swing of the seat, Rebecca felt Anton leaning closer.

"And I should have worn . . . a sweater," she whispered.

"A snowsuit, maybe," he said, and when he laughed, Rebecca didn't know where to look: He was so close, his face angular and chiseled, his chest rising and falling a little with every breath.

"A fur coat," she said, but the words could barely get themselves out, because Anton's face was brushing hers now — his hair tickling her forehead, his nose knocking hers.

His lips pressing hers.

Anton was kissing her, so softly, so sweetly. . . .

And someone was standing right there.

Rebecca gasped, and Anton pulled away quickly.

"There's someone . . ." She stopped. There *was* somebody there, just a foot away, staring straight at them, but it wasn't anyone Anton could see. It was Lisette, standing very still, looking as startled as Rebecca.

"What's wrong?" Anton asked her, scanning the gallery. "Who was here? Where?"

"Oh . . . nobody. I mean, they must have left."

Lisette turned away, stepping up to the French doors and gazing into the busy room. Anton was still looking around, up and down the gallery, out into the yard. The moment between them was broken, Rebecca knew. Maybe Anton thought she'd done it on purpose, invented some excuse to stop the kiss. But she hadn't wanted the kiss to stop. She *really* hadn't . . .

A terrible scream pierced through the party noise. The band stopped playing and the chatter dwindled to a low excited hum, like the sound of insects in a garden.

"It's her!" Helena screamed. She was almost hysterical, standing in front of the French doors and pointing out at the gallery with a trembling, accusing finger. "Mama! Mama, I can see her! The black girl – she's here! I can see her!"

Helena's mother, thin and dark like her daughter, rushed to her side, clutching Helena around her bony shoulders.

"Where, darling – where?" she cried. Someone rattled at the doors, shaking them open.

"Out there! She's *right out there*!" Helena was shrieking, her body quaking with sobs. "Someone DO something! Someone grab her!"

"Are you sure, darling – are you sure?" Helena's mother grabbed her, rocking her back and forth. Whatever else they were saying was lost in the uproar: Men poured onto the back gallery, shouting and running. Anton jumped up, spinning around in confusion.

"There's nobody out here," he said, turning to Rebecca. "*Is* there?"

Male guests rushed all over the yard, searching in the hedges, leaping over the wrought-iron fence, tearing back the lumber stack's canvas covering, shining flashlights hastily supplied by the elderly butler into every corner of the lush garden. If they were looking for Lisette, Rebecca thought, they wouldn't find her: Not a single one of them would be able to see her. Rebecca couldn't even see her now. In the midst of the melee, the ghost disappeared from the porch. Maybe she was inside the house, or perhaps she'd drifted back to the cemetery after Helena spotted her. And how had Helena seen her? Wasn't Rebecca the only one who could see Lisette?

Rebecca stood up and backed against the wall, pulling Anton's jacket around her shoulders. People rushed past her, running to the gallery railings: One woman told another that it was a mugging; someone else shouted that Helena had been shot. Glasses were dropped, crashing onto the gallery's wooden boards. Rebecca wriggled inside, not sure what she should do next. The musicians were packing away their instruments, probably worried they'd get trampled. Someone knocked a whole row of tea lights off the mantel; they shattered on the floor, unnerving one old man so much that he struck out wildly with his cane.

Rebecca stood by the fireplace, trying to make sense of the chaos. Why was Lisette visible to two such very different girls? Did Lisette *know* that Helena would be able to see her? And why did the sight of Lisette make Helena freak out in such an extreme way?

"I think we should go." Anton was back, reaching for her hand; he looked strained and unhappy. "Come on. I have to get you home."

Rebecca nodded, following him through the parlors to the hallway, out the front door, and through the chaos in the yard and the street. Back at his car, he pulled Rebecca's bag out of the trunk, and then stopped, as though he couldn't go any farther or do another thing. He looked as though he was about to be sick.

"What was going on there?" Rebecca asked him. "Why was Helena so upset?"

Anton shook his head, glancing up and down the street. In the moonlight, his face looked more pale and gaunt than usual, sinister in the dark shadows cast by the oak branches stretching above them. He seemed to be struggling, as though he was trying to say something but couldn't. What did he know that he didn't want to tell her? Rebecca knew what *she* was trying to hide from Anton — the fact that she could see a ghost. But what was Anton trying to hide from her?

"What happened tonight . . . it's too hard to explain," he said.

"Please tell me," Rebecca begged. She reached down into the bag, now resting at her feet, and pulled out the sweatshirt she'd packed. She handed back Anton's jacket and pulled the soft fabric over her head. Her teeth were chattering now, a combination of cold and nerves.

"It's just . . . it's just a weird thing to do with the Bowman family," Anton said, leaning back against the tree trunk.

"What weird thing?" she prompted.

"Well, I shouldn't be telling you this." He took his blazer and draped it around her shoulders, even though she had her sweatshirt on. "I really shouldn't. It's something that's only known to . . . well, certain families. Some of the old-line families around here."

"You know I won't say a word to anyone else," Rebecca told

him. This was true: Who was she going to tell? She had no friends here apart from Lisette, and Lisette appeared to be implicated, in some strange way, with the events of the evening.

"I know you won't. The thing is, it just sounds completely insane. You'll probably think I'm crazy when I tell you . . ."

"Tell me what?" she whispered. The shouts from around the corner were dying down. Perhaps the search party had given up their quest.

"That there's some sort of curse on the Bowman family." Anton looked at her, as though he was daring her to laugh. "I know it sounds crazy, but . . . it's just that bad things happen to girls in the family. And it's been going on for, like, a hundred years. Longer, even. And before these . . . before these bad things happen, the girls all see this . . . this ghost, I guess."

A tide of panic swept through Rebecca. Lisette was a harbinger of bad things? An evil spirit, there to play tricks on generations of Bowmans? Something terrible had happened to Lisette, but Rebecca couldn't believe she was evil herself. How could Lisette hurt anyone?

None of this she could say to Anton, of course: Now was really *not* the time to announce she could see this ghost, too. And maybe she was jumping to conclusions.

"What does this ghost look like?" Rebecca asked him. "Do you have any idea?"

Anton nodded, his face disappearing into the tree's velvety shadow. He picked at the bark with one finger.

"She's a black girl," he murmured. "She's sixteen years old and her name is Lisette."

Rebecca's heart sank with a thud, like an anchor hitting the ocean floor.

"The story goes . . ." Anton was saying. "Well, in the Bowman family, they believe that whenever one of the girls sees her, it means she only has a few months left."

"What do you mean, a few months?" Rebecca's chest was tight; she felt as though she could barely breathe.

Anton looked up, his eyes boring into her. He took a deep breath before replying.

"A few months to live," he said slowly. "It means . . . it means Helena only has a few months to live."

Rebecca stared at him. Helena was going to die? And somehow Lisette was involved — her friend, Lisette?

But I can see Lisette, too. Did that mean *she* only had a few months to live? No, she said to herself: This was a Bowman family thing, a New Orleans thing. It had nothing to do with Rebecca.

CHAPTER TWENTY-TWO

REBECCA!" AURELIA WAS LEANING OUT AN upstairs window, waving frantically at her. She and Anton were standing outside Claire's house, Rebecca realized. "What's all the noise about?"

"Nothing — go to bed!"

"*You* go to bed," Aurelia retorted. Claire's round face appeared next to hers in the window. "You're the one who's out late!"

Rebecca pulled her cell phone out of her bag, dislodging her socks, which tumbled onto the ground. She glanced at the time: They had about three minutes before Aunt Claudia would be out pacing the porch and calling the police.

"I have to go," she told Anton.

He swept back his hair with one trembling hand, frowning down at the ground. Rebecca hated just leaving him on the street this way.

"Sure" was all he could say, his voice cracking. He seemed completely traumatized by what just happened at the

Bowmans' house. Rebecca took a step away: She had to go now if she wanted to avoid getting into trouble. She still had to finish getting changed, something she'd planned to do in the bushes in Claire's garden. But now the thought of an angry Aunt Claudia didn't seem all that frightening. Not compared with the story Anton had just told her.

Whenever one of the girls sees her, it means she only has a few months left to live.

"Walk me home," she said to Anton. There were times when you just had to get into trouble, Rebecca decided, and tonight was one of them. "I want you to tell me more."

But as it turned out, Anton didn't have that much more to reveal. Everything he knew about the curse and the ghost, he'd spilled out on that sidewalk on Fourth Street.

It was Aunt Claudia who knew.

Rebecca was still fumbling for her key when her aunt jerked open the front door, so upset she didn't even notice Anton at first.

"What is all this terrible noise in the cemetery?" Aunt Claudia asked, a paisley shawl slipping off her narrow shoulders. "And Rebecca, why are you . . . Anton? Is that you? What are you . . . Good God, child, where are your pants?"

Although Rebecca was wearing her sweatshirt, she was still in her short party dress and sandals, her bare legs prickling in the cold.

"I'll explain everything inside." Rebecca turned to Anton; he was a picture of gloom. "Will you be OK? Without anyone at home, I mean?"

"Don't worry about me," he told her. "I'm sorry, Miss Claudia."

"I don't know what you're sorry for," her aunt said sharply, "but I intend to find out. Rebecca?"

She held the door open and Rebecca trudged in, glancing back at Anton with a rueful smile. She'd rather face the inquisition from Aunt Claudia than go home to an empty house right now.

The inquisition — held at the kitchen table, without even the offer of tea — didn't last long, because Rebecca confessed all of the evening's events: the fake trip to the movies, attending the party, Helena's hysteria, Anton's story. Of course, it wasn't an entirely true confession. To save Aurelia's skin, Rebecca told Aunt Claudia that her little cousin had taken no part in the subterfuge. And she didn't mention a thing about seeing the ghost herself. First she needed to find out what her aunt knew.

"So what is this curse that Anton's talking about?" Rebecca asked. A pensive Aunt Claudia sat stroking her pack of tarot cards, not meeting Rebecca's eye. "Do you know anything about it?"

"No," her aunt replied, but the answer came too quickly, and Rebecca could tell this wasn't the truth.

"I don't believe you," she said. Aunt Claudia kept on stroking the pack of cards. "Anton said some of the families around here know about it. He said it had been going on for a hundred years."

"One hundred and fifty-five," her aunt said softly, looking up at Rebecca at last. No more shouts drifted over from the cemetery, and they sat in silence, gazing at each other. The house was so quiet that a sudden wheeze from the aging fridge made them both jump.

"What happened?" Rebecca whispered, her throat suddenly croaky. Aunt Claudia gave a long sigh, picking her bracelets off one by one and laying them on the table.

"A servant girl was murdered in that house," she said. With one hand, she fanned the bracelets out as though they were cards. "The Bowman house. They told her mother that the girl died from yellow fever, but her mother wouldn't believe it. She knew the girl had already had the fever and recovered. So she came to the house to demand answers, and when she was turned away . . . well, it's said she put a curse on the family."

"Her mother?" This was the first Rebecca had heard about Lisette's mother doing something after her daughter died; Anton hadn't mentioned her at all. And all Lisette had said was that her mother had died not long after that terrible day in August.

"She was from Haiti," Aunt Claudia said. "Well, she was born in New Orleans, but her parents had come from Haiti when they were young, after the revolution. It was called Saint-Domingue in those days, and her family were free people of color. There were things this woman knew — things she'd learned from her own grandmother, I've heard. She said that because her own daughter had died at sixteen, no daughter of the Bowman house would ever see her seventeenth birthday."

"And that was the curse," Rebecca said, thinking of Helena. Her seventeenth birthday was coming up in February — the day after the Septimus parade. Amy and Jessica had told her that, in one of their exhaustive, minutely detailed accounts of the highlights of carnival season. No wonder Helena was terrified.

"A curse, a prophecy." Aunt Claudia got up, scraping her chair back. "Whatever it was, it's come true. In one hundred and fifty five years, not a single Bowman daughter has survived. The sons grow up and marry and have children, but no daughter ever survives her teens."

"Really?" This sounded too melodramatic to be true. Wouldn't the police start investigating if girls kept dropping dead in one particular house?

"There haven't been many girls born to the Bowmans through the years," Aunt Claudia told her, pacing back and forth like a polar bear in the zoo. "But each one dies before her seventeenth birthday. Even the ones who are sent away from the house to live with friends and family in other states."

"And what about this ghost that they say the girls can see?" This was what Rebecca really wanted to know, and the question seemed to snap Aunt Claudia out of her trance. She stopped pacing and stared at Rebecca.

"Have you seen this ghost?" she asked, the color draining from her face. A cockroach scuttled along the kitchen floor, inches from her foot, but Aunt Claudia didn't appear to notice.

"Of course not!" Now wasn't the time to tell her, Rebecca decided. She wasn't sure why she felt this way, why she wasn't ready to confide in Aunt Claudia about everything. Maybe it was because she didn't want anyone telling her who she could and couldn't see, and — from what she'd learned this evening — Lisette had kind of a bad reputation in this neighborhood. "I don't believe in ghosts, you know."

This might have been true a month ago, but now it was a lie. A necessary lie, Rebecca decided.

"You are my own sweet skeptic," Aunt Claudia said, her face relaxing. She walked over, running a soft hand over Rebecca's hair. "That's good. It's a good thing."

"Really?" Rebecca smiled at her aunt. This was the woman who collected voodoo charms and read tarot cards for a living. Maybe Aunt Claudia was admitting she was a fraud.

"Yes, it is. Seeing that ghost . . . well. There's nothing more to say about that. Now, it's time we were both in bed. Far too much excitement for one evening. You were very disobedient to go to that party but . . . but let's talk about all that another time."

"OK," Rebecca agreed, stifling a yawn. She'd save the rest of her questions for tomorrow: Tonight had been exhausting and tumultuous in every way. The kiss from Anton seemed like a distant dream.

In the morning, Rebecca was awakened by rain drumming against the window, and then by what sounded like rain inside the house: It was her aunt, tapping on her bedroom door.

"Rebecca," she whispered, cracking open the door, her frizzy gray hair escaping from the head scarf she always wore to work in the Quarter. "Your father called."

"He's on the phone?" Rebecca sat up, rubbing sleep from her eyes and pushing back the covers. She wondered why her father hadn't called her cell phone or sent her a text the way he usually did when he wanted to get in touch.

"Oh, he's not on the phone now, baby," Aunt Claudia told her. She leaned over to fiddle with the straw doll hanging on the wall, straightening it: Rebecca hadn't even noticed it was back there. "But hurry — you have to get up and get ready. He's just arrived back in New York. He wants you to go home for Christmas."

"Home? New York? Really?" The rain outside was loud, slapping against the gutters. Had she misheard her aunt?

"Yes — now! He's booked you onto the late-morning flight. So hurry and get up. You'll just have to throw some things together. We should leave in . . . oh, half an hour?"

Rebecca was out of bed in a flash, wide awake and practically ricocheting around the room. She pulled the duffel out from under her bed, and started stuffing whatever she could grab into it: sweaters, jeans, underwear, socks.

"I'll fix you some eggs and grits," Aunt Claudia said, closing the door, and Rebecca didn't even bother to tell her — for the hundredth time — that she didn't eat grits. There was no time for talking. There'd be no time to go looking for Lisette in the cemetery, or to talk to Anton again. There was no time for any more confessions or any more questions or any more stories. Rebecca was going home.

CHAPTER TWENTY-THREE

ALTHOUGH SHE'D ONLY BEEN IN NEW YORK CITY for three weeks, Rebecca felt as though she'd journeyed to another world. Sleeping in her small bedroom in the tenth floor apartment, greeting the doorman, riding the elevator, hearing car horns along Central Park West: This was her real life. New Orleans was a strange dream of a place, extreme and claustrophobic, where her universe was confined to a few blocks — school, the coffee shop, the cemetery. In New Orleans, she wasn't just in exile: She was practically incarcerated.

This wasn't something she could discuss with anyone. Her father was so delighted to see her, and so miserable when she was about to leave again, that moaning about her life in New Orleans seemed both selfish and pointless. He didn't want her to be there any more than she did — that was clear. As for her friends, they were more interested in filling Rebecca in on school scandals, romances, and dramas than hearing much about her temporary home in the Deep South. To them, New Orleans was just a place that used to be in the news and the only New Orleanians they were interested in hearing about were Juvenile and Lil Wayne.

So telling them how she'd seen — and made friends with — a ghost was out of the question. Nobody would believe her. Rebecca couldn't really believe it herself. Back in New York, much of the past month seemed incredibly surreal.

One thing her friend Ling said made Rebecca feel a little guilty — not about what she was doing, but about what she *wasn't* doing in New Orleans.

"So," Ling said, stopping on the sidewalk outside the big H&M on Fifth Avenue to count her shopping bags: The post-holiday sales had just begun. "Are you doing one of those Habitat for Humanity things? You know, rebuilding houses or whatever it is they do? I saw something on TV about all these school groups from other states flying down to help, and how all the schools and colleges in New Orleans have to do community service now."

"Um — I don't know about *our* school," Rebecca said. Maybe after the storm Temple Mead girls had volunteered to help gut flooded houses and clean up the debris-strewn parks, but Rebecca was ashamed to admit she'd made no effort to find out if these projects were still going on.

"It could be fun, right?" Ling pulled on her fluorescent orange angora gloves. "You might even get to meet Brad Pitt. He's down there all the time, building eco-houses or something — I saw it on the *Today* show."

Rebecca nodded, promising herself she'd investigate possibilities as soon as she got back to New Orleans. This didn't mean she was looking forward to going back. If it were up to her, she'd stay right here in New York, hanging out with Ling and other people who actually liked her. In New Orleans, Rebecca knew what to expect now — and the prospect of an entire semester as social outcast at Temple Mead wasn't very appealing.

"It's not that much longer now, honey," her father said at the airport. He was trying to smile, but his eyes looked anxious, and he seemed older, somehow, and more stressed. "Before you know it, it'll be summer, and you'll be back home."

"Next you'll be telling me the worst is over," sighed Rebecca, watching her bag sail away and thinking how much she was dreading that first day back at school.

"No." Her father's voice was quiet. The look on his face was grim. "No, I wouldn't say that."

Rebecca stopped shuffling her boarding pass and ID, and looked at him. There was something ominous about his tone of voice.

"I wish I could come down with you," he said, almost to himself.

"But . . . you're going back to China, right?" she asked him. She didn't know what he was talking about. If her father was in the States, Rebecca could just move home to New York. There was no need for the two of them to be exiled in New Orleans.

"Yes, yes," he said. "Of course."

Then he pulled her into a hug so tight it took her breath away.

The New Orleans Rebecca returned to was gray and damp, with a chill in the air to remind its inhabitants that the season was, officially, winter. But her first morning back, walking to school, Rebecca saw the colors of the city were defiantly bright. Front gardens were already dotted with blowsy red or white camellias, and a dense bush of pink azaleas bloomed outside the Vernier house; their scent hung in the still air, pungent and overwhelming. And on the houses themselves, holiday decorations were gone: Now front doors and hedges and fences were decorated in the garish Mardi Gras colors — purple, green, and gold. Mysterious flags hung outside various houses, some sporting a letter, some a symbol, some a crown.

"What does it mean?" she asked Aurelia, pointing to one of these enigmatic banners.

"I guess those people belong to a krewe," Aurelia told her. "That one is Comus, I think. They're one of the . . . you know . . ."

"Old-line krewes," Rebecca said, able to finish the sentence without any problem. Of course the families around her belonged to old-line krewes. They wouldn't dream of joining one of the brash new super-krewes that let in "just anyone," as Amy had explained. "And that one over there?"

She nodded at a flag striped with purple, green, and gold, with a golden crown at its center.

"That's Rex," Aurelia said. "Major-league Patrician. Like, Julius Caesar. But you have to have been a king or a queen to have that flag outside your house. That's the Chesneys' house — Mrs. Chesney was queen."

"Aren't the Chesneys really old?" Rebecca thought she'd seen them sitting on their front porch back in what passed for the fall, on rocking chairs that were chained to the railings so nobody could steal them.

"Oh, yeah." Aurelia nodded, tripping over a lumpy tree root. "She was queen about fifty years ago. That sea horse flag across the street is Proteus, I think."

"And what is that?" Rebecca had to twist her head to make out the silver symbol on a white flag drooping from one pole. It looked like an upside-down ice cream cone.

"That's the Septimus flag," said Aurelia, and they both paused to gaze up at it. That was a strange sort of symbol, Rebecca thought, because it didn't seem to make any sense.

"It looks like it's fallen over," she said.

"Or all burned down," suggested Aurelia, hopping from foot to foot. She shot Rebecca a conspiratorial glance. "I know what the theme is for the Septimus parade this year."

"Do you?" Rebecca was still looking at the flag.

"Don't you want to know?" Aurelia was puzzled. "It's the most top-secret thing ever, but Claire's godfather, this is his first year riding, and he was so excited and all that he blabbed it to her father. If I tell you, you have to *promise* not to say a word. Except to Mama, because I told her already."

"OK," Rebecca agreed, laughing as Aurelia stood on tiptoes to whisper in her ear. This was clearly a big deal.

"It's the phoenix rising from the ashes," Aurelia murmured.

"More mythology!" Rebecca said. "But not Roman, right?"

"Egyptian, then Greek," said Aurelia. "But the Romans knew about it as well. They took all sorts of things from other cultures and made them their own."

Walking the rest of the way to school, Rebecca spotted the Septimus flag several times — including outside the Bowman house and, waving on a flagpole she'd never noticed before, high above the cobbled parking area in front of Anton Grey's house.

Anton. He hadn't replied to a single text or voice message the whole time she was away. Maybe everything between them was over. Maybe he wished that kiss outside the Bowmans' house had never happened.

It wasn't really a surprise. His friends had frozen him out at the Christmas party; his parents probably looked down at Aunt Claudia and her family just like the woman at the party had. There wasn't any old-line krewe flag hanging outside the Vernier house; there was just a tired-looking Mardi Gras wreath on the door, its thin purple ribbon wilting in the humidity.

The first class of the new semester was math, and everyone seemed way too excited considering the time of day, the day of the week, and the subject matter. Before the second bell rang, the Debs were clustered in a corner, talking about the ball they'd attended that weekend: It was January, the height of party season. Someone's older sister was making her debut this year, which meant a whirlwind of party invitations, lunches at Galatoire's, dinners at country clubs, Saturday afternoons at the racetrack, and Sunday afternoon teas at large private homes on Audubon Place or State Street. At this weekend's ball the Debs claimed to have all danced with guys who went to universities like Ole Miss or the University of Virginia or Duke, which was even more exciting, apparently, than dancing with boys who went to St. Simeon's.

"Does anyone here ever do anything *useful* on the weekend?" Rebecca asked Jessica, who was sitting behind her, admiring Amy's new school supplies. "You know, like helping clear out flooded houses?"

Amy wrinkled her nose like a rabbit, tapping her desk with a purple, green, and gold pen.

"I think so," said Jessica, giggling nervously. She wasn't wearing glasses anymore, and her eyes were an unnaturally bright shade of blue. She lowered her voice, leaning forward across her desk. "I saw Miss Hagar once, picking up trash in City Park. We thought maybe she'd committed some crime and was being forced to do community service. But maybe she was just, like, helping."

"Jessica, are you interested in this notebook or not?" demanded Amy. Jessica sat back at once, without another word to Rebecca. And then Miss Hagar herself — dark-haired, stocky, and wearing her usual stained houndstooth blazer — swept into the room, scattering loose papers from the stack of manila folders in her hands. She was one of the toughest teachers at Temple Mead, and Rebecca thought it was extremely unlikely she was a criminal in her spare time.

"Miss Hagar!" Rebecca's hand shot up. "Do you know about any volunteering opportunities — to help rebuild houses and stuff like that?"

Behind her, she heard Amy's low groan.

"Suddenly she's all Miss Community Spirit," Amy said in a stage whisper, clearly intending Rebecca to hear.

"Volunteering in the community, absolutely!" Miss Hagar

gave them a brisk smile. She slapped the stack of folders onto her desk. "I'm glad to hear there's some interest at last. There are a number of organizations in the city who need our help. There are still neighborhoods where many houses need gutting or repairs."

"Like, which ones?" Jessica asked; this question was followed by a pained "ow!" Amy must have kicked her under the desk.

"Well — there are so many . . . Central City, Hollygrove, Gert Town, Lakeview, parts of Broadmoor, Gentilly, the Upper and Lower Ninth, Holy Cross, Mid City, Tremé . . ."

Rebecca felt a flash of recognition. "We could help in Tremé?" she interrupted.

"You can help wherever you want to help," Miss Hagar told her. "Every weekend, organizations like ACORN need volunteers. In fact, we could make it a class project if there's so much interest. . . ."

"Miss Hagar?" Rebecca turned to see one of the Debs waving her hand in the air: Her name was Madison Sherwood, and she was a major Julie Casworth Young wannabe. "My father says that ACORN is a dangerous socialist organization."

"And we're way too busy on the weekends until after Mardi Gras," said another Deb — Rebecca still couldn't remember her name exactly; it was either Katy Lee or Kathy Lee. The initials KL were inscribed in gold on her notebooks, schoolbag, and fountain pen, and this reminded Rebecca of a postcard her father had sent her once from the capital of Malaysia: She always thought of Katy Lee as Kuala Lumpur.

Miss Hagar gave a long sigh, drumming her fingertips against the folders on her desk.

"Maybe we can revisit this topic after Mardi Gras," she said, her voice straining with impatience. Clearly, Miss Hagar wasn't spending her weekends at teas and balls and intimate theme luncheons for forty. "And now, ladies — algebra!"

On her way to the lunchroom that day, Rebecca stopped in the second-floor restroom, in no hurry to do the usual find-a-seat lunchtime shuffle. She could sneak a sandwich into the library, she decided, and spend the break researching ACORN on the Internet.

But before Rebecca could do anything but fix her regulation ponytail, Jessica slid through the door and hurried over.

"Have you heard?" she asked in a half whisper. "About Helena Bowman?"

Rebecca shook her head, combing her long hair with her fingers.

"She's not. Coming. To school. Anymore."

"She's dropped out?" Rebecca found that hard to believe.

"As if!" Jessica's fake-blue eyes widened. The door banged, other girls coming and going. Jessica wriggled closer, lowering her voice to an emphatic hiss. "She's way too sick to come to school. They've stopped all the renovations on her house, because she can't stand any noise. She has to have complete quiet."

"What . . . what's wrong with her?" Rebecca tried to sound nonchalant, but her head was buzzing with the story

Anton had told her before Christmas: *Helena only has a few months to live*.

"Nobody knows. Or nobody's saying. But it must be something really, really bad. Marianne looks like she's about to burst into tears any second. Look, I have to go."

"Thanks for . . . telling me," Rebecca said to Jessica's disappearing back, because she felt as though she had to say *something*. She pulled the tie from her ponytail and started playing with her hair again, just for something to do. What Jessica was saying . . . could it be true? Was Anton right about Lisette being some kind of evil spirit who brought bad things to girls in the Bowman family? Even if Helena wasn't actually sick, she had to be too terrified to leave her own house anymore, even to come to school. Rebecca didn't want Lisette to be evil: She couldn't believe that was true. The Bowman family were the ones who'd done bad things, not Lisette.

On the way, at last, to the lunchroom, Rebecca passed Marianne, though the older girl didn't seem to register her presence at all. Jessica was right: Marianne looked wan and preoccupied, trudging along the hallway alone, her eyes red as though she'd been crying. Part of Rebecca felt vindictively glad that Helena and Marianne were no longer sashaying along the halls of Temple Mead, looking down their noses at everyone else, the self-appointed rulers of the school.

But however rude and stuck-up Helena had acted toward her, she didn't deserve so extreme a fate — either an illness too serious for her to attend school for an entire semester, or a fear so overpowering that her family wouldn't let her leave the house. Rebecca wouldn't be able to stand being locked inside all day, and she certainly wouldn't want to wake up each morning fearing for her life.

The thought of Lisette as a harbinger of death kept nagging at Rebecca all week. The Debs and Plebs might be too busy on Saturdays getting updos and manicures to volunteer with a community organization, but they weren't the only ones with urgent weekend plans. Unless sometime this week she was lucky enough to bump into Lisette, wandering the streets encircling the cemetery, Rebecca had plans of her own for the very next Saturday morning. She needed to track down her friendly neighborhood ghost and ask her some questions.

It was time to hear Lisette's side of the story — about the curse, and all those generations of Bowman daughters. Rebecca knew that whatever Lisette told her, it would be the truth.

CHAPTER TWENTY-FOUR

Aunt Claudia seemed in no hurry at all to get to work on Saturday morning.

"Aren't there lots of conventions in town?" Rebecca asked, trying not to sound too desperate. It was almost eleven, and her aunt seemed more interested in dusting the menagerie of weird carved animals in the front parlor than driving off to the Quarter to set up her card table. "Doesn't it get busy in the weeks before Mardi Gras? Isn't Saturday your really busy day?"

"There's no hurry," said Aunt Claudia breezily. She wafted the molting feather duster over the clutter on the mantel: a gilt clock that didn't work, some carved African statuettes, a slumped Pierrot doll with a broken china foot, and a pile of old green hymnbooks that smelled of must.

There was nothing to do but to try and speed the housekeeping process along. Rebecca vacuumed the hallway and the bedrooms, cajoling a reluctant Aurelia into scooping Marilyn out of the laundry basket and sorting out the no-longer-very-clean laundry. But by the time her aunt decided that the house was more or less tidy and drifted out to her car with her pack of cards and a new, tie-dyed tablecloth, it was almost closing time at the cemetery. Rebecca had never understood why it shut so early in the afternoon, or why it was closed on Sundays — something to do with the city running it, she'd heard her aunt say. It was just another strange thing about this place, she decided, scampering along the street as soon as her aunt's car had disappeared around the corner.

The day was warm but overcast, and in the cemetery Rebecca felt that claustrophobic, short-of-breath feeling she'd come to associate with New Orleans. There was a dampness to the place that Aunt Claudia always referred to as "close" — as in, "it's very close today," usually said while fanning herself with a section of the *Times-Picayune* newspaper. Sometimes Rebecca felt as though the sky was closing in on them, as gray and soggy as the city's other boundaries: the lake and the river and the swamps.

A few people were still wandering the cemetery, cleaning up family graves or taking pictures of the more ornate tombs. The Bowman grave was a favorite with tourists, Rebecca knew, so she wasn't surprised to see a Japanese couple wandering ahead of her down the sandy alley. There was no way Rebecca could talk to Lisette with other people around, unless she wanted to appear completely insane, so she dawdled under a tree, idly scratching her nails against its rough, chunky bark. She'd never seen the Sutton vault, she realized, wondering how close it was to the Bowman tomb. To her frustration, Rebecca noticed that the Japanese couple — both of whom had cameras they were clearly eager to use as much as possible — had been joined by another two tomb-gawkers. Were they trying to walk off the jazz brunch they'd just eaten at Commander's Palace? Didn't they know the cemetery was closing in twenty minutes?

Tired of waiting, Rebecca wandered off in the direction of the Grey family vault. It was so weird to think of Anton getting buried there one day. Or rather, getting *entombed*: You weren't really buried if your remains were stowed aboveground. She wondered if Anton ever thought about it, if it was comforting to know exactly where he'd be ending up or if it freaked him out. But then, so much of his life seemed circumscribed. Maybe it didn't bother him at all.

Out of the corner of her eye, Rebecca saw something: a flicker of dark skirt as someone darted behind a tomb.

"Lisette!" she called, squeezing down the narrow lane between two of the tombs. The ground underfoot was damp and nubby with moss, perhaps because it rarely saw the sun. And sure enough, there was Lisette, leaning her head against the chalky plaster of the vault, her face as gloomy as the shadowy back alley.

"Too many people here today," Lisette complained. Her eyes were red, as though she'd been crying. "All over the Bowman tomb like ants. I'm tired of getting stepped on."

"Does it hurt when they step on you?" Rebecca asked, and Lisette shook her head.

"Some days you just want some peace and quiet," she said. "Though maybe that's not such a good thing, either. I'm thinking about my mama a lot right now. It always seems to happen just before . . ."

"Just before what?" Rebecca shivered, because it was cold

and damp back here, shaded by the dense overhanging branches of a gnarled oak tree. Again Lisette shook her head.

"It's the worst part about being a ghost," she told Rebecca. "You have too much time to think."

"I wanted to ask you about your mother," Rebecca began, but she didn't know how to go on. Lisette looked so sad today, so drawn. How could she begin to ask Lisette about her mother putting a curse on the Bowmans? "My aunt . . . my aunt said your mother went to the Bowman house once."

Lisette shifted her weight from one foot to the other, rubbing her head against the side of the tomb the way Marilyn sometimes rubbed against the table leg.

"Just once," she said softly, not meeting Rebecca's eye. "They let her in. I followed her into the parlor, hoping she could feel me, even if she couldn't see me. But I don't think she could. She never once saw me, the way you can see me."

Lisette looked as though she was about to start crying again.

"This was just after . . . just after you were murdered?" Rebecca said quickly, torn between not wanting to upset Lisette and wanting answers about the so-called curse.

"After she got the message I'd died from the fever. I was surprised they even let her in the house. It must have been the first time a person of color was allowed to sit down on a piece of furniture in that parlor — not that my mother waited for permission. She didn't think of them as her social superiors. Not Mrs. Bowman, not the lawyer man, Mr. Sutton. She was free, just like them."

"What was she like, your mother?" Rebecca asked, and a slow smile crept onto Lisette's face.

"Strong, proud. She wouldn't bow her head to them. She wasn't tall, not as tall as you — but she had a presence. She wore a *tignon* — you know what that is? Once all free women of color had to wear them, because the law wouldn't let them wear hats or veils like the white Creole ladies. That was before I was born. My mother wore one because she said it let people know who she was, a free woman."

"A *tignon*?" Rebecca repeated, and Lisette spelled it for her.

"It was a long piece of material," she explained, "wrapped around her head."

"Like a scarf?"

Lisette considered this. "More like a turban. It was very high," she said, her hand curling up into the air to demonstrate. "And tied in front. It made her seem taller than she was. That day her *tignon* was red like a ruby."

Rebecca imagined the two women facing each other — one pale, dressed in black, the other dark-skinned, wearing her vivid *tignon*. Both of them enraged, because they'd just lost a daughter, and the father of that daughter. One of the women a murderer, the other determined to learn the truth.

"I could see her, but I couldn't talk to her or touch her," Lisette was saying. "She couldn't see me the way you can."

At this, Lisette looked utterly dejected. Rebecca inhaled the dank smell of the mossy soil, the crumbling tombs, this dusky, quiet corner of the cemetery. Now was the time to talk about the curse, but it was hard to muster the courage to ask Lisette directly.

"What . . . what happened next?" she mumbled.

"The lawyer," said Lisette, her eyes bleary, "he told her the story again, the one she'd already heard. About how I'd come down with yellow fever, how I'd been buried already in the cemetery. How they were all sorry, but there was nothing that could be done. How she should respect the lady of the house, who'd just lost her own daughter and her husband, and just go on back home to her own part of the city. And that's when it happened."

"What?" Rebecca's chest felt tight with anticipation.

"Something on her face — Mrs. Bowman's face. Something gave her away. I was watching my mother, but she was watching Mrs. Bowman, and when I looked I saw it as well. There was something in that lady's face when the lawyer man talked about our part of town. Disgust, maybe. Like she was sneering. She didn't feel sorry for my mother — she hated her. I could see it."

"So what did your mother do?"

"She rose up real slow," Lisette said, straightening herself. "And pointed right at Mrs. Bowman. I've never seen her look like that — so furious, so righteous."

Lisette raised her arm, pointing right at Rebecca — mimicking her mother's gesture, Rebecca thought.

"What did she say?" she asked Lisette.

"You've taken my daughter from me. God will punish you for what you've done."

Lisette stopped talking, her outstretched hand trembling. Rebecca was a little disappointed: That was it?

"And then," Lisette said, her voice so soft Rebecca had

to strain to hear it, "she said that this was a place of terrible evil."

"The Bowman house?" Rebecca asked, and Lisette solemnly nodded.

"She said, this is a place of terrible evil, and evil could not go unpunished. That just as her daughter had been taken, before her seventeenth birthday, the daughters of this house would be taken, one after the other. She was talking, on and on, as though she was in some strange, angry trance. It was like a prayer, like she was calling up to God. She was saying, *Lord, I pray that this house will be destroyed, burned to the ground.*"

"Ah!" Rebecca couldn't help exclaiming. So there *was* a curse on the house itself, not just on the family.

"But I couldn't hear everything clearly, because Mrs. Bowman was screaming at her, calling her bad names. And then the lawyer had grabbed my mother, and he was dragging her toward the door, shouting at her to be quiet. He was telling her that her sort needed to be careful these days, that they couldn't just move around the city acting like they were somebody."

"What did he mean?"

"Times were changing," Lisette sighed. "I didn't really understand then, but when I saw what followed, it started to make sense. Our people — the free people of color — weren't welcome anymore in New Orleans. There were new laws, stopping them from meeting in public, even from playing music in public. People were getting arrested. A lot of them moved to other places."

"Did your mother move away?"

Lisette shook her head.

"She died six months after me. Another ghost told me what he'd heard, that she'd dropped dead in the street on the way home from Mass. That day at the Bowman house – that was the last time I saw her. When the lawyer pushed her out the door, I was trying to hang on to her, but my hands just slipped through her, as though she was made of water."

Lisette's body shook with sobs, and Rebecca took a step toward her, wanting to comfort her. But her friend backed away, refusing to be consoled.

"I wanted to say good-bye to her, but I couldn't." She wept, her fingers clawing at the dusty tomb wall. "They just pushed her out of the house, pushed her into the street."

"That's terrible." Rebecca was crying now, too, tears clogging her eyes; she rubbed at them with the back of her sleeve. The thought of Lisette's mother being treated that way by the Bowmans and the Suttons . . . it was disgraceful. *They* were disgraceful. "Did you follow her home? Or couldn't you go back until . . ."

"Who are you talking to?" a boy's voice demanded, startling Rebecca so badly she almost swallowed her own tongue. She swiveled her head to see who it was, though she could tell without looking.

It was Anton Grey, and he was standing right next to her.

CHAPTER TWENTY-FIVE

"WHAT?" SNAPPED REBECCA, WORRIED ABOUT how loud she'd been speaking, how red and tear-stained her face looked. "I mean, what are *you* doing, creeping around the cemetery?"

Anton must have squeezed through the narrow space between the adjoining graves; she was so focused on Lisette's story, Rebecca hadn't heard him approach. Lisette had disappeared into thin air — why, Rebecca wasn't sure. Anton couldn't see Lisette, and he couldn't hear her. All he'd heard was Rebecca talking — to herself, apparently, like an insane person.

"This is my family's grave," he said, his expression puzzled and a little suspicious. Anton looked scruffier than usual, his sweatshirt frayed and grubby, his sneakers scuffed with dirt, almost as though he'd been out all night, sleeping at the foot of one of the tombs. His handsome face was drawn, and there were dark circles under his eyes.

"I'm sorry," Rebecca said, because she couldn't think of anything else to say, and because she *was* sorry, in a way.

Sorry that he'd come across her talking to Lisette. Sorry that she'd snapped at him, when he looked so weary and stressed. Sorry that this was the first time they'd spoken in weeks, and it was in this weird, uncomfortable situation.

"You still haven't answered my question." Anton folded his arms, his eyebrows a straight, dark line. "Who were you talking to just now?"

"Nobody," muttered Rebecca. She wasn't about to tell Anton she could see — and talk to — Lisette. Especially not when he was in such a foul mood.

"Don't lie to me," he said: He sounded contemptuous and angry. Anton had never spoken to her this way before, and Rebecca didn't like it one bit. Where was the Anton who'd draped his jacket over her shoulders, who'd kissed her at the party?

"Really," she said, shaking her head. "Just back off, OK? It's none of your business what I'm doing or who I'm talking to."

"I asked you a civil question."

"Actually, it wasn't *civil* at all."

"So you're just going to stand here and lie to my face?" he demanded. "That's how much consideration you have for someone who's supposed to be your friend?"

"Supposed to be," she said, irritated by his tone. "A pretty strange kind of friendship, when you can't even be bothered to keep in touch when I'm out of town. I haven't heard from you for weeks, and now you creep up behind me and start shouting at me."

"I'm not shouting," Anton said, in a more normal voice. "And I'm sorry I didn't call you back or anything while you were away, but it's been . . . it's been . . . look, you just don't understand."

"I don't understand what?"

"Anything. You don't understand anything."

Rebecca rolled her eyes. Ever since she'd arrived in New Orleans, everyone — her aunt, the girls at school, and now Anton — kept telling her the same thing. How could she be expected to understand anything when everyone was so secretive, when their rituals were so elaborate, when their history was so complex and loaded? How could she get the inside story when everyone did everything in their power to keep her out? The only person who'd ever been honest with her, the only person who'd answered her questions and revealed the secrets and stories of the past . . . well, it certainly wasn't Anton. It was Lisette, and right now she seemed to have drifted away — probably, Rebecca thought, because she wasn't in the mood to hear them argue.

"If I'm so stupid, I'm surprised you're even talking to me right now," she told Anton. She folded her arms, and leaned back against the tomb. "No wonder you can't be bothered to call me. I'm just a dumb outsider, right? Just like your friend Toby told me — I'm a nobody."

A pained expression flickered across Anton's face.

"That's not what I meant, and you know it," he told her. "We're all just worried about Helena. She's in danger, like I was trying to tell you before Christmas. Didn't you believe what I said about seeing that ghost?"

"Of course I believed you!" Rebecca was trying not to feel jealous, but she couldn't help it. Was Anton needed to hold Helena's hand — carry her umbrella, maybe — every hour of the day? Anton never seemed to like Helena that much before: She was just one of his gang. Suddenly, he was so worried about her that he couldn't pick up his phone to call another girl?

"Then you should understand why I've been busy," he said, in a way that sounded as though he was summing up his case in front of a jury.

"I understand that you're upset and concerned," she said. "But blowing me off completely and then blaming it on the whole situation with Helena — that seems kind of convenient."

"Huh?"

"I mean, you talk about me not telling you the truth," Rebecca continued, warming to her argument, annoyed all over again by the indignant look on Anton's face. "But you're not telling me the whole truth, either, are you? Why don't you just admit that you didn't like everyone snubbing you at the Bowmans' party, so acting like I didn't exist anymore was the easy way out?"

"I wasn't acting like you don't exist! I've just been, you know, kind of preoccupied."

"Preoccupied with what other people might think."

"Why won't you listen to me? I'm telling you that an old friend of mine, an old friend of my family's, may be in real danger."

"And I'm not your friend? You can't talk to me about it?"

Anton didn't reply. His silence told Rebecca everything she needed to know. Whatever he'd said to her in the past, however much he seemed to like her, Anton saw her the way everyone else around here did — as an outsider.

"I don't even know why we're having this conversation," she said softly. The sound of a bell was clanging through the cemetery, a signal that the place was about to close. Good: Rebecca wanted to get out of here. The humidity was making her feel short of breath. "You acted like you were different, but you're not. You don't like me any more than the rest of them."

"I *do* like you!" he insisted. "I think I made that pretty clear at the party."

Rebecca felt her cheeks flushing. He'd kissed her, and it seemed as though he'd meant it — but then why had he basically dropped her right after that?

"All you really care about is what your friends will think or what their families will say," she said. This sounded much more cutting and bitter than she intended, but it was too late: The words were out.

"You don't understand anything about our families," Anton said, his voice sharp. He glared at Rebecca, his eyes boring through her. "You don't have our history, OK? You don't see things the way we do."

"Whatever!" Rebecca retorted. They had *no idea* what she could and couldn't see. Irritation surged through her body like a boiling wave of molten lava, and before she could stop herself, Rebecca was snapping back at Anton. "Helena's not the only one who can see things, you know. I can see the ghost, too!"

Instantly she knew it was the wrong thing to say. Anton was staring at her, his mouth open, his face pale as the tomb she was leaning against. This wasn't the time or the place to reveal her secret, Rebecca knew, especially to someone like Anton. Whatever had happened between them, she couldn't trust him anymore. Why hadn't she kept her mouth shut?

"I don't believe you." Anton's voice was firm, but the look on his face told a different story — it was something between horrified and suspicious. Rebecca didn't know what to say. If she said he was right, that she was just making it all up, she'd seem like an immature idiot. But if she stood here arguing, insisting that she could see Lisette as clearly as Helena could . . . well, it would serve no purpose at all. Anton would go racing off to the Bowmans', probably, with this hot-off-the-presses information. And though Rebecca wasn't sure what the Bowmans would do with the news exactly, she certainly didn't want to be a topic of discussion — or derision — in that particular household.

Now the bell was ringing incessantly, its clangs echoing in Rebecca's head.

"We should . . . we should get out of here," she said, but then she remembered Anton had a key for the Sixth Street gate. Unlike Rebecca, he didn't have to play by the rules. And right now, he obviously wasn't in a hurry to go anywhere. He was standing there, staring at Rebecca as though the longer and harder he looked at her, the more likely he was to get out the truth.

Now that the hot tide of anger had subsided, all Rebecca felt was confusion. Part of her wanted to continue this standoff with Anton: She'd said more than she'd meant to, but there wasn't any going back. If she ran away now, Rebecca would look like a wimp and a coward. Anton would write her off as a silly girl and congratulate himself for dumping her so unceremoniously after the Bowmans' Christmas party.

But part of her knew there was nothing else to say. Rebecca wasn't about to confide all the details of her friendship with Lisette to Anton, especially now that he seemed so hostile. Her head was pounding. The shrill ringing bell, the clammy atmosphere, the feeling she had of being surrounded by tombs and trees and high walls . . . everything was oppressing her. If she didn't leave now, she'd be trapped in the cemetery, reliant on Anton's goodwill to get out. And goodwill wasn't quite the way to describe his mood today.

"So that's it?" He sounded incredulous. "You make this insane claim, and then you've got nothing else to say?"

One of the big gates was closing with a creak: Rebecca listened for the slam, for the rattling of the padlock's chain. She felt hot again, but not with anger this time. Just panic, sweeping through her, urging her to escape before the last of those gates was locked for the rest of the weekend. She had to get away from here. She had to get away from Anton.

"I'm . . . I'm sorry," she gasped, sidling toward the gap between the tombs. Once she felt the emptiness of the narrow alley, Rebecca bolted; as she hurried away, her elbows banged against the unforgiving marble walls hemming her in. Anton was calling her name, but she didn't turn around. The Sixth Street gate was already locked, so she ran toward Washington Avenue, where the caretaker, in his khaki uniform, stood jangling a set of keys.

"Just in time," he said in a mock-stern voice, and Rebecca nodded, jogging into the street. She ran all the way home, past the valet parkers outside Commander's Palace, and along the broken sidewalk of Coliseum Street. Her heart thudded with every step, because she knew the Lafayette Cemetery caretaker was right. She'd gotten away from Anton just in time.

CHAPTER TWENTY-SIX

ALTHOUGH IT WAS STILL TOO EARLY FOR parades, Rebecca soon realized that carnival season was already underway. Everyone at Temple Mead was obsessed with the fancy balls they or their parents were attending, chattering in the hallways and the lunchroom about which parades were taking place this year and what the Krewe of Septimus had chosen as its theme.

Septimus was held in particularly high regard in this neighborhood, Rebecca kept hearing, not least because of its unique parade route. Unlike all the other parades, which rumbled through the city downtown to Canal Street, Septimus curled back at Lee Circle and looped its way back along Magazine Street, finishing on Jackson. But those in-the-know, according to Jessica, often ran up to Prytania at the end of the parade, because the floats of the "royal" court kept going, all along Prytania to Louisiana Avenue.

"You get to see them up close, without anyone else around, pretty much," Jessica gushed at the beginning of English: Amy had a dentist's appointment, so Jessica could talk to

Rebecca without getting into trouble. She pulled a recycled paper napkin out of her bag and drew a shaky map of this apparently peculiar route.

"Do you see what I mean now?"

"Kind of," Rebecca said, squinting at the squiggles Jessica had drawn, complete with arrows and scrawled street names. She seemed to forget that Rebecca had never been to a single Mardi Gras parade and had only the vaguest idea about their traditional route — from Napoleon and along St. Charles Avenue, she remembered, thinking of the beads she'd seen dangling from oak trees the day she and Anton took their walk. But Jessica, like everyone else at Temple Mead, obviously thought that the royal progress of a parade was general knowledge throughout the rest of the country.

However out of the loop she was, one thing was soon clear to Rebecca. Because no other parades had this special route, Septimus required dedicated police and barricades and ambulance services and fire trucks and cleanup for stretches of streets unused by any other krewes. And this meant that the people who controlled Septimus obviously had a lot of money, as well as a lot of sway in New Orleans. *That* was no surprise at all.

At lunchtime, nobody seemed to object when Rebecca slid her tray onto the end of the sophomore table — possibly because Amy wasn't there, possibly because they were all deep in conversation.

"I've heard there's no way Helena Bowman can ride this year," someone at the other end of the table announced.

"She's way too sick. Nobody's seen her for weeks and weeks, not even Marianne or Julie."

"Maybe she's got leprosy!"

"Duh — *nobody* gets that anymore. It's probably cancer."

"Maybe she's been bitten by a vampire. What? It's just as likely as her having leprosy."

"Well, I've heard she's mentally unstable. No, really! She went all hysterical at the Bowmans' Christmas party."

"I heard her mother had to slap her."

"I heard that when the ambulance came to take her away, they put her in a straitjacket."

"How do you know? You weren't there."

"Please. I wasn't at, like, the Gettysburg Address, but I know about that."

"Rebecca was there," Jessica piped up. She smiled at Rebecca, as though she was glad — for once — to claim the association.

"What happened *exactly*?" The entire sophomore cabal turned their attention to Rebecca.

"Um . . . not much." Rebecca had no appetite for this conversation — about as much as she had for the sticky grilled cheese. She was too worried about giving anything away. One thing Rebecca had learned from her last encounter with Anton: She had to keep her mouth shut.

"You must have seen something." Jessica was practically pleading with her.

"I saw the band," Rebecca said, wiping her hands on a paper napkin. "They were really good. And I saw a whole lot of champagne and barbecue shrimp. Yum, yum."

Her classmates were not impressed.

The next day, Amy was back, and Rebecca decided to smuggle her homemade sandwich into the library. Nobody else was around yet, so Rebecca checked her e-mail — there was one from her father, who didn't have anything interesting to say about work, and one from Ling, who didn't have anything interesting to say about school — and then spent some time paging through the old map book left open on the big oak table. She liked looking at the maps of Louisiana and the Caribbean, back when France and Spain and Britain were fighting over territory and power. It made her think of pirates and buccaneers, of plantation ladies and dashing explorers — though, she knew, this was a naïve and romantic view.

Back in the days when Haiti was called Saint-Domingue, it was known as the "Pearl of the Antilles," a place of incredible riches where the French produced sugar and coffee and rum for their entire empire. But this was only possible because of the work of hundreds of thousands of slaves. And the brutal treatment of these people led to the slave rebellion and Haitian revolution, which was incredibly bloody and terrible: Rebecca's class had been studying it in history. Anyone with the means to escape Haiti fled the fighting, and thousands of these refugees came to New Orleans — like Lisette's grandparents. With them they'd brought their music and their food and their religion, voodoo. According to her teacher, they changed the culture of New Orleans forever.

And now, since the hurricane, people had moved to the city from Mexico and Central America, to work on rebuilding houses; the city would change again. People like the Bowmans and the Suttons might want everything to stay the same — with them rich and in charge of everything, of course — but that wasn't the way history worked, Rebecca was learning. Anton had told her she didn't understand "their" history, but one thing she was sure of: Cities couldn't, wouldn't stay the same. They moved with the times, whether they were New York or New Orleans.

A strange noise caught Rebecca's attention — a muffled, strangled little yelp. It sounded as though a stray kitten had wandered into the library and was mewing for attention. Rebecca looked around to see if the librarian had noticed, but she couldn't see her anywhere at all. The noise erupted again, from deep in the stacks, a sort of hiccup. Or maybe, Rebecca thought, walking slowly toward the source of the sound, like a sob.

Pacing the length of the towering wooden bookshelves, Rebecca peered down each aisle, looking for the creature making this plaintive little noise. But there were no stray kittens in the library — none that she could see, anyway. There was just a girl, slumped on the floor, wedged between two shelves. Her face was buried in her hands, but Rebecca knew instantly who it was.

Marianne Sutton.

Rebecca stood at the end of the row, not sure what to do. Marianne's shoulders were shaking, and it was obvious that she was crying quite piteously.

"Are you . . . are you OK?" she asked, even though she knew this was a stupid question. Of course Marianne wasn't OK — she was sitting on the floor of the library, sobbing her heart out. She didn't even look up when Rebecca spoke; maybe she hadn't heard her. Maybe the polite thing to do now was walk away before Marianne noticed she had unwelcome company.

"What?" Too late. Marianne had lifted her head; she was

staring at Rebecca as though she couldn't see her clearly. Her chalk-pale face was streaked with tears, and her eyes looked watery and red. Rebecca almost felt sorry for her.

"I just wanted to know if . . . if you were OK. If there was anything I could do." Rebecca took a step toward her, stopping when Marianne flinched.

"No." She shook her head. Her fair hair was a mess, half pulled out of its ponytail.

"OK — well, then . . . see you." Obviously she didn't want Rebecca around, so the only thing to do was back away, leaving Marianne to wallow in her private misery.

"I'm just worried about Helena, that's all," Marianne said. This was surprising — not that Helena's condition was making Marianne anxious and upset, but that she would share the information with an outsider like Rebecca. Her tone was much softer than usual, maybe because Helena wasn't around and Marianne didn't have to act all snooty and rude. Maybe this was the real Marianne, someone who wouldn't be half so objectionable if she were out of Helena Bowman's sphere of influence.

"Do you want me to go get someone?" Rebecca asked her. Marianne would prefer it, no doubt, if she had one of Them to confide in. "Should I try to find Julie?"

She didn't have much idea of where to start looking, but Rebecca was sure one of the J.C. acolytes among the Plebs could help track Julie down. Marianne shook her head, almost dislodging the slipping elastic band.

"It's all right," she said, looking forlorn. "I have to pull myself together before class. Everything's just really starting to get to me."

Marianne wiped her eyes with the back of her hand, brushing back a damp strand of hair.

"I'm sure they'd let you go home," Rebecca suggested. "You know, if you're not feeling well."

In fact, she was sure that the principal would let Marianne go home for any reason whatsoever, even if she was in the best of moods and/or health. That was the thing about being one of Them: You got special treatment, whether you were a student at Temple Mead or a float in the Septimus parade.

"It's all right," Marianne said again, though her voice faltered, and Rebecca wondered if she was trying to convince herself. "I have a French test this afternoon that I shouldn't miss. It's just so hard to concentrate when I'm so worried about Helena, and . . . I mean, we've been looking forward to being maids in Septimus for *years*, and now it looks like it's not going to happen."

"Maybe she'll be feeling better by then?" Rebecca thought that not riding in Septimus was the least of Helena's problems, but she knew how important this kind of thing was to girls at Temple Mead. "Or there's always next year."

This was the wrong thing to say. Marianne's eyes welled with tears again.

"There may not *be* a next year," she said, her voice catching. "That's the thing."

The bell signaling the end of lunch chimed through the loudspeaker. *Saved by the bell*, Rebecca thought with some relief: She just didn't know what to say to make Marianne feel better. All she could do, when Marianne began scrambling to her feet, was extend a hand to help her.

"Thanks." Marianne gave a weak smile, dusting off her

skirt. Rebecca couldn't help thinking that Helena would not approve of this little scenario. She certainly couldn't imagine Helena taking her hand or giving Rebecca any kind of grateful smile. "And . . . Rebecca? You won't tell anyone about this, will you? About finding me crying, I mean."

"Of course not," Rebecca said. She had nobody to tell, but Marianne didn't know that. "Don't worry. Just . . . you know, take care of yourself."

It was pretty lame, she thought, but she didn't know what else to say.

"I will," Marianne said, smiling again. "You, too, OK?"

That was an odd sort of reply, Rebecca thought later, climbing the stairs to her next class, but maybe Marianne didn't know what to say, either. This whole acting-civil-thing was entirely new to them both. Who knew where it would lead?

CHAPTER TWENTY-SEVEN

THAT AFTERNOON, REBECCA DECIDED TO SKIP her usual café routine and walk home with Aurelia. At home, she dumped her blazer and bag in her room and sat down at the kitchen table. She wasn't in the mood for homework just yet, so she had a yogurt and idly picked at a box of crackers, flicking through that day's copy of the *Times-Picayune*.

The society pages were a gallery of debutantes, clusters of tight white gowns and severe updos and anxious smiles, the pictures taken at balls held by various krewes or social clubs. Some of the groups of girls were white and some were black, but — even though their gowns and tiaras were interchangeable — they seemed to belong to segregated clubs and attend entirely separate social events. Rebecca scanned the captions looking for names she recognized, and there were several — probably the older sisters of girls at Temple Mead Academy.

Aurelia had scurried out to the backyard, clapping her

hands to summon the elusive Marilyn, but now the younger girl was back, on the hunt for cookies.

"Re-bec-ca," she said, in a tone that Rebecca had come to know: It was always a prelude to Aurelia wanting to borrow something or beg a favor.

"Au-re-lia," Rebecca croaked back. "What do you want *this* time?"

She was only teasing, but the look on Aurelia's round, angelic face was quite serious. Her cousin leaned against her, gazing down at the beaming faces of the debutantes.

"Wouldn't it be nice," Aurelia said, "if we took Helena some flowers?"

Rebecca shrugged.

"I'm sure she has lots of flowers already. Don't worry about Helena, Relia."

"I know we're not supposed to be friends with her," Aurelia persisted. "But I feel bad about her being sick and all. She's missing all the fun."

Rebecca breathed out a long sigh. Maybe her little cousin was right. Helena wouldn't get to ride in Septimus, and a privilege like that meant everything in the world to a girl like her. Maybe Rebecca was being hard-hearted, only thinking about herself, just as Anton had said. Helena was too sick to go to school, too sick to leave the house. It couldn't be much fun, stuck in that quiet house all day, obsessing about the ghost who crashed your Christmas party and wondering if you were about to die some sudden, mysterious death. Marianne was clearly pretty worried about her, so her condition had to be serious.

"I don't even know where we'd buy flowers," she said, thinking of her walks to nearby Magazine Street: She'd never spotted a flower shop.

"We can take some from the garden." Aurelia sounded excited, realizing, perhaps, that Rebecca was going to give in.

"I don't think there's much in the way of flowers. . . ." Rebecca began, but her cousin had already fished a pair of rusty scissors out of a drawer in the kitchen and was on her way out the back door. A few minutes later she was back brandishing some hacked-off branches, all waxy green leaves and drooping red blooms from the camellia bush.

"So I guess we're doing this," sighed Rebecca, using the society pages to create a taut newspaper cone: The heavy flower heads would plop off en route to the Bowmans' if they weren't supported by something. Aurelia rummaged in the Christmas-wrap box — housed, inexplicably, in the pantry — for a suitable red ribbon, and then raced off to retrieve her collection of glitter pens to make a card.

The warmth and light were already seeping out of the day by the time they walked back up Sixth Street. For once, Rebecca was grateful for her woolen blazer.

"We could just leave them on the front porch if nobody's home," she told Aurelia, half hoping that this would be the case. Rebecca didn't particularly want to see Helena herself, or her mother, both of whom would treat them, no doubt, with pained condescension.

On the sidewalk outside the mansion, they paused, looking up at the somber gray house. Without its Christmas lights, it didn't seem quite so festive. The only concession to

Mardi Gras decorations was the Septimus flag flapping in the breeze. Like many of the grand houses around here, in Rebecca's opinion, the place looked shut up and empty.

The outside iron gate was closed, and when Rebecca tried unlatching it, she realized it was locked. Aurelia rattled the black handle and then, before Rebecca could stop her, leaned on the bell. Almost instantly, the big front door swung open and out stepped the elderly black butler Rebecca had seen for the first time that rainy morning at Temple Mead.

He might have been old, but he was light on his feet, hurrying down the broad brick steps to unlock the gate. But he only creaked it open a little way, blocking their entry, one hand firmly clapped on the gatepost.

"We've brought these for Helena," Aurelia breathlessly announced, thrusting the floppy bouquet up at him as though it were the Olympic torch.

"That's very kind of you, young lady. I'll make sure she gets them." He nodded, lifting the bouquet from Aurelia's clammy grasp, and started pushing the gate closed.

"Can't we see her?" Aurelia squeaked.

"No, Relia," Rebecca said quickly. She didn't want the butler to think they'd come to stare at poor, unfortunate, sickly Helena. "She doesn't want to be disturbed."

"That's right, I'm afraid." The butler shook his head, his face solemn. "Miss Helena needs complete quiet right now. But I'll take your flowers up to her right away, and I'm sure she'll be real pleased to get them. You have a card here, too, I see."

On the card — a square of cardboard cut out from an old cereal box — Helena's name was spelled out in large sparkling letters, with LOVE FROM AURELIA VERNIER AND REBECCA BROWN scrawled along the bottom in gold. Rebecca wondered if Helena would even know who they were.

"Thank you," they chorused, and waited — Aurelia gripping the locked gate as though it was the barred door of a jail cell — until the butler had disappeared back inside the silent, shuttered house. Then they strolled off toward home, crossing the road to walk in the shadow of the cemetery walls. Aurelia was disappointed about being turned away at the gate, Rebecca could tell: Her usually bumptious little cousin wasn't hurdling sidewalk cracks as usual or chattering about her day at school. She was walking slowly, scuffing at the occasional twig dislodged from an oak tree by the brisk wintery wind.

"I've never been in that house," she muttered. "Not like *you*."

"There's nothing much to report," Rebecca said, trying to sound blithe: When Aurelia had asked her about the Bowmans' Christmas party, wanting to know if all the reports about Helena's hysterical fit were true, Rebecca had played dumb. She hadn't heard anyone screaming, she said; people must have been exaggerating. It was a lie, of course, but Rebecca felt the need to try and protect Aurelia — from what, she wasn't entirely sure. Most of the time, Aurelia seemed so blissfully removed from all the nasty dramas and secrets seething in Temple Mead.

"I heard that Helena has a big bedroom on the third floor," Aurelia said, turning around to point back at the Bowman mansion. "It has its own walk-in closet, and . . . look! There she is!"

Rebecca spun on her heels and looked up, following the line of Aurelia's pointed finger. Her cousin was right: Helena was standing at a third-floor window, gazing down at them. The pink tips of the flowers they'd left were just visible; she must have had the bouquet in her hands. Aurelia started waving.

"She wants to say thank you," Aurelia told Rebecca, but although Rebecca murmured her agreement, she wasn't at all convinced that the look on Helena's face was remotely grateful or friendly. In fact, for a moment Rebecca wondered if Helena was going to lift the window sash and hurl the flowers onto the street below, so strange was her expression. She was staring down at Rebecca so intently, the way Marilyn looked when she'd cornered a bird in the yard and was getting ready to pounce.

Helena smiled, much to Aurelia's delight, but it was an odd, tight smile. There was something almost sinister about it, Rebecca thought, shivering as the cold breeze whooshed through the trees. Helena turned her head a little, talking to someone they couldn't see, and then another person appeared at the window alongside her.

Anton.

"I thought that man said nobody was allowed in!" Aurelia was indignant. Suddenly breathless and light-headed, Rebecca grabbed for Aurelia's hand.

"Come on, Relia," she said, tugging her cousin's arm. "We should get home."

Aurelia would have stood there all afternoon, waving up at the local royalty, but Rebecca was taller and stronger than she was, and dragging her around the corner, out of sight, wasn't hard.

This was just horrible: The last person she wanted to see was Anton. Especially in these circumstances. How humiliating, standing around in the street, gazing up at Helena and Anton like peasants gawping at members of the royal family.

No wonder Helena had that strange, thin-lipped smile on her face this afternoon. Rebecca was out in the street; Anton was standing right by Helena's side, exactly where he belonged. Helena wasn't smiling because she felt friendly, or grateful, or touched. There was something cool and spiteful about the way she looked. It was a smile, Rebecca realized, of triumph.

CHAPTER TWENTY-EIGHT

IT WAS A WEEK BEFORE THE SEPTIMUS PARADE, and Rebecca couldn't help getting caught up in all the excitement about Carnival. She stood in the lunch line, waiting for her chicken fajita wrap, wondering how crazy it was all going to be. Tonight, she and Aunt Claudia were planning to walk up to St. Charles to watch three parades in a row: Aurelia was going separately with Claire, because they had some giggle-fest of a sleepover planned that began the second school finished and lasted until they finally conked out, exhausted with chatter, probably sometime around dawn. On the way to school that morning, Aurelia had explained how Rebecca *had* to take a bag with her to the parades, so when she caught beads and other "throws" she could stash them safely away. What she was supposed to do with all this plastic stuff when they got home, Rebecca wasn't sure.

Aurelia had also whispered that Aunt Claudia always took a plastic cup with her, half filled with bourbon and Coke. It was legal to drink in the streets in New Orleans, Rebecca knew, as long as people drank from a plastic cup or a can rather than a bottle. But the thought of her aunt guzzling bourbon in the street seemed both bizarre and hilarious. It was another reason to look forward to her first Mardi Gras.

"Are you going to the parades this weekend?"

Rebecca was so unused to anyone talking to her, she ignored the question at first.

"Rebecca?"

It was Marianne Sutton, standing right behind her in the line, smiling wanly.

"Oh! Sorry. Yes," Rebecca burbled. "I didn't realize you were . . . talking to me."

"It'll be kind of cold," said Marianne, with a little sigh. "Though you're probably used to the cold, being from New York and all."

"Yup." Rebecca grinned. Their exchange was, again, almost civil. In fact, it *was* civil. Just as Jessica was much nicer without Amy around, Marianne seemed to be sort of human without Helena's influence.

"I'm not used to anything real cold," Marianne was saying. "In December it snowed that one day. It's only snowed here three times in my entire life."

"I missed it," Rebecca said, not sure if she should explain that she'd flown back to New York the day after the Bowmans' party. She was so out of the habit of just *talking*. It was all lies, secrets, and accusations these days. Chatting about the weather with Marianne, even if it was just for a few minutes, made Rebecca feel like a normal person again.

That day after school, Rebecca walked home past the cemetery, letting her fingers drift along the rough iron bars of the Prytania gate. She hadn't caught even a glimpse of Lisette in days and days. Possibly she was lying low in the cemetery or hanging around the Bowman mansion driving Helena out of her wits. Or maybe she was avoiding Rebecca, for some reason. After all, if Lisette wanted Rebecca to see her, all she had to do was sidle up to one of the gates. It wasn't as if Rebecca could break into the cemetery or hang around the Bowmans' front porch.

Rebecca paused for a moment, peering through the bars and into the quiet cemetery. The breeze blew an unidentifiable piece of litter along the main avenue, and the trees rustled, papery and agitated, as the wind picked up. Rain was coming: Rebecca could almost smell it in the air. She'd learned this trick here in New Orleans, learned to interpret the strange colors of the sky.

"Rebecca?"

She turned her head sharply, guiltily dropping her hands from the bars, though she'd been doing nothing wrong — not chatting with a ghost, at least. Marianne stood a few feet away, swinging her leather schoolbag. Rebecca couldn't help feeling nervous. The last time she'd been confronted by a member of the Sutton family outside the cemetery, it hadn't gone very well.

But Marianne was smiling again. That was the hardest thing to get used to, Rebecca thought. Apart from acting like a decent person to Marianne that day in the library, Rebecca hadn't done anything to deserve all this friendliness, any more than she'd done anything to deserve the hostility of last semester. She was the same old Rebecca. It was Marianne who'd changed.

"I think it's going to rain," said Rebecca, hoping that Marianne wouldn't ask her why she was staring into the closed cemetery. "It's pretty windy already."

"I guess." Marianne shrugged. "As long as it doesn't rain *next* Friday night, I don't mind."

Rebecca smiled at her but said nothing. There was only so much weather she could discuss.

"You *will* be here, won't you?" Marianne continued. Her blue eyes widened. "For the Septimus parade?"

"Oh, sure," said Rebecca. She was kind of looking forward to it, despite herself. Jessica had told her that the costumes were amazing, and that the special throws were as sought-after as the hand-decorated shoes bestowed by the Muses krewe, or the famous Zulu painted coconuts. None of this meant much to Rebecca yet, but she got the general idea: You could catch good stuff at Septimus.

"Great!" Marianne beamed at her. "Because I had this idea and . . . and I don't know what you think about it, and I know it's not much notice, but . . ."

Rebecca followed Marianne's gaze. She was looking over at the Bowman mansion on the other side of the street. There was no sign of Helena in the window today, Rebecca was relieved to see.

"What?" she prompted. The oak trees shook in a sudden burst of breeze, and the noise seemed to break the spell; Marianne snapped back to attention.

"My mother and I were talking, and I was telling her how you're a really similar height to Helena."

Rebecca raised her eyebrows. Where was Marianne going with this?

"And usually, it's a superbig deal to be picked as a maid, because you get to go to all these parties and the queen's luncheon, and things that have already happened. So it's not really fair for a girl to just get asked at the last minute like this, because then she's missed ninety percent of the honor. But then we thought that maybe *you* wouldn't mind, because you don't really go to the balls or anything, do you?"

"No," Rebecca replied, puzzled, not sure what she was agreeing to, or disagreeing with. Marianne wasn't making herself very clear.

"That's what I thought." Marianne looked relieved. "You're just visiting New Orleans and all, right? So it's not as though you could get this chance again."

"This chance to do what?" Was Marianne really asking her to be a maid — to be Helena's stand-in? Marianne went a little pink, swinging her bag even harder.

"Would you like to ride on the float with me next week? You just have to stand there and wave and throw beads. There'll be someone to hand you the beads, because you won't be able to move much — they have to anchor our gowns and headdresses, because they're so big and heavy. You'll see. Maybe you could come over now to take a look? We have our own dressmaker, and she's been working on the two costumes at our house for, like, months. She's there right now — that's why I thought it would be a good time to . . ."

Marianne was talking on and on, which was just as well, because Rebecca didn't know what to say. She and Marianne appeared to be walking along the street together, back in the direction of Temple Mead. This was the most bizarre turn of events. She, Rebecca, would be riding in the Septimus parade. Wearing Helena Bowman's costume. And right now she was walking to the Suttons' house for some kind of fitting.

"I'm not sure about this," she told Marianne, her heart thumping. "I've never even been to a parade before. I don't know that I could do . . . whatever it is I have to do."

"Oh, you'll love it," Marianne said, picking up her pace. "It's going to be so much fun!"

"But I thought you had to belong to Septimus? I mean, that your father or grandfather or whoever had to be a member. And doesn't it cost thousands of dollars to get your daughter onto a float like this?"

Some of Amy and Jessica's tutorials had stuck in her brain.

"They can waive the rules." Marianne sounded completely unconcerned. "And Helena's father has already paid for her costume and throws and everything. He's hardly going to ask *you* to pay him back."

This sounded a little ruder than maybe Marianne intended, Rebecca thought, loping along the sidewalk toward the Sutton house on First Street.

"The costumes are just amazing," Marianne was saying. "My mother's going to be so happy you said yes! I told her I was going to ask you. We've been totally racking our brains about who could step in."

"Your mother's home now?" Going to the Suttons' house might mean seeing the vile Toby, and Rebecca didn't want to be under the same roof as him. But she couldn't say this to Marianne.

“My mama and our dressmaker. Toby’s at soccer practice.” At this, Rebecca almost wheezed out a sigh of relief. “So we’ve got the place to ourselves.”

And some place it was, Rebecca thought, climbing the pristine white front steps. The Suttons’ house was as grand as the Bowmans’ and more beautiful in some ways, painted a rich terra-cotta, with black cast-iron gallery railings as ornate as fine lacework. The garden surrounding the house was subtropical, like a lush jungle, though it wasn’t messy and overgrown like Aunt Claudia’s. And inside the house, with its dark wooden floors, soft rugs, and dark green walls, Rebecca felt as though she was in some orderly, peaceful sanctuary, like the Temple Mead library on a much larger scale.

“This must be Rebecca!” A thin, middle-aged woman with smooth platinum blonde hair — a much more fake version of Marianne’s blonde mop — came padding out of another room. She wore slim-fitting velour sweatpants and a soft-pink sweater, and Rebecca thought she recognized her vaguely from the Bowmans’ Christmas party, though Mrs. Sutton was interchangeable with any number of the mothers who lined up in their cars outside Temple Mead or dropped into the Café Lafayette for a skim iced latte. They had perfect tans, taut faces, big diamond rings, even bigger shoulder bags, and cars as large as studio apartments in New York.

“Nice to meet you, Mrs. Sutton,” Rebecca said, suddenly a little bashful.

“You just call me Miss Karen,” said Marianne’s mother, flashing a giant crocodile smile. However warm she was acting, there was something chilly about her. The look in her ice blue eyes wasn’t truly friendly, Rebecca decided. She was appraising this new friend of her daughter's, looking her up and down as though Rebecca were an item on sale in a store.

"Wasn't I right?" Marianne dropped her bag onto one of the silk-cushioned chairs, but Rebecca was hesitant to follow suit. All of this furniture looked expensive and breakable, kind of like Miss Karen. "She'll fit Helena's costume, I'm sure."

"Well, let's just see about that right away." Miss Karen gestured toward the stairs, and Marianne bounded up. There was nothing to do but follow her. "Shirley has everything set up and waiting for you. Rebecca honey, I hope you're not shy!"

At the top of the stairs, Marianne raced down a long corridor and disappeared into a room at the back of the house. It overlooked the broad back garden, though it was some time later when Rebecca even thought to look out at the view. There was far too much to look at in the room itself. Not furniture, because there was nothing in there aside from a small writing desk and a couple of gilt-edged chairs. Not decoration, because it was a fairly plain room, with butter yellow walls and white moldings, the cream-colored curtains heavy and tied back with simple cords. And not people, because the only person in there was the dressmaker, Shirley, who was dressed in unflattering mom jeans and was busy crawling around on the floor picking up pins.

What was transfixing in this room were the two costumes, standing upright as though worn by invisible models. Both were dazzling, awash with sequins and fake jewels, their ball gown–style skirts falling to the floor and fanning out like glorious flower petals. One of the dresses was a dramatic black and silver; the other was made up of vivid reds, oranges, and golds. Against one wall lay vast feathered objects, which at first Rebecca thought might be giant fans; just as she was wondering how they'd be able to pick them up, Marianne told her they were headdresses.

"They'll be fixed to stands, honey," Miss Karen said. "So they don't crush your poor little skull! And show her how the dress works, Shirley."

Shirley hastily stuck her fistful of pins into the black pincushion she was wearing like a bracelet and explained that Rebecca would have to show up that day in leggings and some kind of glittering leotard top. She wouldn't step into the dress itself until she was on the float: It was easier to get those over-the-top constructions in place and have the girls climb in, rather than ask them to negotiate the steps while in costume.

"It's perfectly safe," Miss Karen reassured her. "You just want to make sure you take one more powder-room break before you get onto that float. Because once you're in, you're in. And you're not getting out until someone lifts you out!"

"Which one is mine?" Rebecca whispered. She'd never worn something so extravagant and ridiculous and extreme before in her life. The idea of wearing it in public, while traveling on some kind of lurching float, was both exciting and kind of scary.

"The red one," Marianne said. "The theme for this year's parade . . . Mama, can we tell her?"

"It's top secret," Miss Karen said with a wink. "Can we

trust you, Rebecca? You can't say a word to any of your friends at Temple Mead."

"Phoenix rising from the ashes," Shirley said, before anyone could stop her. *So Aurelia was right!* "And that's what Miss Marianne is, the ashes."

"And Rebecca will be the flames!" said Miss Karen, frowning at Shirley. Rebecca got the feeling that Miss Karen had planned on revealing this allegedly top-secret information but — judging from the number of times Shirley checked the fob watch hanging from her pocket — the dressmaker hadn't wanted to waste any more time. "You lucky girl! I'm sure half of Temple Mead would cut off their right hands to get an invitation like this."

Rebecca thought of Jessica and felt a little bad. It would mean so much more to her. Maybe Rebecca should decline the honor and suggest Jessica instead.

"But it's been so hard to find someone exactly Helena's height and size," Miss Karen was saying, and Rebecca realized that Jessica, who was much shorter and stockier than Helena, would never fit into the costume.

There were two other maids, according to Marianne, and their costumes would represent water and wind. They'd ride on another float, with their own stewards to hand them beads. Rebecca would be standing on a pedestal-like platform at the back of her float, with Marianne on another pedestal at the front.

"Just move from side to side a little." Miss Karen acted it out. She looked like some kind of mechanical Barbie doll. "Waving and smiling, waving and smiling. Shirley, help Miss Rebecca climb into this thing. Do we need the stepladder?"

Rebecca had long enough legs to render the ladder unnecessary, though she did have to take off her school skirt and blouse — that was why Miss Karen had hoped she wasn't shy, she realized, clambering into the costume wearing nothing but her underwear, and half wishing that she wasn't wearing the camisole set Ling had bought her as a joke at Christmas: the words NYC CHICK were plastered, in red letters, across her backside.

Shirley draped the scratchy, heavy folds of the top over her, pinning and grunting and darting away to make notes on a small pad of paper. It wouldn't itch, Marianne assured her, when they had their leotards on; Miss Karen had them on order. Rebecca couldn't feel the skirt at all: It was so wide and sprawling that it missed her legs altogether. She loved the vibrant colors of her gown and the way it glittered when the sun hit it.

"We'll try the headdresses next week," declared Miss Karen, flicking open her cell phone and closing it again. "I have to go pick up Toby. Can you come back on Monday after school, honey?"

Rebecca walked home as fast as she could; it was already growing dark, and the first drops of rain were splattering onto the sidewalk. She couldn't wait to see the look on Aunt Claudia's face when she told her all this. Sure, she wasn't supposed to hang out with the Bowmans and the Suttons et al, but this had to be an exception. The chance to ride in a Mardi Gras parade, especially one as exclusive and prestigious as this, in such a glamorous costume, with no cost involved whatsoever . . . her aunt had to say yes.

But Aunt Claudia didn't look shocked at all when Rebecca found her sitting in the semidarkness of the front parlor, a book lying open and facedown in her lap. Maybe she'd been napping, Rebecca wondered, because at first she didn't seem to react to Rebecca's announcement at all.

She simply reached for her reading glasses, which were lying on top of a brass dish etched with Arabic letters.

"What night is the parade?" she asked slowly, her face grave.

"February twentieth," Rebecca told her.

"I'll just have to . . ." Aunt Claudia began, heaving herself up from the low-slung armchair. She padded out of the room and down the hallway, Rebecca following her. She wanted to get a definite answer on the parade now, and not let her aunt dither about it for days. There wasn't time for that. She'd already been fitted for that amazing glitter-flame costume. And secretly, she couldn't wait for the near-hysteria sure to break out at school when word of her maid-of-Septimus status got out. Legions of Debs would be fainting in the hallways, overwhelmed by jealousy and outrage. Mean Amy would be struck dumb. That, at the very least, made the whole thing worth it.

Her aunt walked into the kitchen and straight to consult — surprise, surprise — her ad hoc oracle, the wall of odd calendar pages. Carefully she peeled one day off, fingering its corners. This was the first time Rebecca had ever seen Aunt Claudia actually remove a page from its spot on the wall.

"What's wrong?" she asked, leaning in from the doorway, trying not to sound impatient.

"I'm . . . I'm not sure if the parade is a good idea." Her aunt's voice was creaky and strained. "I mean . . . well, I just don't know."

"Don't know what?" This was beyond ridiculous. Rebecca could see the page in her aunt's hands, and sure enough, it was February twentieth. What, was her entire life going to be controlled by these stupid pages stuck on the wall? Just because that date happened to be ripped out of a calendar at random didn't mean Rebecca should suffer. This was her one chance to take part in a big carnival parade. Other girls would fight tooth and nail to be in her spot! Why her aunt was such a killjoy, Rebecca didn't know.

"We'll talk about it later." Aunt Claudia slithered past her, walking back up the hallway to the parlor. Enraged, Rebecca stared at what was left on the Wall of Nonsense. She wanted nothing more than to rip every stupid white date off and throw it in the trash. It was just coincidence that the date of the Septimus parade matched one of the pages. It didn't mean anything.

Rebecca grabbed the closest page at hand. October twenty-fifth . . . OK, that wasn't random. It was the day she arrived in New Orleans. And the next October page: Wasn't that the first night she slipped into the cemetery to spy on Anton and Helena, the night she fell over and saw Lisette for the first time?

She clutched at another page, ripping it as it pulled free from the grease-stained, peeling wall. The Saturday after Thanksgiving: That was the day she'd walked to Tremé with

Lisette. The date in December was the night of the Bowmans' party — the real date, not the one she'd told Aunt Claudia. The other day in February was Helena's birthday, the day after the Septimus parade. The only date Rebecca couldn't account for was the one in March. She tore it from the wall and, grasping her damp pile of pages, marched along the hallway to find her aunt. She wanted answers — straight answers — and she wanted them *now*.

CHAPTER TWENTY-NINE

IN THE PARLOR, HER AUNT WAS SITTING DOWN again, but she wasn't reading. Her glasses were folded and set aside on a cluttered table. Her book was lying open and upside down on the frayed Turkish rug. The only thing in Aunt Claudia's hands was the calendar page for February twentieth, and this she was absentmindedly turning, rubbing its edges between her thumbs. In the twilight of the room, it was hard to make out the expression on her face.

"What do these mean?" Rebecca demanded, brandishing her handful of calendar pages. "I know about some of these days but . . . what is this date in March about? Why did you stick all these dates up on the wall?"

Aunt Claudia looked up at her, and now Rebecca could see how weary she looked, how strained. She wasn't even wearing any jewelry today, just a floaty caftan of nebulous ethnicity.

"I just knew they meant *something*," she said, motioning to Rebecca to sit down on the chaise longue. "But when I first pulled them out of the calendar . . . well, baby, I knew what some of them related to. Some of them were a mystery. They just spoke to me, that's all. I know you don't think much of my psychic powers, but there are some things I can see, even if I don't understand them altogether."

"So that's the Septimus parade." Rebecca wriggled forward on the silky chaise longue, and pointed to the sole page in Aunt Claudia's hands. "And this one is the Bowmans' Christmas party. And this one is the day I arrived."

"And what about the other dates?" Aunt Claudia squinted at the pages Rebecca was clutching. Rebecca opened her mouth to reply and then closed it again. So far she'd never said a word to her aunt about Lisette. Actually, she'd lied, saying she'd never seen a ghost. She wasn't sure if this was the right time to admit her secrets and lies: Aunt Claudia might get annoyed, and clam up about everything else.

"Baby, you have to tell me everything you know." Her aunt sat forward in the collapsing armchair so her knees were almost touching Rebecca's. "You have to tell me everything that happened on the days I don't know about. And then I'll tell you everything I know, and we'll see where it all leads. I want to be straight with you, but you have to be straight with me, OK?"

"OK." Rebecca was still reluctant. She was going to have to own up to a lot of things. But this mystery, she sensed, would be solved only if she and her aunt worked together. "That one day in October . . . well, it was the night, really."

"The night?" Aunt Claudia looked startled. "You were home that night."

"I went out," Rebecca said in a small voice. "To the cemetery."

"To the cemetery at night?" Rebecca nodded, trying not to be deterred by her aunt's horrified tone.

"I went in to see what Anton and all his friends were doing, but on the way out, I bumped into . . . I met . . . I saw, for the first time, without knowing . . ."

She trailed off, gazing down at the clump of pages in her hands, unable to look Aunt Claudia in the eyes.

"You saw the ghost?" Her aunt sounded surprisingly calm. But when Rebecca glanced up, she realized Aunt Claudia wasn't calm at all: She was white as a sheet.

"I didn't know she was a ghost until later," Rebecca stumbled on. "And then, after Thanksgiving, we went for a walk together. Through the city, to her house in Tremé."

"I see." Her aunt didn't sound angry — just terribly, terribly sad. It was almost as though she had known or suspected it all along. Since she was telling the truth at last, Rebecca decided she may as well tell her aunt everything.

"After the Bowmans' party, when I told you I'd never seen the ghost . . . I had. I'm really sorry I lied. But then I didn't know what it all meant. Actually, I still don't. I don't understand what's going on, or why Helena and I can see something nobody else can see."

"Of course you don't understand." Her aunt spoke softly.

"And that date you have there — the Septimus parade," Rebecca went on. "Why is that a special day? Why did you say I shouldn't take part in the parade?"

Aunt Claudia crumpled the piece of paper in her bony hand.

"Because that," she said, "is the day the curse will be lifted. Or so I think."

"Really?" Rebecca tossed her stack of pages onto the chaise longue. "What makes you think that? Wasn't the curse in . . . in perpetuity?"

She thought of Aurelia telling her that when she first arrived in New Orleans.

"People think that," said Aunt Claudia. "At least, those people who know a little about the curse, and there are too many of them around, as you've gathered, I'm sure. But long ago, the Bowmans found someone who could tell them more about the curse, and the story's a little different."

"Really?" Rebecca's mind was swimming. "Who? When? What did . . ."

Aunt Claudia held up her hand.

"Over a hundred years ago," she said. "Let me go back a little, so you'll understand. After the curse was placed on the family, it was some years before another Bowman daughter reached her teens. She was about to turn seventeen, sometime in the 1880s, when she contracted pneumonia and died. This girl was the granddaughter of the original residents of the house, the Mr. Bowman who died of yellow fever and his wife."

"The woman who murdered Lisette," breathed Rebecca. Aunt Claudia nodded.

"Their son had inherited the house after the Civil War, when his mother died. This girl was his only daughter. But he scoffed at the idea of a curse, and he and his wife wouldn't believe it had anything to do with their daughter's death. His two sons grew up and married and had many sons of their own, but one of the sons had a daughter. Just before her seventeenth birthday, she was up in St. Francisville visiting friends, when she was killed in a riding accident."

"And that's when they started taking the curse seriously?"

"It could have been coincidence, but the family began to get very, very nervous. There'd been just two girls born into the Bowman family since that terrible day in 1853, and both had died suddenly, practically on the eve of their seventeenth birthdays. The new mistress of the house didn't want to take any chances. She wanted the curse to be lifted."

"But Lisette's mother was dead by then," Rebecca told her aunt. "She dropped dead in the street a few months after Lisette was murdered. And anyway, she would have died of old age by then, right?"

"Probably, if she wasn't dead already — 1905 was the year they tried to take the curse off the house. The new Mrs. Bowman invited anyone she could think of to help them — all sorts of self-proclaimed voodoo queens and mystics. Someone who called himself the High Priest of Hoodoo. A priest was even asked to perform an exorcism, I hear."

"Did any of this work?"

"Not a thing. But one day someone came to visit them, someone they hadn't invited. She was an old Creole woman who lived down by the river on the other side of town — Miss Celia, everyone called her. She'd been born in Haiti early in the previous century, people said, during the revolution there, the daughter of free people of color. Her family had fled to New Orleans in 1809, escaping the bloodshed and political turbulence on that ravaged island. So the day she came to call on the Bowmans, she was a very old lady, over a hundred years old, and half blind. But still famous, in certain parts of the city, for her powers of second sight."

"Did she know Lisette and her mother?"

"Oh, yes. She'd known Rose Villieux very well. She'd lived in Tremé for fifty years after she arrived in New Orleans, and she knew both Marie Laveaus . . ."

"I didn't know there was more than one." Rebecca had only a vague idea about the famous voodoo priestess.

"She knew Marie Laveau and her daughter, the one who mysteriously disappeared. She'd known Dr. Jim Alexander, and Eliza Nicaud, who were famous in voodoo circles here for years. And, of course, she knew all about the curse on the Bowman house. The very day Lisette's mother came to the house, she'd returned home to Tremé and summoned her closest friends, Miss Celia included. These were women who knew about these things, because many of them were refugees from Saint-Domingue, or the daughters of these refugees. That night, they came together in her house on St. Philip Street and prepared an altar. They carved the name "Bowman" onto seven black candles, and Rose repeated the curse she'd made. She wanted to make sure the family would suffer, the way she was suffering."

"And Miss Celia was there?" Rebecca asked, even though her aunt had already told her this.

"She was." Aunt Claudia nodded. "So the Bowmans were very interested in what she had to say. The curse had taken its first victim almost immediately, she told them. . . ."

"But wait a minute," Rebecca interrupted. "Didn't you say that the first Bowman daughter didn't die until after the Civil War? Like, in the 1880s?"

"That girl wasn't the first victim," said Aunt Claudia quietly. She looked warily at Rebecca. "The first person the curse killed was Lisette's mother. To make a curse so strong and so brutal . . . well, there's a price to be paid. Karma, if you like, if you don't mind mixing religious traditions. As you know, I'm not a stickler about these things."

Her aunt cast a wry glance around the living room, with its mixture of Buddhist statuettes, African masks, pictures of saints, and brass Indian gods.

"Rose knew she wouldn't survive long after inflicting so cruel a curse," she continued, "but she had nothing left to live for, Miss Celia said. The man she loved was dead. Their daughter, Lisette, had been killed, without any consequences for the murderer. And things were starting to get very bad in the city for her community. They were seen as a subversive presence, fueling the discontent of the slave population. Rose must have decided that she had nothing to lose but her life, and that it was worth it, to take revenge for her daughter's death."

"Who *told* you all this? About what Miss Celia said, I mean?" Aunt Claudia looked old, but she couldn't be more than fifty, at most, Rebecca decided: There was no way she could have been alive the same time as this strange old crone, Miss Celia. She seemed totally averse to having anything to do with the Bowmans. So where did she get all this inside information?

Her aunt seemed in no hurry to answer. She picked up one of the carved wooden elephants from the side table and scratched at some dust gathered in the thick folds of one of its ears. Then she put it down again, wheezing out a tired sigh.

"I never met Miss Celia," she said. "But I feel as though I know her well. My grandmother was her great-granddaughter and a favorite of the old lady's. Miss Celia was so close to her that she told her the whole story when my grandmother was just a child. Frightened my poor Maw-Maw half to death. And when she died, Miss Celia left every penny of her savings to my grandmother, including the money the Bowmans gave her for telling them more about the curse. And with that money, my grandmother eventually bought this house. During the war, like I told you. She left it to me when she died. We needed to keep an eye on things, she always said. One day, she told me, we'd be of service again."

Rebecca could not believe her ears. Aunt Claudia was a descendant of one of the Haitian refugees? This strange little house was part of the Bowmans' story? All those months when her aunt wouldn't tell her a thing . . . when she knew more than anyone, practically, in the neighborhood.

"So you're . . . you're . . ." She wasn't even sure what she was trying to ask. "You really *are* a descendant of a voodoo priestess?"

"A spiritual advisor," Aunt Claudia corrected her. "That's how she preferred to be known. I haven't inherited many of her powers, I'm ashamed to admit. Miss Celia had second sight, as they say. She was the one who said it would all end the day of the Septimus parade."

"So she came to the house and just said that to them?" Rebecca asked. This strange old Miss Celia sounded as secretive and eccentric as Aunt Claudia. "I don't get why she waited so long to tell them, if she was prepared to just turn up and blab all the details."

"I don't think she knew in advance." Aunt Claudia got up and walked to the window, twitching the heavy lace curtain as though it was out of place. She peered out into the street, in the direction of the cemetery. "It was only when she went to the Bowman house that she started seeing things."

"Like what?" Rebecca prompted, because her aunt seemed more interested in looking out at the street than finishing her story.

"My grandmother told me she walked into that house, and went straight to the staircase, bending down to touch it."

"That's where Lisette was killed!"

Aunt Claudia nodded.

"And then she walked out of the house and across the street to the cemetery, with the Bowmans trotting along behind her. She headed straight for their family vault, like she knew exactly where it was located, even though later she swore she'd never been there before in her life."

"Weird."

"And it was when she stood on the steps of the tomb that Miss Celia could really see things. *Flames coming down*, she said."

"The house on fire!" Rebecca said, thinking of the curse.

"Darkness and light." Aunt Claudia turned sharply to stare at Rebecca. She looked nervous, as though she was afraid of something. "People in masks and colorful costumes, shivering in the cold — that's why she thought it was the night of the Septimus parade. A flame tumbling from the sky. A girl falling to the ground. The seventh Bowman girl to die, and the last. Once she fell, the curse would be complete."

"And Helena . . . is she the seventh girl to die?" Rebecca's stomach lurched when her aunt nodded. For the first time, she really felt sorry for Helena. "It's so awful."

And so unfair, she thought, that more than a hundred and fifty years after Lisette's murder, a girl still had to pay with her life. However odious Helena Bowman acted most of the time, it wasn't her fault that Lisette had been killed.

"And another girl." Her aunt's voice, shrill all of a sudden, cut through the dead air of the parlor. "Miss Celia saw another girl, high above. She pointed up to the stone angel on top of the tomb, and at first the Bowmans thought *that* was the second girl, that Miss Celia must be talking about the angel. But she told them there'd be another Bowman daughter, of the same age. That night the two girls would come face-to-face, lit by torchlight. One girl would live, and the other would die. And the curse would die with her."

"But Helena doesn't have any sisters," Rebecca protested. This didn't make sense at all. "And even if she did, they wouldn't be the same age. Are you sure Miss Celia wasn't talking about the angel?"

Aunt Claudia shook her head, clutching at pieces of furniture as she made her way back to her seat. The room was very dark now; they needed to turn on some lights, Rebecca thought. But she didn't want to break the spell of the story.

"Maybe she meant Lisette?" Rebecca suggested. After all, Lisette was a Bowman daughter — the only other Bowman girl Rebecca had ever met — and she was sixteen, just like Helena. In a permanent state of sixteen, in fact.

"Lisette is already dead," her aunt pointed out, her voice

soft again. "And you're right, Helena doesn't have a sister. But she does have a first cousin, born just a few weeks after she was."

"Really?" Rebecca sat up straight. "Who? Does she live in New Orleans, too?"

Aunt Claudia looked at Rebecca, green eyes blurring with the beginning of tears.

"Baby," she said, starting to say something and then swallowing it back.

"What?" Rebecca's skin was tingling with anticipation. This story was getting more and more strange. Who was Helena Bowman's mystery cousin? And why was talking about this making her aunt so upset?

"I have something to tell you," she said, reaching out a hand to stroke Rebecca's arm. "Helena's cousin, the other girl . . . oh, Rebecca. It's you."

CHAPTER THIRTY

REBECCA COULDN'T SEE STRAIGHT. SHE STARED into space, the room's furniture and clusters of tired knickknacks disappearing into the gloom. She could be in the cemetery now, so mysterious were the dark shapes of the parlor, so oppressive its claustrophobic atmosphere. Aunt Claudia was talking on and on, but nothing she said made sense.

Helena Bowman had a first cousin; their birthdays were just a few weeks apart. This girl was the daughter of Helena's uncle, Paul Bowman. Paul had left New Orleans as a young man and never returned; he'd married a girl named Sarah in some other city. Very few people in New Orleans knew where he'd gone or that he was married; very few knew this daughter even existed, because Paul and Sarah had raised her elsewhere. They'd hoped somehow to defy the Bowman curse by leaving behind the city and the mansion and the family's terrible history — even though it meant Paul, the older of the two Bowman brothers, was turning his back on his considerable inheritance and all the advantages of being part of one of New Orleans's most powerful families.

Rebecca shook her head: Her ears felt clogged, as though she'd been bowled over by a wave while swimming in the ocean.

"But I don't know anything about this Paul and Sarah!" she protested. "And I wasn't born just a few weeks after Helena — I'm almost a year younger than she is!"

Aunt Claudia reached over to the lamp on the side table and clicked it on: A sickly pool of light illuminated their corner of the parlor.

"Paul and Sarah moved all around," she said, her voice quiet but very firm. "They were determined to lose all contact with the Bowmans, all connection with the past. Paul grew a beard, so he'd be harder to recognize, and before their daughter was born they changed their names as well. To Michael and Millie Brown."

Rebecca wanted to cry out, but she couldn't make a sound. Everything she knew about her life and her parents and her family — could it really be a lie?

"And," Aunt Claudia continued, reaching out to grasp Rebecca's hand, "through a friend in the CIA, they even managed to change their daughter's birth certificate, taking more than a year off her age. She was given the birthday of June twenty-eighth, 1993. But actually, she was born in 1992, on March twelfth. That's your real birthday, Rebecca. You're almost . . . you're about to turn seventeen."

Rebecca drew her hand away from her aunt, and shuffled through the calendar pages lying on the chaise longue. There it was: March twelfth. The day she was born. Her parents had lied to her. All these years, her father had kept the truth from her. She felt sick to her stomach, unable to speak. A fat, hot tear rolled down her face, and Rebecca wiped it away with the back of her hand.

"They were trying to protect you, Rebecca." Aunt Claudia could read her mind. "If Miss Celia was right, then this terrible curse still has one victim to claim. That's why your father's done all he could to keep your very existence a secret."

"Then why has he just dumped me here now?" Rebecca spat out, her voice shaking, "If it's so dangerous for me to be here?"

"I talked him into it," said Aunt Claudia calmly, and suddenly she didn't seem so batty and eccentric anymore. This woman Rebecca barely knew . . . she was holding Rebecca's life in her hands! "He's spent all your life trying to dodge this curse, trying to hide you from its power. But I made him see there was no escaping it. Bowman girls have died in other places, far from New Orleans. Staying away wouldn't save you. The curse needs to play out, just as Miss Celia predicted. I'm doing everything I can to protect you."

"But he should be here," Rebecca said, barely able to listen, sobs welling up in her throat. She missed her father so much. "Why is he in China, when he should be here?"

"Rebecca, baby." Aunt Claudia's voice was gentle. "He *is* here. He was only in China for a little while, when you first came in November."

"I got another postcard from him, just last week!"

"Someone sent it for him. He left a stack for a colleague to mail to you. When you came back to New Orleans after the holidays, he flew down on the next flight. He's been here, watching over you as well."

"I want to see him," said Rebecca through a sob. She needed her father to tell her this whole story was true, to reassure her that everything was going to be OK. But Aunt Claudia was shaking her head.

"It would be very dangerous for the two of you to be seen together. Although it's a long time since he lived here, and he looks very different these days, there's always a chance someone will recognize him. He has to keep away from this neighborhood. Believe me, *I* don't even see him, though he's staying somewhere in the Quarter. It's just too risky."

"If he can't do anything, then why is he even here?" Rebecca felt irrationally angry with him right now.

Aunt Claudia patted her hand, as though she was trying to calm Rebecca down.

"Your mother died trying to protect you," she said. "The two of you were crossing that street in Paris, hand in hand, and when Sarah saw a car heading for you, she flung you out of the way, not even thinking about saving herself. Your father insists he'll do the same. I keep telling him to stay away, because right now nobody has any idea that you're a Bowman. You look more like your mother, thank god."

"You knew her?" Now Rebecca really wanted to cry.

"I never met her." Aunt Claudia smiled sadly at Rebecca. "But I saw her photograph."

"I had a picture of her in my wallet, but it disappeared."

"Your father took it. He didn't want anyone here to see it — to see him with you, and put two and two together. After losing your mother, he couldn't bear the thought of losing you as well." Aunt Claudia leaned forward, brushing Rebecca's hair away from her hot, damp face.

"So how do you know my father?" Rebecca demanded. She couldn't understand why her father was putting so much faith in someone who read tarot cards for a living.

"I was the one person in New Orleans he'd kept in contact with. He's a few years younger than I am, and I used to babysit him a lot when he was a child. We would explore the cemetery together, and I would scare him with stories about Miss Celia. I swore him to secrecy about them, because I thought I might get into trouble with my mother or his, and I needed that babysitting money. Paul never told a soul. And even though years passed and our lives moved in very different directions, we knew we could always trust each other. I was his eyes and his ears here, trying as best as I could to take up where Miss Celia left off."

"And that's why you went to see him in New York that time," said Rebecca, trying to piece it all together.

"Yes, that's why. I had to remind him that you would be at risk wherever you lived, whatever name you had on your birth certificate. The curse doesn't care about pieces of paper. And now, the fact that you can see the ghost, just as Helena can, proves that the spirit world knows exactly who you are, even if nobody else here has a clue."

"But I still don't get why I have to be here," Rebecca said sulkily. "Helena is the seventh girl — when she dies, the curse will end. Isn't that what you said?"

She realized this sounded incredibly mean and selfish, as though she was wishing death on Helena, but she couldn't stop herself.

"Miss Celia had a very specific vision of the end of the curse," Aunt Claudia reminded her. "Remember? She saw two girls on the night of the Septimus parade. Meeting each other face-to-face by torchlight. For the seventh girl, it will end in the cemetery — and you're right, Helena is the seventh girl. You're several weeks younger than she is. And your taking part in the parade . . . well, maybe it's a good thing."

"A good thing?" Rebecca was incredulous at her aunt's sudden change of heart.

"Septimus is a nighttime parade, so the route will be lit by the flambeaux. And because they park on Louisiana rather than Jackson, the floats of the royal court drive along Prytania. Past the Bowman mansion — you see? Even if Helena is too sick to attend, she'll be watching out the window. There'll just be you and Marianne on your float, so she won't be able to miss you. Miss Celia's prophecy will come true — the two of you will see each other by torchlight."

"But what about the burning house and all that other stuff?"

Aunt Claudia tapped one finger against her mouth.

"That one had me stumped for a while," she admitted at last. "Until Aurelia told me about the theme for the parade — the rising phoenix. I guessed that one or more of the floats would be decorated to resemble a burning building. Everything Miss Celia saw related to the parade."

"*My* costume is designed to look like flames," Rebecca told her. "And Marianne's is all dark, like smoke and ashes. The other two maids are wind and water, I think, but I haven't seen their costumes — they're on another float. Everything's about fire and rebirth, Marianne told me."

"So this might be it!" Aunt Claudia looked relieved. "Helena *is* very ill — I heard two of the maids talking about it at the grocery store just a week ago. She's too sick to leave her bed most days."

Rebecca decided not to mention seeing Helena standing in her bedroom window the other day, Anton by her side, gazing down at Rebecca with snooty contempt. Clearly Helena wasn't so ill that she couldn't struggle to the window. She *had* looked pale and drawn, it was true, but then, she'd been inside the house for weeks.

"And we have this page." Aunt Claudia pointed at the March twelfth sheet lying next to Rebecca. "That means you'll be here to see your birthday — your *real* birthday."

"I hope so." Rebecca was overcome by everything she'd learned tonight. Her father . . . her father was a Bowman! And he was right here, in New Orleans, hiding from everyone. Hiding from *her.*

"The prophecy will play out, just as Miss Celia saw it," Aunt Claudia was saying. "Everything will happen just as she said. And you'll be safe at the end of it all — you mustn't worry, Rebecca. When the parade ends, I'll be waiting to help you off the float and take you home. Then it'll all be over."

"For Helena," Rebecca whispered. It was so hard to believe that she was really going to die.

"Poor girl," said Aunt Claudia, shaking her head. She gathered up her glasses and pushed herself up out of the low armchair. "This curse has been a blight on our community for too many years. It's made too many people secretive and fearful. I feel terrible for poor Helena Bowman, but I just want all of this to end."

Neither of them were in the mood for parades that evening. They ate a dinner of warmed-up leftovers, and then, after she'd washed the dishes, all Rebecca wanted to do was sleep. Or lie in her darkened room, at any rate, trying to process all this new information. Aunt Claudia followed her along the hallway as though she were reluctant to let Rebecca go.

"Say nothing to anyone about this conversation," she whispered, pulling Rebecca close for a bony hug. "Don't let Marianne think you're anything other than excited about taking part in the parade. Just act the way you always act at school. And whatever you do — don't tell a soul that you can see the ghost."

"All right," Rebecca murmured, wriggling free of her aunt's grasp the way Marilyn the cat squirmed away from Aurelia. She slipped into her bedroom and closed the door, her heart thundering.

Don't tell a soul you can see the ghost.

But she'd already blabbed about seeing the ghost. She'd told Anton, that day in the cemetery. Maybe he thought she was joking, or lying, or just trying to show off. Or maybe he'd gone straight to the Bowmans and told them all about it. There was no way Rebecca could find out, because something told her she wouldn't be seeing or hearing from Anton again.

Once upon a time, Rebecca had thought he was on her side. But then, she'd thought that about Lisette as well. And Lisette must have known all along what it meant when Rebecca could see her — that Rebecca was a Bowman as well, and a potential victim of this curse.

Her father, Anton, Lisette . . . there was nobody Rebecca could trust anymore. They all told her half-truths. They all tried to keep her in the dark.

But one thing was crystal clear to Rebecca. Tomorrow she was going to walk back into the cemetery, to look for the ghost causing all this trouble. The Septimus parade was just days away, and she wanted the truth from Lisette. The whole truth.

CHAPTER THIRTY-ONE

On Saturday morning, dark clouds still rolled in the sky, threatening a more severe downpour than last night's intermittent showers. Rebecca shivered, a damp cold invading her bones as she marched past a yawning tour group — all in rain jackets, conventioneers' plastic lanyards hanging around their necks — and toward the Bowman tomb. It was strange to think of her father playing here when he was a child — long before he was "Michael Brown," in the days when he was still Paul Bowman. This was the place Aunt Claudia had told him her creepy stories; this might even be the spot where he first learned about the curse on the Bowman family and the prediction Miss Celia had made all those years ago. All this time, Rebecca had thought of the cemetery as her own secret place, in a way, but her father and her aunt knew it as well. Knew it more intimately than she did, probably, because they'd grown up looking at it every day. She wondered where her father's bedroom used to be in the Bowman house. Maybe he could have gazed right into the cemetery from his window, the way Helena could now.

Because she was so lost in thought, Rebecca managed to trip over a tree root and stub her toe on a shattered tomb plate en route to the Bowman tomb. But one thing she didn't miss: the sight of Lisette huddled on the cold steps of the Bowman tomb, staring up at her, looking about as miserable as Rebecca felt.

"I know what's going on," Rebecca said, stalking up to the ghost and stopping a few feet away. However dejected Lisette looked, Rebecca wasn't going to allow herself to melt with sympathy or let Lisette off the hook in any way. "You haven't been honest with me."

Lisette leaned back against the base of the tomb, her dark eyes dull with sadness.

"I've told you my story," she said softly. "You know what *I* know."

"That's not true!" Rebecca was trying to keep her voice down, but it was hard when she was so upset. "There are other things you could have told me — should have told me. Like the old lady, Miss Celia, coming to the cemetery and making her prophecy. You *must* have been here for that!"

"I was." Lisette stroked her long braid, gazing up at Rebecca. "But there were lots of people who came and went and said things about the curse. Lots of crazy ladies, and a priest, and some kind of Indian who was chanting and rattling something all around the tomb. They all said they could see into the future."

"And you know more than they do, right? You're just not willing to tell me."

"I don't know anything!" Lisette looked wounded. "I've told you everything I know. I have no idea when the curse will end. *You* know as much about all this as I do."

"Yeah, right," hissed Rebecca. She crossed her arms, glaring down at Lisette. "With one major exception. That first night, when you found me here in the cemetery, and I looked up at you — when I could *see* you! I didn't know what it meant, but you did — didn't you? You've known all along."

Lisette took a long breath; she said nothing. She wasn't admitting anything, but she wasn't denying it, either.

"The only people who can see you," Rebecca continued, "are other ghosts, and girls from the Bowman family. Girls who are your age, just about to turn seventeen. It's been that way for the last hundred and fifty-five years, right? The girls can see you, just before it's their turn to die."

"No!" Lisette shook her head. "I mean — that's the way it's been in the past. But I thought this time maybe it meant something else. Helena was my age, she belonged in the big house. You're not from here. You're not old enough. You didn't scream when you saw me, the way the others always did."

"But you must have known," Rebecca insisted. "Why didn't you warn me? If the only girls who can see you are the ones about to die . . ."

She choked up, unable to finish her sentence. This just wasn't fair. Even if her father had lived here years and years ago, he'd changed his name and renounced his inheritance. Rebecca wasn't part of this place. She didn't belong here. The curse had nothing to do with her, but somehow she was at risk from it, just as Helena was. For all Aunt Claudia's reassurances last night, Rebecca felt incredibly nervous about next Friday. What if *she* was the one the curse decided to take?

"I just don't know if I can trust you anymore," she finally managed to say. "Maybe everyone else has been right all along — you're some kind of evil spirit."

"I'm your friend!" Lisette protested, jumping up from her seat on the steps. "You know that!"

In the distance, Rebecca could hear the murmuring of the tour group, the high-pitched voice of their guide, the crunch of their footsteps. Lisette must have heard them as well, because she reached out a hand to Rebecca: If Rebecca took it, she'd be invisible.

But she didn't want to take Lisette's hand. Rebecca just didn't trust her anymore. Maybe Lisette always told Bowman girls she was their friend — right before they died.

"I don't know anything anymore," she muttered, sniffing away the tears dribbling down her face. "I don't even know who I am."

"I can prove to you I'm your friend — let me show you!" Lisette took a step toward her; Rebecca backed away. "Maybe I can help you somehow! Maybe I can . . ."

The tour group rounded the corner, headed toward the Bowman tomb. Lisette glanced at them, and Rebecca decided this was her cue to leave. She turned, walking as fast as she could without breaking into a jog, refusing to look back to see if Lisette was following. All she had to do was get through the gate and onto Sixth Street as quickly as possible, because that was a place Lisette could not go.

The gate was in sight now, just a few paces away. But someone was stepping out from behind the Dumpster filled with trash and sawed-off tree limbs, moving in front of the open gate.

Anton.

He must have been lying in wait for her. There was something menacing about him today: He was all in black, and his face looked drawn, sunken beneath his high cheekbones. He loomed over her like some kind of sinister vampire, blocking her escape route.

"Rebecca — I need to talk to you." He placed one hand on the gatepost to stop her from squeezing past.

"Then why don't you just call me, like a normal person?" she demanded, using her sleeve to swipe the tears off her face. She was in no mood for another interrogation from Anton. "Or how about you come knock on my front door? Please get out of my way."

Rebecca tried to duck under his arm, but she was too tall, and he was too strong; she just bounced back into the cemetery. He was breathing hard, she noticed. His pale face looked haunted, as though *he* was the one who could see ghosts.

"I know why you're here in the cemetery," he blurted, the words running together. "I know you can see the ghost, OK? I believe you. You were talking to her at the Bowman tomb just now, weren't you?"

So he was spying on her and following her, not just lying in wait. Rebecca was incensed: She couldn't trust herself to speak. Did Anton want her to know he "had" something on her?

"I didn't believe you at first," he said quickly; there was panic in his eyes. "But just now — I heard you. I know I shouldn't have been sneaking around. . . ."

"No, you shouldn't."

"Look, I'm just really stressed-out and worried right now."

Worried about his friend, Helena, thought Rebecca.

"Would you let me pass, please?" If she had to punch and kick her way out of this cemetery, she would. "I have to get home. Unless you just want me to get into trouble again."

Anton hung his head.

"Don't ride in Septimus," he muttered.

"What?"

"Don't ride in Septimus."

"Why shouldn't I?" Rebecca was outraged. Who did Anton think he was, telling her what she could and couldn't do? Was she such a leper, such an outsider, that her very presence on a Septimus float would sully the parade?

"I . . . it's just that I have a bad feeling about it. I can't explain." His eyes bored into her, so intense they were almost manic. "Tell Marianne you can't ride."

"Are you insane?" The parade was in less than a week. It was too late to pull out, simply because Anton had some unspecified "bad feeling." Probably a bad feeling that Rebecca didn't have enough family money or blue-blooded connections. If only he knew who she *really* was! She had just as much right to ride in that parade as Marianne and Helena.

And anyway, she had to ride: Aunt Claudia had said so. Miss Celia's prophecy would be fulfilled when Rebecca's float passed Helena's house, when Helena looked out and saw

Rebecca in her costume of glittering flames. The curse would end — Aunt Claudia was convinced of it, even if Rebecca wasn't. She could tell Anton none of this. He didn't deserve any honesty from her; he was as unreliable and shady as Lisette.

Anton was staring at the ground now, opening and closing his mouth as though he wanted to say something but didn't know how to get the words out.

"You've said what you wanted to say," Rebecca told him. "I have to go."

"Please!" Anton looked up at Rebecca, his eyes red, his face twisted in some secret pain. "Please don't ride in the parade."

"Whatever." Rebecca was too exhausted to feel angry anymore: She just wanted to get home and shut the door. She was tired of people pushing their secret agendas, of hiding the whole story. Obviously Anton — who seemed tongue-tied all of a sudden — wasn't going to explain himself. Maybe he thought that seeing Rebecca ride in her place would be too much for poor, fragile Helena. No wonder he was reluctant to say more. *Please don't ride in the parade, Rebecca — the sight of you makes Helena sick!*

Helena, Rebecca thought. *My cousin*.

Anton sighed, staring over Rebecca's head at something in the distance — maybe someone walking in the Washington Avenue gate on the other side of the cemetery. Now was her chance. She slithered under Anton's arm and ran down the street, relieved that she'd left the door unlocked. She didn't look back, so she had no idea whether Anton was following.

She should have listened to Aunt Claudia that first night

in New Orleans. *Stay away from the cemetery.* It was the place Rebecca had come to associate with the two people she really cared about here, Lisette and Anton. And she couldn't trust either of them anymore. In fact, she'd been a fool to trust them at all. This place had brought her nothing but secrets and sadness and confusion. Rebecca was sick of it. Today, she decided, would be her last visit to Lafayette Cemetery.

CHAPTER THIRTY-TWO

Although Septimus did not roll until seven P.M. on Friday night, Rebecca couldn't go to school at all that day: There was too much to do. Miss Karen waved away Aunt Claudia's objections, telling her Principal Vale wouldn't mind one bit, and of course Miss Karen was right. The Krewe of Septimus took precedence over the teaching staff of Temple Mead. And anyway, Rebecca and Marianne weren't the only ones who needed to get ready. The school's dance team — the Temple Mead Tappers — and majorette squad were marching in that night's parade, leading out the St. Simeon's band, so they didn't have to come to school, either.

Rebecca was told to arrive at the Suttons' house by eleven, to get her hair sprayed and backcombed into giant geisha-like rolls, after which layers of thick, theatrical makeup would be applied by a guy in paisley pajamas and velvet slippers who called himself Mr. Stevie Jay.

In Marianne's serene, sky blue bedroom — its walk-in closet as big as Rebecca's room on Sixth Street, decorated with Audubon bird prints rather than voodoo talismans — Rebecca changed into her leotard, black with red-sequined flames hand sewn down each sleeve. The bodice of her maid's costume would be pinned to this on the float itself; the vast, glittering skirt was transported in the back of a van that afternoon. Once she was lowered into the dress, Rebecca would not be able to move at all.

"Remember, girls — no potty breaks!" Miss Karen trilled: She was overseeing the preparations with an unnecessary amount of nervous energy, Rebecca thought, darting in and out of the impromptu hair salon set up in the guest bedroom, pausing only to pat Marianne's now-huge blonde pillow of hair, or confer with Mr. Stevie Jay about the right shade of orange for Rebecca's eye makeup. "Once you leave the house, that's it! And don't drink too much water today — you're on the float a long time."

Aunt Claudia raised a sardonic eyebrow. She was sitting in a corner, reading her book. Miss Karen had told Aunt Claudia that she didn't have to stay at the Suttons' all day. In fact, she'd been adamant that there was *no need at all* for Aunt Claudia to do anything more than drop Rebecca off. Although Miss Karen was smiling like a beauty pageant contestant the whole time she was talking to Aunt Claudia, Rebecca caught the looks she was exchanging with Marianne and the hairdresser — as though Aunt Claudia's caftan and bangles and knotted gypsy head scarf were more ridiculous than the over-the-top costumes Rebecca and Marianne were about to get swallowed up in.

This made Rebecca feel tense and uncomfortable. Today was her one chance to play the role of Garden District insider, honored — to the consternation of Amy and the entire Roman class system at Temple Mead — by getting asked to ride in Septimus. She couldn't help wishing that her aunt would just go home, or go to work down on Jackson Square, or go *anywhere* that wasn't this house.

But then Rebecca was ashamed of herself. Her aunt was here for a very good reason, she knew: to watch out for Rebecca, and make sure nothing stopped her from getting on that float this afternoon. She wouldn't leave Rebecca's side until the float lurched up Napoleon Avenue, beginning its long and winding progress past the thousands of people lining the route. And eventually, hours later, when the floats and marching bands reached Louisiana Avenue, Aunt Claudia would be waiting for Rebecca, to extricate her from her elaborate feathered headdress and acres of spangled skirt, and then to walk her home. And the very next day, Aunt Claudia had promised, Rebecca would be able to see her father.

In Marianne's bedroom, in front of the full-length mirror, the girls stared at their transformed appearances.

"You look amazing," Marianne told Rebecca. In fact, Rebecca could barely recognize herself. A mask of spiky flames, red and gold and orange, was painted around her eyes; her lips were a sparkling gold. Her dark hair was piled so high, she felt taller than ever. She reached up a hand to pat it gingerly: It was stiff with hair spray.

"My hair feels so weird," she said. "And it looks even weirder."

"It has to act as a cushion for the headpiece," Marianne explained, her voice faint and tremulous. Maybe she was nervous about the parade. "But most of it gets hidden inside the cap, I think."

Marianne's hair had been sprayed with streaks of silver, and her eye makeup was a dramatic cloud of black and gray. Her false eyelashes, tipped with silver, kept sticking together, and Rebecca was glad she didn't have to wear them as well.

"I'm worried about throwing the beads and everything," Rebecca said. She was excited about the parade, and this made her want to chatter about anything and everything. "I'm glad you're in front of me on the float — I can just copy you."

"Yes." Marianne's blue eyes were glazed; she was staring into the mirror, Rebecca thought, but not really looking. "I'll be in front of you. The whole time."

"Good," said Rebecca. She picked at the sequins on her leotard, wondering if Miss Karen wanted them to try on the long evening gloves they had to wear. "I'm trying to get my head around throwing beads for four hours. Won't our arms get tired?"

"You'll be exhausted," Marianne replied, frowning at her own grotesque reflection. She turned away abruptly and stalked out of the room. This had to be hard for her, Rebecca decided. Tonight's parade was supposed to be this exciting experience she shared with her best friend, Helena, and instead she was stuck with a near stranger, Rebecca.

But after they pulled up in Miss Karen's Porsche Cayenne at the assembly point, the sprawling parking lot of a supermarket right on the river, Rebecca discovered there'd been a change in plans. She would be riding in the front of the float, with Marianne on the pedestal behind her: That was where their respective skirts and giant headdresses had been positioned, and nobody wanted to change that now. Because her movement would be so restricted, Rebecca wouldn't be able to take her cues from Marianne. The only person she could rely on was her steward, who wore a black tuxedo and — incongruously — a sinister, expressionless mask; his job was to hand her beads and make sure she, and the feat of engineering that was her costume, didn't topple over.

"I know it feels cold now," Aunt Claudia was saying to her, walking behind Rebecca up the steps of the float. "But you'll be hot inside that costume."

"I hope so!" Rebecca was wearing nothing but her leotard, a pair of khaki shorts, and her Converse sneakers, clutching her pair of gold lamé evening gloves. The weather forecast for this evening was for true winter cold, and the wind gusting off the river was bitter.

The two stewards on their float were busy lifting Marianne into her tentlike skirt, one of them grasping for the cord to secure around her waist. Rebecca stood gazing around the scene in the parking lot, which was clogged with giant floats. Some were two stories high and as long as a truck, all decorated with brightly colored papier-mâché shapes — she could see birds, flowers, waves, flames. Men in satin tunics and pantaloons, either holding or already wearing those same blank masks, bustled on and off the floats, shouting to each other and loading bags of beads and other throws, as well as boxes of beer. Some were already drinking from cans or out of plastic cups, their masks tilted back a little. Rebecca didn't recognize any of the men, of course, but she suspected the Suttons' father was here, and Anton's father, and maybe even

Helena's father. Rebecca's uncle. Her father's brother. Now *that* was a weird thought. Rebecca wondered where her own father was.

The green tractors that would pull each float were backing into position. The floats were named and numbered: Nearby was number 17, *Blowing in the Wind*, decorated in whorls of blues and grays; and behind it was number 18, *Burning Down the House*, its fake flames rising like lurid spikes. Rebecca glanced at Aunt Claudia to see if she'd noticed this particular float, and by the look on her face — something between relief and anxiety — Rebecca thought she must have. Her aunt was right: Miss Celia's vision would be realized, in every detail, during tonight's parade.

The queen's float was parked nearby as well, swarming with little girls in blonde wigs and white dresses, the teenaged queen herself a fairy-tale vision in a bridal ball gown. She was a Temple Mead graduate, Rebecca had heard, some sort of cousin of Julie Casworth Young's; she'd transferred to LSU this year from the College of Charleston so she could be closer to New Orleans and take part in all the required social events. Rebecca had missed the special "queen's luncheon" and wondered if they'd get to talk at all — probably at the end of the parade. Right now everything was too crazy.

Yellow school buses parked along Tchoupitoulas off-loaded band members in their faux-military uniforms. Dozens of schools had to be taking part in this parade — some all white, some all black — and many had sent their cheerleaders or majorettes as well. The luckier girls were in shining Lycra bodysuits, protected a little against the cold night air, but most were in short pleated skirts, with only thick pantyhose to keep their legs warm. Some girls practiced routines in a corner of the parking lot, or twirled their batons high in the air; drummers knocked out an ad hoc rhythm, while musicians warmed up by blowing random notes on their tubas or flutes. It was all costume and cacophony, whichever way Rebecca looked. She felt as though she were taking part in some kind of circus, especially when some tortured note erupted from a nearby trumpet: It sounded like an elephant, getting ready to charge.

Anton had to be here, she thought. Didn't he say he always got to ride on one of the floats? In their masks and costumes, all the men looked more or less the same. Sure, some were more rotund than others, but it was impossible to tell who was young and who was old. The sallow masks made them all look equally sinister and anonymous. Some men, in velvetlike breeches and dark capes, were climbing onto horses; they wore cocked hats as well as face masks, heavy gloves obscuring their hands.

These were the captain and the dukes, the most important men in the Septimus organization, Rebecca knew; they were among the richest and most powerful people in New Orleans. The decision about who was admitted to the krewe, who was chosen as that year's king, whose daughters were chosen to be the queen and her maids — that decision was theirs to make. They must have approved her stepping in for Helena, she thought, just as they'd approved Claire's godfather riding for the first time, after years of paying his dues — though he was stuck way back, Aurelia had told her, in the very last float. For the first time, Rebecca truly realized how prestigious, and how unprecedented, her invitation was. These were people who only looked after their own, people who spent large amounts of money and time and effort sticking together and keeping the riffraff out. Like Miss Karen had said, Rebecca was a lucky girl.

The saddlebags slung onto the horses were brimming with doubloons, fake coins embossed with the krewe's name and the parade theme. This week, despite all of Amy's loud sighs and sniffs, Jessica had spent one entire lunchtime explaining "throws" to Rebecca, even bringing in a handful of doubloons — gold, silver, purple — from previous years for her to examine. The special thing about this year, Jessica said, was that all the doubloons would be black.

"Your turn," the other steward told her, and the two tuxedoed men lifted her by the armpits — a little roughly, she thought — to maneuver her into the dress. She caught one last glimpse of Marianne, who was a dramatic pyramid of black and silver at the back of the float, but soon Rebecca couldn't look anywhere but straight ahead and, with effort, from side to side. Aunt Claudia fussed around her, helping her pull on the evening gloves, getting in the way when Rebecca was lassoed to her post.

The men known as flambeaux were assembling next to the maids' floats. They were all black, Rebecca noted, and dressed in T-shirts and jeans. They didn't wear masks, but several of them were shrugging on long black robes. The torches they carried, strapped on for support, were dangerous-looking, kerosene-fueled, metal contraptions that spewed flames and dripped oil. These men would light the way, dancing and dipping and collecting coins from appreciative people in the crowd, just as they had every year for nearly a century and a half.

"How does that feel?" Aunt Claudia was asking, and Rebecca realized that her headdress, mounted on the end of a pole, had been levered into place. She settled her head, with its ridiculous pile of hair, into the soft cap, glancing at the brilliant feathers curling down around her. With her towering feathered headdress in place, Rebecca felt almost seven feet tall.

"OK, I think," she told her aunt. The stewards had disappeared, and Aunt Claudia was busy pinning her sequined bodice to the leotard. Her aunt and Miss Karen were right: It was already hot inside the stiff casing of the dress. She tried turning her head from side to side and was relieved to discover that the pole pivoted with her. But there was no denying that this was going to be an uncomfortable ride, and a long one.

"Now, I'll be waiting for you on Jackson," Aunt Claudia told her. "I'll help you get out of all this."

"And where do I have to look for Aurelia?"

"She and Claire will be at Sixth Street and St. Charles, on the neutral-ground side. Claire's parents have ladders."

Most families, Rebecca had learned, lined the route with ladders, boxes hammered onto the tops to provide seats for their children. Aurelia and Claire made out like bandits at parades, easily catching the showers of beads, soft toys, plastic cups, and other throws that rained down from each float. Last Saturday night, when Rebecca had joined them, she'd been hit on the head over and over with plastic bounty, though she'd barely been able to see the floats at all through the wall of ladders.

"Now promise me," Aunt Claudia said in a low voice, leaning in close, "that you won't move from this spot until I come to get you."

"I *can't* move," Rebecca whispered back. This was true. For the next four hours or so, she was a prisoner of her costume.

"I'll be waiting," Aunt Claudia promised. "And I'll bring your jeans and coat, so you don't freeze to death. Though I think you'll find throwing beads is very hot work."

"I'll do my best." Rebecca grinned. She intended to fling beads as far and as fast as possible, especially if that meant making her steward work harder.

"And one other thing." Aunt Claudia wasn't smiling. "Remember to look. When you . . . you know."

Rebecca nodded. She knew exactly what her aunt was talking about. When her float passed the Bowmans' house, she had to be sure to look up at the windows. *That night the two girls would come face-to-face, lit by torchlight.*

The flambeaux fired up their torches, shouting to each other. One of the dukes trotted past, calling to the captain that it was nearly time. The flashing blue light of a police car pulled into view; it would lead the parade onto Napoleon. Aunt Claudia, mindful of Rebecca's makeup, blew her a kiss and climbed down off the float.

Septimus was about to roll.

CHAPTER THIRTY-THREE

"HAIL, SEPTIMUS! HAIL, SEPTIMUS!"

Between the cacophony of the bands and the clamor of the people lining the streets, the parade felt as loud as a rock concert to Rebecca. All along the route, the citizens of New Orleans were screaming and waving and jumping in the air, pressing in toward the float from both sides.

"Throw me something!"

"Over here! Here!"

"THROW – ME – SOMETHING!"

The steward passed her handfuls of plastic necklaces, and Rebecca hurled them into the crowd; but however fast she threw, it was never fast enough. The crowd roared and bellowed, always wanting more. Children perched on ladders, hands outstretched, shrieked at her, and though she was looking out for Aurelia and Claire, Rebecca never saw them in the blur of faces and flailing arms.

In fact, before long she couldn't tell one cross street from the next: Between all the crowded balconies and porches, the thicket of people on the sidewalk, and the oak trees already festooned with wayward beads, the entire parade route was a chaotic carnival. The strings of beads she threw were every color of the rainbow, and in the crowd, many people were dressed in costume or in lurid nylon wigs, their faces painted and their necks swaddled in beads or fluorescent necklaces or garish plastic pendants.

Everyone on the street seemed to be having a great time, but to Rebecca the whole experience felt increasingly surreal, and at times almost sinister. Her float was both led and flanked by men on horseback, surveying the parade through their expressionless masks. The crowd greeted them with cries of "Hail, Septimus!" and the dukes tossed doubloons to them, splattering the street with the small, shining black discs. The way people scrambled onto hands and knees to pick up these fake coins made Rebecca think of medieval peasants, groveling at the feet of the high and mighty, grateful for any act of charity. There was something contemptuous in the casual way the doubloons were thrown, and something desperate and eager about the way they were grabbed up. It was as though these men were acting out, in pageant-style costume, the way they saw their role in the city: as smug lords and masters, generous only when they felt like it, socially superior to everyone else.

In front of the float, flambeaux twirled and dipped, their flames streaking the night sky. Occasionally they paused — when someone pushed through the crowd to hand them some change or a folded dollar bill — but most of the time they were on the move. The kerosene was pungent, and fumes from the tractor pulling the float belched into Rebecca's face; cigarette smoke wafted over from the crowd.

Between twisting from side to side, as best she could, to throw beads, and being surrounded by the constant movement of rushing bodies, waving arms, trotting horses, and dancing flambeaux, Rebecca started feeling flustered, sweaty, and dizzy. They seemed to have been rolling for hours, but they were still on St. Charles Avenue.

A couple of times the parade ground to a halt for unknown reasons.

"Why have we stopped?" Rebecca asked the steward the first time; she had to strain to look over her shoulder at him.

"Don't know." He was very brusque, preoccupied with ripping open bags of beads and tearing the paper fastener off each bunch. The empty plastic bags he just tossed onto the road. "Some float's hit a tree, maybe. A tractor might have broken down. Or maybe someone got run over."

This last thought seemed to amuse him.

At least these stops gave her a chance to get her bearings, though they also provided an opportunity for people to rush the float, reaching up to her with imploring hands, begging for whole bags of beads. The dukes muttered to each other, and the flambeaux adjusted their holsters, dripping black oil onto the road. Then, abruptly, they'd be off again. Behind her — stretching for miles, she guessed — all the floats packed with krewe members were dispensing beads and other throws; Rebecca could hear the roar of the crowd as floats passed and school marching bands played. But all she could see was the float ahead of her — it was carrying the two other maids, dressed as water and wind — and the flambeaux and dukes on horseback encircling her float.

After the parade rounded Lee Circle and entered downtown, the parade-goers seemed even more boisterous. *Maybe they're drunker,* Rebecca thought, *because they've been waiting such a long time.* Her arms ached from throwing; her neck was stiff with the effort of twisting, and she couldn't move the lower part of her body at all. The steward kept thrusting string after string of plastic beads into her hands, and she did her best to smile and keep throwing. Why the girls of Temple Mead thought this particular role a glamorous one, she didn't know. It was utterly exhausting, especially when the floats turned onto the craziness that was Canal Street. The entire city had to be out tonight, cramming every inch of sidewalk and neutral ground, screaming and whistling and clamoring for throws.

It was a relief, after the parade began wending its way back along Magazine Street, to start recognizing landmarks closer to home — even though, as the crowds thinned, Rebecca could feel the cold wind blowing off the river. Her feathers rippled in the stiff breeze, and her hands, protected only by the thin gloves, felt numb and weary. The sound of one of the marching band's drums made her head pound. She stifled a yawn — it had to be getting close to midnight. The sky was black as ink, the stars diamond-sharp.

But now wasn't the time to feel tired. The royal floats of Septimus were turning onto Prytania at long, long last: The parade was over. Soon her float would pass the Bowman mansion. This was the vital moment, Rebecca knew: She had to look up at the Bowman house, look for Helena. She wanted to make absolutely sure that Miss Celia's prophecy was played out to the letter, however terrible the consequences. It was important not to be distracted or to look away.

As her float rolled nearer and nearer to the Bowman mansion, the white walls of the cemetery visible on the other side of the street, a knot of anxious anticipation grew in the pit of Rebecca's stomach. She turned her face to the right, staring up through the fortress of oak trees. The gray walls of the Bowman house were in sight. Any moment now, Rebecca would be looking straight at it.

Now! Rebecca's gaze swooped from the empty gaslit porch up to the third-floor windows, but she couldn't see anybody. The blinds were down, the curtains were drawn. Apart from the light beside the front door, the house appeared to be in total darkness. Panic made her heart beat faster: Where was Helena?

The tractor pulling her float seemed to be picking up speed. Suddenly the Bowman house was behind them. Rebecca grasped her fistful of beads, ignoring the shouts of the thin scattering of parade-goers gathered here, hoping that some of the royal floats still had leftover throws to unload. She couldn't believe she'd messed up.

Maybe everything was OK: Helena might have been inside the house, looking out, and Rebecca simply couldn't see her. Maybe she'd been peeking through a gap in the curtains. Still, this wasn't the result Aunt Claudia had wanted. The first thing Rebecca had to do when her aunt got her out of this concrete boot of a costume was tell her what had — or rather, hadn't — happened.

Her float made the wide turn onto Louisiana Avenue, trundling toward the river. As it turned, Rebecca glimpsed the first floats in the long procession — the king's, the queen's, the captain's — slowing down, preparing to stop. She felt too agitated to be tired now, the wind sharp against her cheeks: She wanted to get off this float and to talk to her aunt.

Rebecca let the beads in her hand drop and was glad that the steward was no longer bothering to pass her more.

"We're stopping soon, right?" she asked him. There was no reply. When Rebecca tried to glance over her shoulder, all she could see was the vast, bright canopy of her feather headdress, billowing in the wind.

The tractor slowed again, flanked now on each side by one of the dukes on horseback. And then, to Rebecca's surprise, it began to turn again, heading back into the Garden District down a narrow side street where all the streetlights were out.

"Where are we going?" she asked — still no response. "Hello? Why are we . . ."

A hand slapped across her mouth, pressing so tight Rebecca could barely breathe. What was going on? Who the hell was gripping her head so tightly she couldn't turn it at all? She squirmed, trying to shout, trying to move, but she was pinioned in place by her costume, its ropes and safety belt, and whoever was trying to keep her quiet.

The houses along the street were all dark and silent; not a soul was about. The horses' hooves clicked against the asphalt, their riders never once glancing back at Rebecca. In the distance, she could hear the faint sounds of drums and tooting horns: The parade was coming to an end on Jackson Avenue. The musicians and baton twirlers would pile back into school buses; the krewe members would pour off their floats, throwing their empty bags and cans into the street, pulling off their masks. Nobody would hear her shouts — not them, not Aunt Claudia — even if this man took his clammy hand off her mouth. Terror rose in her throat. What was happening? Where were they taking her — and why?

And suddenly, she understood.

Up ahead, white walls glared at her, bright as lights. The float was headed for the Coliseum Street gate of the cemetery.

And, like one of the gladiators of the ancient world, Rebecca was being taken there to fight for her life.

CHAPTER THIRTY-FOUR

Through the cemetery gate, masked men poured: Some carried flaming torches, smaller than the ones toted by the flambeaux. Others climbed onto the float, detaching Rebecca's headdress and pulling her roughly out of her pinioned skirt. She struggled, kicking her legs wildly at them, lashing out with her arms. Writhing and twisting, she could see that Marianne was no longer on the float; the stewards were gone as well. There was just her, the immobile costumes, and these ominous, silent men in masks and dark capes.

One big man lifted Rebecca off her feet, throwing her over his shoulder as though she were a sack of potatoes.

"No!" she screeched. "Let me go! Help! Help!"

She tried to kick him in the stomach, but the toe of her sneaker just thudded against his rock-hard leg. The path illuminated by the men with torches, the little procession — totally silent apart from Rebecca's outraged cries — made its way through the dark cemetery.

Cold prickled her bare legs — Rebecca was wearing nothing

now but her shorts and leotard — and she drummed her hands against the man's back, though this seemed to have no impact on him.

"Put me down!" she spat, trying not to cry: Her voice was cracking, and she wanted to sob with rage and frustration and fear.

Without a word, he did as she asked, dumping Rebecca hard onto the ground. She lay sprawled, blinking in the semidarkness until her teary eyes could focus.

She was surrounded, hemmed in by tall white tombs and more than a dozen men, every one of them wearing a mask. Some were in costumes she recognized from the floats before the parade began; others wore the more ornate garb of the dukes on horseback. Some people simply wore heavy coats, as though they hadn't taken part in the parade at all. The identical blank-faced masks were turned toward her, alien and expressionless. Beyond them were shadows fading into darkness, the spreading canopies of oak trees like black clouds hanging low in the sky.

Glancing around in desperation, Rebecca could see there was nowhere to run: Every possible route, even a narrow sliver between vaults, was blocked by a masked onlooker. She scrambled back, bumping against the steps of a tomb. The Bowman tomb.

"Aunt Claudia!" she screamed, but her voice was squeaky, breaking the words into two. Who knew if her aunt was still looking for her among the floats on Louisiana — or if she too had been grabbed by masked men?

She pulled herself up the steps, waiting for her back to knock against the gravestone fixed to the front of the tomb:

Instead she bumped into legs. A girl's legs. Rebecca looked up: Helena!

Helena Bowman stood leaning against the family vault. She was dressed in a heavy black coat and jeans; her pale, peaky face looked scared. The stone angel on top of the tomb loomed above her, and for the first time Rebecca realized that the object in the angel's hands was the mysterious emblem on the Septimus flag — an upside-down torch.

"Let me go!" Rebecca bleated, though she knew nobody here had any intention of letting her go anywhere, any time soon. "Please! I haven't done anything!"

"Shut up!" a woman's voice spat at her, and Rebecca thought she recognized the speaker as Mrs. Bowman. The woman — in a mask and long black coat — stepped forward, wrapping her arms around the shivering Helena.

"Move away, Terri," a man ordered her in a booming voice: Rebecca started, because she couldn't tell who was speaking. Everyone looked exactly the same. But one thing she was sure of: They were all Bowmans and Suttons and their closest allies.

Helena started whimpering, clinging to her mother.

"I want it to be *over*," she said in a petulant voice. "I want it over with *now*!"

"No!"

Another man's voice, but a younger one this time: Someone was pushing through the small crowd until he stood in front of the tomb, in the flickering light cast by the torches. He pulled off his mask, throwing it onto the ground.

"Anton!" Rebecca gazed at him, and everything inside her ached with sadness at the sight of his stricken face. She couldn't stop herself from crying now, her body convulsing with sobs. The guilty horror on his face told the whole story: He had betrayed her. He must have told his family — or the Bowmans, or both — that Rebecca could see the ghost. Whether he realized what that meant or not was immaterial. Someone else had grasped the truth: Rebecca *had* to be a Bowman daughter, the second girl seen in Miss Celia's prophecy all those years ago.

"Get back," a man growled at Anton, pushing him away.

"Rebecca," he cried. "I never meant to . . ."

"Be quiet!" It was Helena's mother's turn to rip off her mask, hurling it onto the steps. Her face was quivering with anger. "You should remember *who you are*!"

Someone grabbed the shoulder of Rebecca's leotard, hauling her to her feet and ripping off a scattering of red sequins in the process.

"Step away now, Terri," another man said. Mrs. Bowman hugged Helena, then slowly backed down the stairs, inadvertently kicking her mask. Rebecca wanted to throw up. Everything from the prophecy was in place: the cold night, people in masks and costumes, the flames on her dress, she and her cousin standing together, face-to-face, by torchlight. Two daughters of the Bowman house, both sixteen years old.

One girl would live, and the other would die. And the curse would die with her.

A masked man, one of the dukes who'd ridden alongside Rebecca's float for the whole parade, stepped forward. He was holding a gun, his gloved hand shaking.

"No!" she gasped, shivering with terror. There was no way to escape, nowhere to run. In desperation Rebecca grabbed

Helena's arm; the other girl tried to shake her off. The look on Helena's face was that of pure contempt. As she struggled to push Rebecca away, Helena's mouth pressed into that same tight, malicious smile Rebecca remembered from the day they'd delivered her flowers. It was almost as though she was enjoying Rebecca's terror, getting some twisted satisfaction from what was about to happen.

"I don't like this," the man with the gun said; he was still holding it low, not pointing it at Rebecca. "We've never intervened in fate before. The curse just has to take its course."

"No!" screamed Helena's mother. "We have to save Helena! Do you hear me?"

Another tussle was going on at the foot of the stairs: Anton had surged forward again and was being dragged away by one of the men.

"Get him out of here!" someone shouted, and Anton was silenced, swallowed up by the crowd. Helena had pulled free of Rebecca's grip, wriggling far enough away to give the man at the bottom of the steps a clear shot.

"Rebecca!"

That was Lisette's voice! Rebecca looked around wildly, trying to spot her, but all she could see was the circle of expressionless masks.

"Get away!" Helena shrieked, and Rebecca twisted, following Helena's gaze. Lisette was lying flat on the domed roof of the tomb, crawling tentatively toward the edge. "Get her away from here!"

Helena stabbed an accusing finger in the air, but nobody below them moved. They'd just think she was pointing up at the angel, Rebecca thought: Nobody else could see the ghost up on the Bowman tomb's roof. Only Helena and Rebecca could see and hear Lisette.

"What is it, darling?" Mrs. Bowman cried.

Lisette stretched one arm down, reaching toward Rebecca. "Take my hand!" she pleaded. "Quick!"

For a split second Rebecca hesitated — Could she trust Lisette? Was this all part of this sick ceremony of death? — but she had no choice: Any moment now she was going to be shot, right here on the steps of the tomb. She turned her back to the masked crowd, standing on tiptoes, her whole body stretching so she could reach Lisette's hand. Just one more inch . . . there!

The loud communal gasp she heard had to mean one thing: Rebecca was now invisible to everyone. As far as they were all concerned — the men in masks, Helena's mother, the man with the gun, even Anton — she'd just vanished into thin air.

But one person could still see her.

"She's here!" Helena shouted, her voice choking and enraged. "For god's sake, shoot her! Shoot her now!"

Helena tugged at Rebecca's outstretched arm, trying to pull her free from Lisette's grasp. Lisette was dangling perilously off the edge of the tomb, now with two hands holding Rebecca. With her free hand, Rebecca pushed at Helena, trying to fight her off.

"She's right here — shoot! Shoot!" Helena sounded as though she was possessed, and she must have looked that way as well, grappling with a person nobody else could see.

“I can’t . . . I can’t see her,” said the man with the gun.

“You can climb up,” Lisette told Rebecca. “I got up right from where you’re standing — put one foot on the top of that stone there.” Rebecca managed to haul herself up part of the way, but it wasn’t easy: She felt as though she was about to get torn in two. Above her, Lisette was tugging her right arm out of its socket, and below her, Helena was pulling and clawing at Rebecca’s bare legs, trying to drag her back down.

“On the count of three, pull me as hard as you can,” she said to Lisette, breathlessly kicking out with one leg at Helena, whose nails felt sharp as razors. This was her only chance to get away. Even if it took a superhuman effort, she had to break free from Helena and get onto the roof of the vault. “OK? One, two, THREE!”

Lisette pulled hard and, with all her might, Rebecca swung her free hand up to the pedestal holding the stone angel. If she could only get ahold of it, she might be able to haul herself up. Her fingers slithered around the base, searching for a grip, her free leg flailing in Helena’s face and managing to get one decent kick in.

“Ow! Up there! She’s getting away!” Helena was furious.

Lisette gave another massive tug, this time nearly dislocating Rebecca’s right arm, and that was it: Rebecca’s fingers dug into a small gap at the back of the base, and although the angle was awkward, it might give her the leverage she needed.

“Just . . . one . . . more,” she gasped, looking into Lisette’s dark eyes and knowing, in that instant, amid the utter panic of the moment, that she was wrong ever to doubt

Lisette. The ghost had been true to her word, coming to help Rebecca — the one nonspirit friend she'd had in a hundred and fifty years — when Rebecca needed her most.

"Ready?" Lisette murmured, and Rebecca nodded. With another giant, desperate burst of effort, Rebecca tugged on the base of the angel, trying to let it take as much of her body weight as possible, heaving herself up. But the gap into which she'd dug her fingers was growing: The angel was rocking on its base, coming free from the roof of the vault. The more she gripped it, the more the pedestal rocked — until suddenly, almost without a sound, the angel and her upside-down torch tipped forward, rocking and then toppling toward the ground.

Helena screamed, letting go of Rebecca's leg; still, it was all Rebecca could do to hang on to Lisette and the remains of the pedestal, her face turned to see the angel fall.

And then there was a sickening crack. Not the sound of the stone angel shattering on the steps of the tomb, but of the stone slamming into Helena, striking her on the skull and knocking her to the ground.

"Helena!" shrieked her mother, and the crowd pushed in, pulling the broken pieces of stone away from her crumpled body, the stone torch lying smashed on the steps just above her head. Helena's face was white, her skull crushed and bloody. Her eyes were closed.

Rebecca dug her feet into the grooves of the tomb and hauled herself onto the roof, lying exhausted and panting next to Lisette. People were crying and shouting below them, swarming like insects around Helena's prone form.

"Do you think . . . do you think she's going to die?"

Rebecca whispered to Lisette. She felt sick with fear and worry. She hadn't meant to kill Helena: She was just trying to get away.

Lisette looked back at Rebecca, a quizzical expression on her pretty face, as though she didn't quite believe it all, either. Something approaching a smile — a slow, sad smile — appeared, and then it faded. Or rather, she was fading. Lisette was disappearing, right in front of Rebecca's eyes.

"Good-bye, Rebecca," Lisette whispered, and just like that, she was gone.

"She's dead!" Mrs. Bowman wailed. "My baby is dead!"

Helena Bowman lay dead on the steps of the family tomb, the seventh Bowman daughter to die. The ghost of Lisette Bowman was gone, her spirit no longer forced to haunt Lafayette Cemetery.

The curse was over.

CHAPTER THIRTY-FIVE

REBECCA'S MIND WAS IN A DAZE — HELENA WAS dead, Lisette was gone; how had this all happened? — but she knew she had to get away. Mrs. Bowman was beside herself with grief and rage. With Lisette gone, Rebecca was visible again. Any second now, the people clustered on and around the stairs could look up and see her, and who knew what they would do? It was her fault that Helena was lying dead and broken at the foot of the tomb.

"Give me that gun!" A familiar gruff voice was shouting, and Rebecca's heart soared. It was her father! There he was, pushing through the cluster of masked men, pulling off his own mask. Maybe he'd been there all along, waiting for his moment. Someone tackled him, dragging him to the ground, but Rebecca's dad was strong: He was fighting back, flailing and punching.

She opened her mouth to cry out, but it was too late — she'd been seen. One of the men must have scaled the tomb: Someone was tugging at her arm, trying to pull her back into the shadows. Rebecca was too scared to even look around. They knew she was up here; they were overpowering her father. It was all over.

"Come on!" She swiveled: It wasn't a masked man up here on the tomb with her. It was Anton, his eyes wild, half hanging off the back of the tomb. He tugged hard on her arm again. "Quick!"

Silently she wriggled back, out of sight, slithering down the back wall of the tomb into Anton's arms. Her feet hit the ground. She was shaking so much she could barely stand up.

"This way," he whispered, but Rebecca hesitated: This was the person who'd betrayed her. If Anton had kept his mouth shut, none of this would have happened tonight.

"My father . . ." she began, and Anton shook his head.

"While there's a distraction — quick!"

He was right, she knew: She had to get out of here, and Rebecca knew she needed help. Her entire body felt limp and chilled to the bone. Anton took her hand, dragging her through a narrow, damp cut between the tombs and all the way to the cemetery's dark perimeter. He was running, keeping his head down, and Rebecca staggered in his wake, wanting nothing more than to collapse in a heap. They passed what she thought was the Prytania gate, darting into the shadows in case someone spotted them. By the disused wall vaults on the Washington Avenue side, Anton paused.

"If I push you up onto the box here, do you think you can get over the wall?" he asked. Rebecca nodded, though she wasn't sure if she had the energy left for any more climbing. Anton knelt, signaling to Rebecca to climb onto his shoulders. Swaying, he rose to his feet, Rebecca clutching handfuls of his hair to keep her balance. It wasn't a bad thing for him to suffer a little, she decided, though she did feel a twinge of sympathy when he crashed one shoulder into the cemetery wall. With a few kicks and some help from a now-battered Anton, Rebecca was able to straddle the top of the wall, waiting to help Anton up, as best she could, before they both slid down into the street.

"This way," he said, taking Rebecca's hand again before they crossed Prytania; she'd jarred her ankle hitting the sidewalk, so he was half dragging her.

"I want to see my father," she wheezed. Her ankle was stinging, and she was shivering miserably in the cold. "We have to . . . go home."

"Not yet — it's not safe on Sixth Street yet," Anton told her. "Everyone's way too upset and angry."

He didn't understand that Rebecca wasn't talking about *that* home: She meant New York. All she wanted was to find her father and get out of here, as fast as possible. But right now she couldn't do anything fast. Rebecca hobbled after Anton down Washington, where the heavy tangle of oak branches almost obscured the moonlight.

"Here," he said. He peeled off his sweater, and Rebecca pulled it over her towering hair and mangled leotard, lowering herself onto the lumpy, exposed roots of one of the oak trees. She was too tired to walk another step, her body rebelling against everything she'd put it through tonight — the hours standing on the float, all that kicking and pulling and climbing — and her mind felt as though it was about to shut down. She was wracked with guilt for bringing that stone angel down on Helena's head: Rebecca had never meant to hurt Helena. She was just trying to get away. And then

Lisette — her only friend — had vanished. Rebecca wanted her father. She wanted Aunt Claudia. She wanted someone to tell her that the curse was really over and that everything was going to be all right.

Anton crouched next to her, his back against the trunk of the tree.

"I never meant for any of this to happen," he told her, running a hand through his thicket of hair. "You have to believe me."

Rebecca shook her head.

"You said you wouldn't tell anyone," she managed to say, though her teeth were chattering uncontrollably. "You . . . you lied to me. And because . . . because of that . . . look at what happened."

"I didn't tell anyone! Please . . . listen!" Anton slid to the ground. "I wasn't the only one in the cemetery the other day — the day I accused you of being able to talk to the ghost."

"What?"

"Toby was there. Toby Sutton. He followed me, because he thought I was meeting up with you. He was hiding behind that stupid Dumpster, and he heard everything we were saying. He told his parents, and they told my parents. And the Bowmans."

Toby's parents. Miss Karen — she knew. And Marianne must have known as well. All day today, when they were getting ready for the parade, they knew what was in store for Rebecca — a gunshot in the head, late that night in the cemetery.

"But it was my fault," Anton went on, looking down at his scuffed shoes. "In a way. I can't just blame Toby."

"What do you mean?" Rebecca wasn't sure what Anton was trying to do – shift the blame onto someone else or admit to something himself.

"Before Toby said anything, they were already suspicious. After the Christmas party, I asked my mother something about the ghost. If it was possible that someone else could see it. I was thinking about when you and I were sitting out on the gallery at the Bowmans', and you jumped, like you saw somebody. And right after that, Helena started screaming."

"You told your mother about that?" Rebecca felt herself blushing, thinking about that night. About Anton kissing her. Maybe he was thinking about it as well, because he met her eyes — quickly, nervously — and then looked away.

"I didn't tell her anything," he said. "Not about . . . anything that happened that night. But right away they seemed to want to know everything about you. My father told me you might not be . . . well, who you claimed to be. They said I had to ask you questions, get information out of you. But I didn't want to. That's one reason I never got in touch with you after the party. I told my parents you weren't answering my calls or e-mails."

"You could have still talked to me," Rebecca pointed out, unwilling to let Anton off the hook. "You just didn't have to tell anyone, that's all."

"I guess. It was just so much pressure. That day we had the argument in the cemetery, just after you got back from New York? Someone else saw you going in that day. I got sent in to interrogate you. I had to, even though I didn't want anything to do with it."

"That was the day I told you I could see Lisette," Rebecca murmured. She wrapped her arms around her bare legs, huddling to keep warm, wishing she could stop trembling. This was her fault as much as Anton's — she should have kept her mouth shut.

"I never said anything to them," Anton said quickly. "And somehow they *knew* I wasn't telling them the whole truth. That's why they sent Toby in to spy on us. That day I tried to warn you about riding in the parade — you just wouldn't listen."

"Why didn't you just *tell* me, instead of dropping all those vague hints?"

"You ran off before I had the chance to explain!" he protested. "And anyway, I was real confused. My parents and friends were all saying one thing. . . . I've known Toby and Helena all my life. Everyone kept telling me that Helena's life was at stake. I just didn't know what to do."

"So you did nothing." Rebecca didn't know if she could forgive Anton. All this week he'd known what they were planning for her, and he'd said nothing. "You just left me to . . . to get murdered tonight!"

"I didn't have a choice," he said. "Toby had heard what I was saying to you, telling you not to ride in the parade. Everyone was beyond angry with me. They emptied my pockets — got my phone off me, everything. They even took me out of school! I had to go to a fishing camp in Mississippi with two of my uncles. There was no way to reach you. We only drove back to the city this afternoon, because they were riding in Septimus. They're both dukes."

The men on horseback, thought Rebecca. Anton's family. It wasn't just the Bowmans and the Suttons in the cemetery tonight.

"I was locked in my room this evening," he was saying. "My dad only came to get me so I could witness the end of the curse in the cemetery. He thought it was important because . . ."

"Because why? Your family likes seeing girls getting killed?"

Anton shook his head.

"We were part of it. All those years ago, when Lisette died . . ."

"Was murdered, you mean."

"When Lisette was murdered. Our families were friends then. It was my ancestor who talked to Mrs. Bowman and to Mr. Sutton, who was her lawyer. It was his idea to hide the body in the Bowman family vault and to tell her mother she'd died of yellow fever. He and Mr. Sutton carried Lisette's body to the cemetery the night she was killed. Don't you get it? We have her blood on our hands as well. And the blood of all those Bowman girls who died. If they hadn't lied to Lisette's mother, this curse would never have happened. It was the Greys and the Suttons who tried to cover it all up, and the result was . . . well, you know better than anyone. Girls dying, one after the other. All the way down to tonight. God, I just can't believe Helena is dead."

Anton rubbed at his face: He looked exhausted as well, Rebecca thought. She almost felt sorry for him. She wanted to believe him — wanted to believe that he'd tried to protect her, that he'd lied to his family rather than expose her, that he'd been kept away all week so he couldn't warn her of what was about to happen.

"At least it's all over now, right?" He glanced up at Rebecca. "That ghost is gone."

"She was my friend," Rebecca told him. Even though Lisette would be with her mother now, it was hard not to feel sad. Rebecca would miss her.

"I'm your friend as well," Anton insisted. "You have to believe me! I wouldn't do anything to hurt you, I swear. That's why I never said a word to anyone, even though it meant choosing you over Helena. I didn't want to be part of this any more than you do."

"Too bad, buddy." A sneering voice from somewhere in the darkness spoke up, and Rebecca almost fell off her tree root. She knew exactly who was speaking before he stepped out of the shadows.

It was Toby Sutton.

CHAPTER THIRTY-SIX

TOBY STOOD, HANDS ON HIPS, GLARING AT THEM. In his parade costume he looked like a malevolent clown.

"You're part of it whether you want to be or not," he told Anton. "And we've got some unfinished business to take care of."

"Get out of here, Toby." Anton scrambled to his feet. "It's all over now, OK? Helena's dead, and there's nothing we can do about it."

"Nothing we can do?" Toby parroted in a bitter, mocking tone. He sneered down at Rebecca as though he'd like to spit in her face. "Your girlfriend here murdered Helena — and our lame-ass parents just let her father walk away."

Rebecca gasped: Her father was OK — thank god. Toby shot her a look of contempt.

"Well, excuse me if I'm not in the mood to play happy families," he said. "Nothing's over until *she* pays."

"Nobody's *paying* for anything." Anton took a step toward Toby; he was much taller than his friend, and for that reason, maybe, Toby warily backed away. "Haven't we just had a hundred and fifty years of people paying for something that shouldn't have happened? Isn't that why Helena died tonight? That's it — the curse is over. Helena's death was a bizarre accident, like all those bizarre accidents and illnesses that killed all those girls. It's not Rebecca's fault. There's no more unfinished business. Just get out of here and leave us alone."

Toby gave a theatrical sigh, taking another few steps backward.

"I guess I'll have to do this alone, then," he said. He was fingering something, Rebecca noticed — something small, obscured in one hand. The moonlight caught it, and it gleamed. Not a gun, she thought! But no, it was too small.

"He's got something," she warned Anton, standing up to face Toby. "In his hand, he's got something."

"She's a genius, your girlfriend." Toby looked smug. He opened his palm, and there lay Anton's silver lighter. "Your father left this lying around, and I thought, *Now* that *could come in useful.*"

"You're talking nonsense," Anton said impatiently. "Give it back, and get out of here. I'm not in the mood for your stupid games."

"Whatever," said Toby. He was walking backward to the corner now, a vile smile cracking his face. "All I know is, a house has to burn tonight. And it's not going to be one of ours."

"No!" Rebecca clutched Anton's arm. Toby had disappeared around the corner. "He's going to . . . we can't let him . . ."

Her mind was a fuzzy mess. Why was Anton just standing there? If Toby wanted to burn a house down tonight, there was one prime target: Aunt Claudia's house on Sixth Street. The stories about Toby's pyromania weren't just idle gossip: He'd probably doused the place with gasoline already.

"We have to stop him," said Anton, and he took off down the street, skidding as he skirted the corner of Prytania. Rebecca pounded after him, running as fast as her numb, shaky legs would allow. Toby was way ahead of them: He'd had too big a head start. All he needed was seconds to light that fire. Aunt Claudia's little house was a dry wooden box; it would go up instantly. And for all Rebecca knew, her aunt and her father were inside.

"Stop!" she shrieked, but she knew this was just as futile as all her pleas on the steps of the Bowman tomb. Except this time there was no Lisette to save her — or to save the house. Toby was right: There was a burning house in the prophecy. Rebecca and Aunt Claudia had never imagined that it might be *theirs*.

Anton ran in long, loping strides, and he was gaining on Toby. Rebecca pushed herself on, willing Anton to catch him. The boys had reached the Bowman mansion when Anton threw himself forward, tackling Toby around the legs. Toby fell hard onto the sidewalk, and the two of them started rolling like one long, angry snake, thrashing on the ground. They were punching each other, Rebecca saw as she ran up. Toby kneed Anton hard, and for a moment it looked as though he was going to get up and run off again.

But Anton surged forward again, dragging Toby back, and then he smacked Toby straight in the face. Both of them reeled, Toby flopping onto the ground. Anton staggered over to the low iron railings along the Bowmans' front yard.

"This is the house that'll burn!" he shouted, blood trickling from his nose. His eyes were wild. "This is where it's all going to end — right here!"

"No, Anton!" Rebecca couldn't believe he was really going to do this. Anton had the silver cigarette lighter in his hand; he was striking the wheel, flicking up a flame. He crouched, reaching through the railings.

A large plastic tarpaulin heaped with lumber and other building supplies stretched across the yard to the side gallery. Anton lowered the flame to the frayed edge of the tarp. Toby eased himself up: He was leaning on his hands, his mouth an *O* of amazement. He couldn't believe it, either, thought Rebecca. He couldn't believe that Anton was prepared to burn down the Bowmans' house to save Rebecca's.

She couldn't see the lighter anymore, or its tiny flame, but moments later it was clear that Anton had made contact. The tarp was alight, crackling with flames. Fire licked at the pile of lumber, and then it must have reached something much more flammable, like a can of paint: With a "pop" the fire suddenly tripled in size, dancing toward the house.

Anton stood up slowly, looking at what he'd done. Then he hurled his lighter hard, throwing it onto the gallery. It wasn't too late, Rebecca thought, looking around — someone could still stop this. All she had to do was dial 911, and a fire engine could race up and put this out. But she didn't have her phone with her: It was too bulky for her shorts pockets, so she'd given it to Aunt Claudia this afternoon.

"Call the fire department," she ordered Toby, though he appeared too dazed to hear her. "For god's sake, before it's too . . ."

She was interrupted by a louder, more explosive series of pops: There had to be paint cans lining the side gallery. The flames licking at the posts now ran in longer and longer lines as though someone was drawing them along an invisible string. An acrid smoke filled her lungs, and the heat of the fire sizzled her cheeks and bare legs. Fire darted up the side of the building, obscuring the chimney; a window exploded. Anton seemed to wake from his stupor.

"We have to get back," he said to Rebecca. "This place is going to blow."

Toby, still on the ground, was laughing and shaking his head.

"You're crazy, man," he told Anton. "I thought I was meant to be the bad one. What the hell have you done?"

Anton took Rebecca's hand and pulled her onto the street. She could hear doors opening and slamming, the murmur of voices. Lights were going on up and down the street; in the distance, the whine of a siren sounded.

"Move unless you want something to fall on you," Anton said to Toby.

"Don't worry." Toby pushed himself off the ground, then stood wiping the blood off his face. "I'm out of here. This is all yours, bud."

"Come on," Anton muttered to Rebecca. The Bowman house was ablaze, flames shooting into the sky, its gray façade crackling into a ridged, papery black. Smoke billowed into the street, and flying smudges of ash showered onto their heads. A door in the old slave quarters opened, and the elderly butler ran into the driveway; he was clutching a damp towel to his face, making for the side street, as far as Rebecca could tell. There were people running in the street, shouting; the sirens were getting closer. Nothing was clear anymore, the street a thick smoggy gray.

Anton was leading her past the cemetery and down Sixth Street, both of them coughing and spluttering. Aunt Claudia: Was she safe? Had they taken her somewhere? The door to the leaning yellow house was locked, and Rebecca didn't have a key. She pounded on it, but nobody answered. Without any discussion, Anton tugged a loose brick from the rickety steps and slammed it into the window. The pane shattered, and he used the brick to knock the remaining jagged pieces of glass onto the floor of the parlor.

"Miss Claudia!" he shouted, lowering his head to peer in.

"Can you see them? Can you hear them?" Rebecca was almost hysterical. The usually quiet neighborhood was roaring with noise now, flashing with police lights and sirens, unnaturally lit up by the burning Bowman mansion.

"No," Anton told her, reaching in to fumble for the window latch. "How do I get this thing open?"

He answered his own question by wildly smashing another pane.

"Be careful." He pushed up the window sash and helped Rebecca climb in. "There's glass everywhere."

"Oh my god!" Rebecca crunched across the room, making her way to the hallway. Lights were on there, but the kitchen was empty, everything exactly where they left it earlier in the day. Anton opened each of the bedroom doors in turn.

"I can't see anyone," he called. "Have you looked . . . what?"

The splintering sound of exploding glass in the distance made them both jump. The front door rattled, as though it was giving way, being forced open.

"Rebecca!" It was her father, roaring for her. "Are you in here?"

"Yes!" She threw herself into the hallway. Her father stood just inside the front door, his face bruised and scratched, Aunt Claudia pressing in behind him.

"She's here, Paul," her aunt said. "I knew she'd be here."

"Thank god you're all right," he said, and Rebecca hurtled into his arms, burying her face in his heavy coat. "It's all over, honey. It's all over."

She could hear Anton's footsteps, slowly thudding up the hallway.

"Thank you, Anton," said Aunt Claudia. "Thanks for bringing Rebecca home."

"The Bowmans' house," Anton said, his voice cracking with emotion. Rebecca lifted her head to look at him. He was wiping at his face with the back of his hand. "Is it . . . is it too late?"

They moved onto the front porch in a dark clump, Rebecca still clinging to her father. The night sky glowed a burnished orange. Rebecca's eyes stung with smoke and tears and ash, and she couldn't trust herself to speak at all. In the distance, flames danced from the roof of the Bowman mansion, shooting into the sky. Anton gripped the railing, staring out at the fire. Marilyn the cat scooted up the stairs, weaving around Anton's legs and rubbing up against the post.

"Mama!" A breathless Aurelia was running toward them, thundering down the sidewalk. She stopped at the other side of the gate, beckoning wildly. "We've been out watching the fire! You can see much more up on Prytania — come on!"

"We'll stay right here, thank you," Aunt Claudia said firmly. "And I think you should come up here as well, out of harm's way."

"But, Mama," Aurelia pleaded. "It's fine up there, really. Claire's parents are there and everything. It's like . . . it's like Rome is burning! The barbarians are at the gates!"

Rebecca rested her head on her father's shoulder, and they stood there together, in silence, watching Rome burn.

EPILOGUE

On a sunny Saturday in mid-May, two teenagers made their way into Lafayette Cemetery. One was a seventeen-year-old girl, tall and dark, carrying a simple wreath of pungent olive leaves. The boy was even taller, his hair brushing his collar, his fingers paint-stained and cut. The school year was over, and they'd spent the last week working on a house in Tremé. It was an old Creole cottage, one of the oldest homes in the city of New Orleans. With the help of a local charity, and a group of enthusiastic volunteers from their schools, they'd managed to gut the house, clear out all the rubble from its collapsing roof, and give the exterior a fresh coat of pale blue. Work on its renovation would continue throughout the summer, even after the girl returned to her hometown, New York City.

In Lafayette Cemetery, its calm ruffled by the usual Saturday morning tour groups, the stone angel still lay in broken pieces at the foot of the Bowman tomb. One of the tour guides steered her group of half drunk convention-goers past that particular alleyway, lamenting the grave's recent state of disrepair. She pointed to the blackened ruins of the Bowman mansion and told them how the famous curse on the house had finally come true. A terrible and mysterious fire had taken place there, the night of the Septimus parade — terrible because it had destroyed one of the finest houses in the Garden District, and mysterious because the fire department seemed to have no idea at all how it started.

The boy and girl waited until the tour group drifted away before walking up to the Bowman tomb, carefully picking their way around the stone shards littering its steps. The girl reached forward, leaning the wreath against the door.

"Good-bye," she said, and took a step back. The boy reached for her hand, and they stood for a moment in silence among the broken wings and shattered torch of the toppled angel, reading the name recently carved into the marble sealing the vault's door.

LISETTE VILLIEUX BOWMAN

1836–1853

One of the city's oldest curses had ended. At long last, one of the thousands of ghosts of New Orleans was resting in peace.

ACKNOWLEDGMENTS

Special thanks to Richard Abate at Endeavor, Aimee Friedman and the team at Scholastic, and two excellent readers — my husband, Tom Moody, and my niece, Rebecca Hill, who helped me so much with this story.

Readers interested in learning more about the rich and complex history of New Orleans might want to start with Ned Sublette's *The World That Made New Orleans: From Spanish Silver to Congo Square*. And anyone keen to help rebuild and renew this unique American city should visit www.makeitrightnola.org or www.habitat-nola.org.

Don't miss Paula Morris's next thrilling and haunting novel,

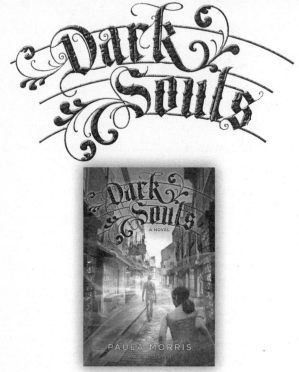

According to Miranda's cell phone, it was just after three in the morning. She'd woken up feeling a little sick – too much rich Indian food, she thought ruefully. In Iowa right now it would only be nine in the evening. If she could send texts, she could see what the girls were doing, maybe. But her phone couldn't send anything to the US or receive anything, either, as she and Rob had discovered in Manchester airport. And anyway, what would the girls back home have to say? What happened on *Glee*

that night, maybe. Who was and wasn't going to Matt Angeli's holiday party. Nothing that meant anything. Everything back home seemed more than thousands of miles away: It felt totally irrelevant.

The attic bedroom was stuffy and too hot. Miranda kicked off her quilt, swung her legs out of bed, and padded over to the window. She pulled back a curtain, and peered out. Nothing but silence and darkness. The Christmas streetlights were out, and no stars were visible in the sky. In the attic across the street, Miranda couldn't make out anything in the room beyond the window. It was just too dark.

She moved to twitch the curtain back into place, but something stopped her. A light flickering – the tiniest light. A candle.

The ghost was there.

Miranda froze, still clutching one of the curtains. He looked even more breathtaking this time, his face like chiseled marble. She was staring at him, she knew, but it was like staring at someone up on the screen of a movie theater. He was an idol, someone to gawk at, to admire. What he was thinking when he looked at her, Miranda wasn't sure. She was just a teenage girl wearing pajamas from the Garnet Hill catalog, her auburn hair messy and her eyes crusted with sleep. But there was something about his intense gaze that made her feel special. Picked out, in some way. Only a few people could see ghosts: That was what Nick had said. The way this ghost looked at her – it was as though there was something between them. As though he knew her.

The ghost held up his right hand, just as he had last time, and a burst of cold, an injection of it, seemed to pierce her through the glass. Miranda pressed her own hand against the window. She knew what to expect now, the surge of cold playing through her veins, from her fingertips to her toes. And this time she wasn't overwhelmed by shock; she had enough sense to notice details about the ghost. The sleeves of his shirt drooped, like a pirate's shirt. She'd thought his fingers were dirty, but it was really just his fingertips, as though he'd been dipping them in something like ink – or blood. The wound across his neck, clearly visible, was a purple line.

Tonight he wasn't smiling at all, but his eyes were warm, velvety dark. Miranda wished there weren't two closed windows – and a stretch of very cold open air – separating them. She wanted to talk to him, like she'd talked to that little girl ghost, Mary, in the street. Maybe, like Mary, he had something to tell her. She'd seen him three times now: That had to mean something. When she saw Nick again – if she saw Nick – she'd ask him.

The ghost opened his mouth: Was he trying to say something? Then the flame of the candle leapt, just for an instant, and died. Everything was dark again – inside, outside. He was gone.

Miranda peeled her hand off the glass and staggered back to bed. The sharp jolt of cold had stopped as soon as the candle went out, but she still felt shivery. She pulled the quilt back up onto the bed and snuggled down, her heart racing. What was he going to say to her? What did he want her to know?

To Do List:
Read all the Point books!

Airhead
Being Nikki
Runaway
By **Meg Cabot**

Wish
Wishful Thinking
By **Alexandra Bullen**

Top 8
What's Your Status?
By **Katie Finn**

Sea Change
The Year My Sister Got Lucky
South Beach
French Kiss
Hollywood Hills
By **Aimee Friedman**

Ruined
By **Paula Morris**

Possessed
Consumed
By **Kate Cann**

Suite Scarlett
Scarlett Fever
By **Maureen Johnson**

The Lonely Hearts Club
Prom and Prejudice
By **Elizabeth Eulberg**

Wherever Nina Lies
By **Lynn Weingarten**

To Die For
By **Christopher Pike**

The Vampire's Promise
By **Caroline B. Cooney**

Clarity
By **Kim Harrington**

Girls In Love

Summer Girls

Summer Boys

Next Summer

After Summer

Last Summer

By **Hailey Abbott**

And Then Everything Unraveled

And Then I Found Out the Truth

By **Jennifer Sturman**

Hotlanta
By Denene Millner and Mitzi Miller

Hotlanta

If Only You Knew

What Goes Around

In or Out
By Claudia Gabel

In or Out

Loves Me, Loves Me Not

Sweet and Vicious

Friends Close, Enemies Closer

Love in the Corner Pocket

The Comeback

By **Marlene Perez**

This Book Isn't Fat, It's Fabulous

This Girl Isn't Shy, She's Spectacular

By **Nina Beck**

Kissing Snowflakes

By **Abby Sher**

Breakfast at Bloomingdale's

By **Kristin Kemp**

Secret Santa

Be Mine

Spring Fling

By **Sabrina James**

21 Proms

Edited by **Daniel Ehrenhaft** and **David Levithan**

Point

www.thisispoint.com